THE GIRLS
WEEKEND

THE GIRLS WEEKEND

JODY GEHRMAN

TORONTO • NEW YORK • LONDON
AMSTERDAM • PARIS • SYDNEY • HAMBURG
STOCKHOLM • ATHENS • TOKYO • MILAN
MADRID • WARSAW • BUDAPEST • AUCKLAND

WORLDWIDE™

ISBN-13: 978-1-335-66933-9

The Girls Weekend

First published in 2020 by Crooked Lane Books, an imprint of The Quick Brown Fox & Company LLC.
This edition published in 2021 with revised text.

Copyright © 2020 by Jody Gehrman
Copyright © 2021 by Jody Gehrman, revised text edition

This edition published by arrangement with Harlequin Books S.A.

For questions and comments about the quality of this book, please contact us at CustomerService@Harlequin.com.

Harlequin Enterprises ULC
22 Adelaide St. West, 40th Floor
Toronto, Ontario M5H 4E3, Canada
www.ReaderService.com

Printed in U.S.A.

THE GIRLS
WEEKEND

In loving memory of Jan Wolf.

ONE

LIKE MOST CLUSTERFUCKS these days, it starts with a group text.

I'm lounging on my couch, peering out at the steel-blue sea in the distance. Iron-gray clouds skulk along the horizon. My window's open a crack; a ribbon of salt breeze, tangy with rain, winds through the stuffy room.

My phone chimes, and there it is.

A text from Sadie MacTavish.

The sight of her name there, glowing on my screen, stirs something so old it feels primal.

Hello, my fabulous friends! How are you? I've missed you so much. I hope you'll agree that a Fearless Five reunion is way overdue. What better excuse than throwing an amazing shower for our dear Amy? She's due in early July. I've already looked at Cabrillo's calendar, so I know Moody's done teaching May 22nd. How about we gather @ my place June 3–7? It would mean the world to me if you'd come. xoxo Sadie

I reel back, heart pounding.

Reading her words, I can hear her voice in my ear, see her beautiful face, those green eyes, the lush black hair. I recognize the exact note she's hitting, perky and upbeat, but also commanding. She looked up the college calendar; there's something both flattering and off-putting about her taking that extra step, making sure I won't have to work. That's always been her gift: serving a cocktail of bossy and sweet into frosty martini glasses. She can seduce, beguile, and manipulate all in one deft pour.

I stare out the window again, my eyes on the tiny strip of sea that counts as my ocean view. The Santa Cruz coastline is fringed with fog. Wind pushes against the wavy glass like something trying to get in. I shiver and close the window.

We were tight back in college—all five of us. Em and I are still pretty close, but I haven't talked to Sadie, Amy, or Kimiko in years. The thought of a reunion makes me squirm with both delight and dread.

They were some of the best friends I ever had. When I think of them, I picture all the times we laughed so hard we couldn't breathe. We were caught in that magical golden bubble between childhood and adulthood— four years spent trying on different personas, exploring futures with reckless optimism. We knew each other in a way I took for granted. Our favorite songs, our favorite foods, our favorite colors—we could rattle off one another's with the speed and confidence of auctioneers. It was more than just an encyclopedic knowledge of each other's quirks, though. It was love. We knew secrets about one another weighty as grenades. We were there for each other without question. I've never had a circle of friends like that before or since.

My phone chimes again. I pick it up.

It's from Em: Are you going?

When I don't respond: Come in, Moody.

After another minute of silence: Call me! We need to discuss.

Obediently, I phone her. She picks up on the second ring.

"Oh my God, finally." She's someplace noisy—a mélange of voices, festive and bright, a bass beat. There's a slamming sound, and the party soundtrack disappears. "So, what do you think? Want to go?"

"Did you know Amy was pregnant?" I ask, deflecting.

"Amy's not on Facebook, but I saw when Sadie posted about it. Didn't you?"

I hesitate before answering. "I've been trying to stay away from Sadie's online empire."

"Yeah?" Her tone goes cautious. "Why's that?"

I sigh. "You know. Her life is so amazing twenty-four/seven—yoga classes with celebrity trainers, organic gardens, book tours, annual get-togethers with Tim Burton. It just gets to be a bit much."

I try to make my tone light, airy, like it doesn't really matter. The truth is, I found myself tuning in to Sadie's Instagram and Facebook feeds with the sick relish of an addict pulling out her drug of choice. I couldn't look away from the bright, beautiful world she inhabits. When I caught sight of myself in baggy sweats and an ancient sweat shirt, my self-esteem plummeted. My world looked gray and deflated next to the magical hot-air balloon Sadie MacTavish floats around in.

"You need to get over this." Em says it with an air of impatience.

"Get over what?" I know what she's talking about, but I want to hear her say it.

A car honks in the background; I hear footsteps as Em moves away from the source of the noise. "Your thing with Sadie."

I get up and put on the kettle, but immediately turn it off. It's after five. Prime drinking time. Reaching into the freezer, I free a cube of ice from the tray and deposit it in a highball. As I pour Maker's over the cube, it emits a satisfying crackle. "Can you define *thing*?"

"You know what I'm talking about. You're convinced her life is so much better than yours."

"Um, it kind of is." I'm not being petulant, just factual.

She groans. "You don't know that."

"I'm not saying my life sucks—"

"Of course it doesn't suck. You've got me."

"True…but come on, Sadie's got everything: the best-selling children's book trilogy, the movie franchise, the hot man, the gorgeous daughter, the organic garden—"

"Stop."

I do. My breath has grown shallow. I take a swig of my drink. "I'm just saying…"

"Come with me. Please."

"I don't know, Em. The last time I saw Sadie was ten years ago, and—"

"At Kimi's wedding?"

"Yeah." I sigh, remembering how gorgeous Kimiko looked that day, her hair a wild mane of black curls, her wedding dress a violet satin number that showcased all her curves. It was out on Orcas Island, at a cute little B and B with an expansive garden.

My eye catches on a note stuck to my refrigerator, a

quote from Oscar Wilde: *Always forgive your enemies. Nothing annoys them so much.* With one finger, I caress its edge.

Em exhales. I can picture her in some alley behind a trendy bar in SoMa, still in her work clothes, watching hordes of chic San Francisco hipsters stream from their offices. "What happened at that wedding? I remember you were upset."

I was having a great time until Sadie and I started talking. We'd always been competitive, but I figured we'd outgrown that dynamic by the ripe old age of twenty-eight. Still, after five minutes in her presence, I felt all my hard-won confidence, my scrappy self-esteem, slipping away like sand in an hourglass. Sadie's a lot like family in that way: I think I've come so far, that my progress is undeniable, but all it takes is one Thanksgiving dinner to put me right back at the kids' table, watching my adult self fall away like a cheap Halloween costume.

"I just get so insecure around her, Em." I sip my drink. "She's my kryptonite. I'd love to see Amy and Kimiko, but—"

"It won't be like that now. You're a grown-ass woman."

I cradle the cold glass. "We're like oil and water. She only asked me because she had to. She doesn't even like me."

"She doesn't *dis*like you. She won."

The truth of this shoots through me, an unwelcome stab of clarity. "Wow. Okay."

"You know what I mean." She softens her tone. "This is your chance to prove to Sadie—and Ethan—

that you're over it. You've moved on. You're doing just great."

The thought of seeing Ethan and Sadie playing lord and lady of the manor sounds painful. I'd rather endure a slow root canal in a Thai prison. Ethan and I have too much history for that to be anything but pure torture. But then I think of Kimiko's husky laugh and Amy's party-girl abandon, and I ache to be surrounded by my girls again. It sounds like going home. It's just unfortunate that the whole thing is a package deal.

"Come on. I know you're curious," Em prompts.

She's right, of course. In the years that have elapsed since I last saw Sadie and Ethan, I've tried to picture them many times. I've got a tragically active imagination, so my film reel of their lives comes easily enough. The maddening part is never knowing which versions are closest to the truth. I recall the *Vanity Fair* article that ran years ago. The article featured a massive photo spread of Sadie and Ethan's island estate and their shiny, perfect lives. The family looked like Greek gods, kayaking, surfing, cuddling up by their massive fireplace. It was like a car crash. I couldn't look away. This chance at front-row seats to their reality holds a voyeuristic allure. I want to see them. I just don't want to be seen.

Em changes the subject. "I wonder how Amy's doing. I thought she didn't want kids. Kimiko told me Sadie's been working with doctors, trying to get the meds right, but it's hard to find something strong enough to even out her moods without hurting the baby."

"That's got to be tough—on both of them," I say.

Amy was diagnosed with bipolar disorder back in college, after a pretty hairy incident our sophomore year. The five of us threw some legendary parties back in the day, and Amy was always at the heart of them, effervescent and charismatic. She was like nobody else I'd ever known. Her crazy, uninhibited love of adventure was infectious. She sparkled—she really did. I admired her balls, her willingness to dive into life headfirst. She did everything with gusto. Sadie planned the logistics, but Amy was the stick of dynamite that set the room on fire. Her nickname used to be Crazy Amy—sometimes shortened to Cramy.

Amy's always been a handful, though. Her moods could swing from ecstatic to woeful in seconds. It hurt so much, seeing this bright, vivacious spirit robbed of her verve. It used to scare me. I was never the one tasked with prying her from the jaws of depression, but I always felt like I should be able to come up with a remedy for her bleak days, throw down the rope ladder that could guide her out of that hole. It wasn't possible with her, though. Once she was down there, nothing and no one could get her out. No one except Sadie—forcing her to get out of bed, take a shower, eat something. Sadie always did the heavy lifting when it came to Amy.

Since they're family, I suppose Sadie feels a different level of obligation. Amy and Sadie are cousins, but they grew up more like sisters. Amy's parents died in a car accident when she was seven, so Sadie's family took her in and the two of them grew up together.

Sadie's always looked after Amy, but I wonder how Sadie feels about Amy having a baby. We're all in our late thirties. Sadie and Ethan's daughter, Dakota, has to be seventeen by now. Rather than contemplating an empty nest, I'd guess Sadie's faced with the prospect of parenthood-by-proxy. Now she can either step away and let Amy fend for herself, or she can spend another eighteen years providing Amy's kid with stability. Not that she'd adopt—nothing as overt as that. But Amy relies on Sadie financially and emotionally. From what I gather, she lives with them and doesn't have a job. If she checks out, Sadie will probably be the one to step in.

Em's tone turns thoughtful. "Sounds like the whole pregnancy's been a roller coaster. I think this girls weekend might be Sadie's way of asking for help."

"Sadie doesn't do 'help.'"

Em hesitates. "Nobody has it easy, June. Even bestselling authors need friends."

I don't reply. The static on the line crackles.

"Don't we have some level of obligation here?" She changes tack. "The five of us were close once upon a time. The least we can do is show up."

I sip my drink. "You think Kimiko will go?"

"Probably. She's in Seattle. It's only like an hour drive for her."

I circle back to her earlier point. "Even if this is an SOS from Sadie, how is a girls weekend going to fix anything, Em?"

"It won't." She hesitates. "But we do have history."

I catch the flicker of memory under her words. The five of us shared so many adventures: running naked across the quad at midnight, taking mushrooms at Fragrance Lake, stage diving at a Spice Girls concert—all questionable escapades. We're bound by them, a shared history that's not all that unusual, I guess, but it feels sacred because it's ours.

Em lowers her voice, speaking close to the phone.

"Don't old friends owe it to each other to answer the call of the tribal drums?"

I swirl the whiskey in my glass. Outside, the rain clouds have started to close in. The wind chimes on my balcony clang a mournful tune. "Maybe."

"Think about it." Em knows me well enough to recognize when to back off.

I nod, even though she can't see me.

Long after I've put the phone down, I stay there, staring out at the gathering storm, mentally listing all the reasons going to Sadie's is a bad idea.

I TRY NOT to think about Sadie in the weeks that follow. There's a flurry of responses from the others. Plans begin to coalesce in the vague, scattered fashion typical of group texts. I don't respond, hoping my silence won't seem too glaring amid the cacophony of friendly female noise.

This is wishful thinking. I'm the elephant in the room. I can feel my nonresponse being noted and avoided, like a smear of dog crap everyone minces around on the sidewalk.

Just to be sure I won't give in to group pressure, I plan a camping trip with my boyfriend, Pete; we decide to leave a couple of days after school gets out. We'll drive down the coast, with stops in Big Sur, Cambria, Pismo Beach, and Santa Barbara. He surfs, so it's not too hard to sell him on the idea.

In the meantime, I focus on my classes, feeding off the steady, easy love I feel for my students. I teach English at Cabrillo, a community college just south of Santa Cruz, a beautiful campus with a view of the sea. It's a dreamy job, in many ways. My colleagues are smart and full of surprises, my students doubly so.

It's April, and the weather's all over the board. Santa Cruz springs can give you nothing but soupy fog for weeks. Then—bam—out of nowhere, this balmy, tropical day lands in your lap like a valentine. On a Wednesday toward the end of the month, just such a day appears. My English 201 class is abuzz with the spring weather, restless and eager for release. I let them go ten minutes early, unable to fight the pull of blue skies outside our classroom windows. It's not a day for discussing the finer points of semicolons.

When I get to my office, I sit in the silent wreckage, feeling unsure about where to start. Stacks of essays compete with folders of notes from meetings.

I hear a knock at my door.

"Come in," I call.

Sarah Madsen opens the door a crack. She shoots me a shy, darting look as she hovers inside the doorway. "Do you have time to talk, Professor Moody?"

"Of course." I gesture at the chair across from me. "Have a seat."

She sits, her thin body curled like a comma, her restless hands pulling at the sleeves of her sweater. "I wanted to talk to you about my manuscript."

"Okay. Sure."

"It's just…" She looks around, scanning the walls, her eyes swimming behind thick glasses. "I wrote a story about this girl who's in the class, and I'm worried she might not like it."

"Oh. Okay." I try to read her furtive glance. "Is it an unflattering portrait, then?"

Sarah snorts. "You might say that."

"Will she know it's her?" I lean back in my chair. "I've written stories based on people I know, and most of the time they don't recognize themselves."

"Well, it's about Astrid Lund." She licks her lips. "And I named the character Astrid Lund."

Astrid Lund is one of those powerful, larger-than-life girls who moves through life like a tropical storm. I can see why shy, meek Sarah might want to write about her. It's easy to see things will always fall apart around Astrid. At the same time, you know she'll emerge from the wreckage, a phoenix blossoming from the ashes again and again.

"That could be... Maybe you could change the name?"

Sarah looks wounded. "Aren't you always saying you can't compromise your art to make your audience comfortable?"

"You might fictionalize a bit, is all." I pause. "I mean, the class is called Fiction Writing."

Her expression is doleful. "I don't know."

"It's taking life and turning it into art."

This pleases her. Almost as quickly, though, her face falls. "She'll probably assume I'm jealous, if she does figure it out."

"Why would she think that?" I keep my tone neutral, curious.

Sarah shrugs. "Really, it's satire. The character's a cannibal."

I put my hand to my mouth, trying not to laugh. A glint of dark humor flashes behind Sarah's glasses.

"But most people don't get satire. They'll say I'm a

lesbian who's obsessed with her." She looks at the floor. "Either way, I can't win."

"So why do you want to workshop it?"

She looks lost for a moment, considering. "I don't know. I guess because I like it. The story, I mean. I feel like it says something true."

I nod; this idea resonates like a guitar string inside me. "Then you should put it out there. If other people don't get it, screw 'em."

She lets out a startled bark of a laugh. "Exactly."

Something occurs to me. "Have you ever tried writing something from Astrid's point of view?"

"No." Sarah wilts, her shoulders sagging. She could be pretty, but she carries herself like a person expecting to be kicked. "I have no idea what she thinks about."

"Might be interesting. As an exercise."

"I mean, she gets everything she wants." Sarah picks at her nails. "Where's the tension in that? If conflict drives the story, she's got no story."

"Maybe her life is more complicated than it looks." It comes out as barely more than a whisper. The echo of my conversation with Em is uncanny. "Nobody knows what someone else is carrying."

Sarah's young, serious face regards me with interest. "Um, Professor Moody?"

"Yeah?"

"I was trying to find your book. I really want to read it."

"Oh." I can't hide my pleasure at this. "That's sweet."

"I couldn't find it anywhere."

"Yeah." I hope I'm not going to blush. "It's out of print."

"Out of print?" She looks puzzled.

I breathe out a puff of air, wishing I didn't have to say this. Sarah looks so trusting, so sincere in her belief in me as a bona fide author. "It was published by a tiny, obscure publisher; they did a small print run, and—anyway, I have a copy at home somewhere. I'll lend it to you, if you're really interested."

She nods, her face earnest. She stands, one hand snaking out toward the door. "That would be great. I'll take good care of it."

Sarah spots a photo on my wall. It's from Kimiko's wedding, the Fearless Five clutching champagne flutes and smiling at the camera.

"Oh my God. Is that Sadie MacTavish?"

I blink, surprised. Sometimes I forget what a celebrity Sadie's become. "Yeah. We were friends in college."

She gasps. "Do you think she'd sign my copy of *Dakota's Garden*?"

I try not to look as pained as I feel. Something in my gut twists. "She's pretty busy."

"Sorry. I shouldn't have asked." She deflates, turning toward the door.

My voice comes out eager in spite of my misgivings. "Let me see what I can do."

She jerks back around, flattening herself against the door. Her breathless joy is half comical, half heartbreaking. "That would be so amazing."

I force a smile. "Looking forward to reading your story."

She returns my grin. Hers is edged with secretive delight. I know that smile. It's the one we writers wear when we believe, deep inside, we've created a masterpiece; we also fear it's a steaming pile of crap. I feel a protective urge, an unreasonable longing to shield her from the slings and arrows she's sure to face. Sarah's already been kicked around; that much is clear. She'll be kicked around a lot more before her life is over. There's nothing I can do about that. I can only provide her with a small haven now and then, a place where she can feel visible and appreciated.

A FEW DAYS before the semester ends, I decide it's time to corner Pete and nail down some details about our camping trip. He's not a planner, which is fine, but I'm not going to get stuck doing all the prep work. Most of the places we're planning to camp are first come, first served, so we don't need reservations, but we do need to shop for food and sketch out a basic itinerary. Sitting in my apartment with a glass of wine Wednesday evening, I send him a quick text. What's up? Want to come over and plan our epic adventure?

Blue dots chase each other on my screen. They seem to go on forever. That's odd. Pete's not a verbose guy. The longest message I've ever gotten from him was probably five words. When the text comes through, I have to read it several times before my brain will compute its meaning. I don't know how to tell you this, June, but I can't do this anymore.

My stomach drops twelve stories inside me, an elevator plummeting. My fingers tremble as I write, Can't do what, exactly?

Another interminable pause. I try to swallow and find my mouth has gone dry.

Before I started dating Pete, I tended to connect with guys on dating apps and met them "over the hill," as we say, in the South Bay or San Francisco. They were Silicon Valley creative types, mostly—designers, not programmers. We'd meet at wine bars and trendy, exotic restaurants where I had zero chance of bumping into a student. If I liked the guy enough to go home with him, I did, but I rarely repeated the experience. Online dating was a simple supply-and-demand exchange of goods. When I felt the heat building in my bones, needed an outlet for my angstier urges, I'd find someone I liked the looks of whose profile didn't make me want to retch and spend the night with him. A little human contact went a long way for me back then. One decent encounter could last me a couple of months.

Then I met Pete. He taught the guitar class I took at Cabrillo. He wasn't very organized, but he was charismatic and playful. On our second date, he played me a song he'd written called "Moody June." Nobody had ever made such an effort to woo me. I was a goner.

My phone chimes at last.

I've met someone.

Are you seriously breaking up with me via text?

I'm sorry. I'm in Amsterdam.

I almost drop my phone. There's a surreal, dreamlike quality to this conversation, a nightmarish disorientation that has me gulping more wine. You're in Amsterdam?

I moved here to be with someone.

I search my memories, trying to recall my last date with Pete. The past couple of weeks have been crazy at work. With effort, I dredge up a memory of our most recent hookup: dinner at his place a week ago. He seemed a little distant, hard to read, but I figured he was just in one of his moods. He gets like that sometimes—unreachable. I chalked it up to Pete's artistic temperament. I had no idea he was planning to swan off to Amsterdam with a mysterious love interest. Serious plot twist.

Fighting the urge to hurl my phone against the wall, I type, You're just now telling me this?

I'm sorry. You're a great person and I wish you well.

Ew. Seriously? That's the kind of thing you say to someone you barely know, someone you desperately want to get rid of, not the woman who's indulged your sexual peccadilloes for over a year.

Fuck off, Pete.

I scroll through my contacts until I find Em's number.
"What's up, buttercup?" Em sounds impossibly normal.
My breathing is shallow, like my lungs have shrunk to half their normal size. I try to find words and can't.
"You okay? What's going on?"
I can't get enough breath to fuel the words. Maybe pain will snap me out of this. With my fingernails, I dig into the flesh of my arm. The sting soothes, but not enough to slow my breathing.
"June? Babe, you there?"
"Pete broke up with me in a text," I blurt.

She sighs. "Oh, God. I'm sorry."

It takes me a second to realize what's wrong with her response. Not enough surprise.

"You want me to kill him? I'll do it. I'll choke him with his own intestines."

A weird, wobbly laugh escapes me. "He's in Amsterdam. He's met someone and *moved* there."

"That *asshole*!" Now she's not just trying to make me feel better. Em's fierce when someone messes with her people. "I had a feeling he'd screw this up."

"I'm an asshole magnet." I swig more wine.

"You want me to come over? I could get in the car and be there in an hour."

Tears push at the backs of my eyes, making them tingle. Until now, I haven't felt like crying. "No, I'm okay."

"Does this mean you're coming to Sadie's?"

"Pete and I were supposed to go camping." I sigh, thinking about the misery of wallowing in my apartment alone. It will be the worst possible start to my summer: endless cartons of Häagen-Dazs, bad movies, too much booze, and not enough leafy greens. Some women go on self-improvement kicks when a guy dumps them. I know myself well enough to accept I'm not that girl.

"I know," Em says. "I'm taking advantage of you when you're at your lowest."

I can't help guffawing. Em always knows how to talk me out of a funk. She's the perfect person to help me nurse my wounds. But going to Fidalgo Island means facing Sadie in all her glamorous splendor. Am I up for The Sadie MacTavish Show when I feel this down?

I grasp at the first excuse I can find, stalling. "It's

kind of shitty to spring an extra guest on Sadie last minute."

"Are you kidding? Everyone will be thrilled. It's not the Fearless Four reunion. It's the Fearless Five."

"Even if the fifth is mopey and miserable?" I ask, my voice small.

Em's tone goes soft and cajoling. "Getting away will be good for you. Nothing heals a breakup faster than talking smack with your girls over copious amounts of booze."

I glance at my fridge, reading the Oscar Wilde quote again. Next to that is a magnet Em gave me. It shows women dancing in a field over the words *Friendship is about finding people who are your kind of crazy.*

If I stock up on ice cream and mope around the apartment for weeks on end, that will set the tone for my entire summer. Going to Sadie's will be like jumping into an ice-cold lake. Even if I'm miserable, it will be an excellent distraction—an emotional reset button that will allow me to skip weeks of self-destructive brooding.

"Okay." I stand up. "Let's do it."

"Yeah?"

"Why not? We're going to Sadie's."

"About damn time."

It occurs to me as I hang up that Em didn't sound the slightest bit surprised. She knew I'd end up going to Sadie's, just like she knew Pete was an asshole who'd break my heart.

TWO

THERE IS NOTHING sweeter than driving through a glistening forest listening to Ani DiFranco with your best friend. We have the windows down, the damp air pushing against our faces. "Falling" plays from Em's stereo at a volume so massive, I feel it deep inside my chest. The day is all blinding blue skies and lemony sunlight.

We drove to Eugene yesterday and spent the night. Now we're on Highway 20, the final leg of our journey. The redwoods shimmer with rain. The highway hairpins through primordial forests. We've got Starbucks in each cup holder. Em's tiny yellow Fiat purrs as it penetrates the dappled shadows. The branches filter swaths of sunlight, casting an intricate lacework across the windshield. When I close my eyes, I can see the shadows racing between quick starbursts.

Em's put together an epic playlist. Right now, we're listening to "Chick Singers Who Make You Want to Shave Your Head." It's all midnineties, folksy, pseudo-lesbian singer-songwriter stuff; the mood careens from angry to rebellious to tender abruptly enough to induce whiplash. The women line up in their combat boots: Ani, Jewel, Sinead O'Connor, Melissa Etheridge, Joan Osborne, Alanis Morissette, Sheryl Crow. All the tunes we gorged on back in college. She's even peppered it with the odd Hole song, as a nod to everything else going on around us at the time. We lived at the epi-center of grunge. None of us were into it, but it was there—pounding from dorm stereos, tearing through the quad. For us, it was all stripped-down girl stuff all the time. We knew the flannel-shirt crowd loved their distortion, but we didn't deal in that currency. We lived in a world of our own making. Its soundtrack was fe-male, angry, and acoustic.

Beside me, Em drives with the focused intensity she brings to every task. Her short dark hair is mussed by the steady stream of air pushing through the window. I'd never say this, because it's precisely the sort of com-ment Em would take the wrong way, but she reminds me of a seal: great liquid black eyes, dark hair kept pelt-short, gray sweater, and sleek black pants. She has a seal's agility, too—passing trucks and RVs, darting from lane to lane when she needs to. Not aggressive or showing off, just deft and competent. There is noth-ing I like better than riding shotgun with Em. It pains me to think I've gone without the pleasure for months.

Em and I were roommates back at Western Wash-ington University in Bellingham. From the first day we met, I felt that click—an almost audible snapping into place, connecting with effortless precision. Until then all my relationships had been functional, satisfactory, but never intimate. Growing up in Lakeport, a small working-class town in Northern California, I saw the people around me as comrades more than soul mates. My parents, the circle of friends I'd forged in school—they were all fellow survivors, important because of what we had endured together more than who we were. We drifted through our days in a well-equipped lifeboat, waiting to be rescued or to wash ashore someplace better. The day I met Em, I knew I'd left that lifeboat behind, had stepped onto terra firma. In that new world, mutual survival was no longer the only criterion for connection.

Em guns it up a hill. The shadows dapple her face and body, striping her skin and sweater as they glide over her.

She throws me an inquisitive look. One hand turns down the volume. "You okay?"

"Yeah." I say it too quickly, though.

Her eyes catch on mine before returning to the road. "You sure?"

Em and I have drifted some in the last year. I could blame it on Pete, but that wouldn't be accurate. She never trusted him, never got what I saw in him. Her suspicion was like a splinter: small but irritating. If she'd been off base in her assessment of him, that would have been easier, but it was the niggling sense that she saw him more clearly than I could that made me awkward around her. She didn't pull away, though. Em's too loyal for that. If we're being honest, we both know I'm the one who got sloppy.

It's not that I avoided her or shut her out—nothing so dramatic. But gradually, the effort it took to climb into my car and brave the tangle of traffic to go see her in San Francisco started to seem like more trouble than it was worth. She came to see me about once a month, but after a while we felt the strain of that imbalance.

Then she moved in with Reggie; he's wonderful and eccentric and perfect for her. They met at Google, where they both work. Seeing them together only made me more aware of all the ways Pete and I don't fit. We became the sort of friends who text a few times a month, get together rarely. If I'd seen into that future back when we were at Western, I'd have been appalled. The changes we swear to fight off with savage claws in our twenties end up creeping over us like a rising tide in our thirties.

I look at her, a quick pang of gratitude shooting through me.

"You weren't surprised about Pete, were you?" I ask.

She hesitates only long enough to check her rear-view mirror. "No."

Neither of us says anything for a moment. The hum of the wind through the windows, the tinny, turned-down music, fill the car as we both consider this.

"You wish I'd warned you?" Her tone is half sheepish, half defiant.

"I wouldn't have listened."

"I know it doesn't seem like it now"—she raises her voice above the wind—"but this really is a good thing. You're going to feel so much lighter now that you've shed his dead weight."

An image of my replacement—she has a name now, Allegra—flashes through my mind. I've stalked them online, but I've promised myself I won't look again. She's twenty-three, tops. In every photo she's smiling, her honey-colored hair glowing in the Amsterdam sunlight. Her cheeks are ripe peaches, her throat a pale, creamy stretch of perfection. The stupid thought reappears like an irrepressible cork bobbing to the surface: how smooth and silky her skin must feel under his fingertips, so flawless compared to mine.

"It's not just that he broke up with me. I keep thinking… what does this say about my life? The longest relationship I've been in for ages, and he breaks it off with a text? It's so juvenile." As soon as I've said it, the alarming truth of it hits me. "I'm almost forty, and what have I got to show for it? No soul mate, no kids, no stellar career."

"You're an amazing teacher," Em protests. "You love your job."

"You know what I mean." I tug at the seat belt, feeling confined all of a sudden. "Isn't this the classic midlife crisis? Where you look around and ask, *Is this all there is?*"

She gives me a side-eyed look. "This breakup says way more about Pete than it does about you."

"Come on, Em." I can hear the doubt in my voice.

"I'm serious. You deserve more than what he offered. Way more. All you have to do is accept that and move on." She accelerates up a hill, her brow furrowed in concentration.

I can't help thinking this is easy for Em to say. She and Reggie seem to have the perfect relationship. They laugh about the same things. They both love hiking and concerts in the park, throwing dinner parties; they have kick-ass careers, plenty of money. She's won the relationship lottery, while I keep stumbling from one ill-fated hookup to the next.

For the hundredth time since I made the impulsive decision to come along on this trip, I wonder if I've made a mistake. Aren't reunions basically the Comparison Olympics? Here I am, already measuring my life against Em's; I know there will be a whole lot more of that in the days to come. Kimiko's divorced with a twelve-year-old son, Amy's pregnant, and Sadie—well, Sadie's got it all. The hot Scottish husband, the world-class career, the beautiful daughter, the lavish estate in Puget Sound. If there's one person in the world I've always compared myself to, it's Sadie. We were friends back in college, but there was always a competitive subtext to our relationship. Our need to one-up each other egged us on, gave our friendship its edge. Now I'm seeing her again for the first time in a decade, and my self-esteem is anemic. It's like going into the ring against Ali when all I've done to train is eat doughnuts and binge-watch *Rocky*.

Em seems to sense my growing trepidation. "I know you're not in the best place, okay? And I get that this trip might be hard because of that."

I nod, feeling a lump in my throat.

"But you know what?" She puts a hand on my knee, squeezes quickly before turning her attention back to the road. "You're way cooler than you realize. You've traveled all over the globe, had amazing adventures. You published a novel; you've got an awesome job." She shoots me another quick look, assessing whether or not I'm hearing her. "Also, you have the prettiest feet in the world."

I laugh. Years ago, on an outing at Lake Padden, the five of us lined up our recently pedicured feet and tried to determine whose were the sexiest. We even enlisted a hapless judge, some random German tourist. He declared me the winner. It's the last time I beat Sadie at anything.

"Thank you." I put my bare feet on her dash. "They are pretty stunning, I must say."

"Dazzling," Em agrees.

"You know when you said on the phone that Sadie 'won'?" I hear myself asking.

"Yeah…" She adjusts her rearview mirror.

"What did you mean?"

She licks her lips, thinking before she speaks. "Maybe I'm wrong, but I suspect that's how she sees it. You two competed for Ethan's attention all those years. That summer after senior year, I know he proposed to you first, but *she* doesn't know that. In her mind, she got her man, plain and simple. She won."

Ethan MacTavish was once a focal point of the competition between Sadie and me. He was a grad student when we were at Western; he taught our freshman English class. With his hypnotic Scottish brogue and his flashing blue eyes, we were both infatuated from the very first class. We spent four years vying for his attention, though most of the time he treated us like benign kid sisters. Until I had my chance with him.

I think back to that summer. Ethan and I spent three incredible months together. We were so into each other. He took me sailing every chance we got on his friend's boat. We'd feast on elaborate picnics on Chuckanut Island, feeding each other rich cheeses and succulent slices of melon. We hiked along misty bluffs, through ancient forests, stopping every few miles to kiss or just to gaze at one other, besotted.

Then he asked me to marry him, and I freaked out.

It wasn't the most natural proposal. We'd been dating only a few months. The truth was, he needed a green card. He'd finished his PhD, and his student visa would expire soon. If he wanted to stay in the States—and he did, desperately—he needed a wife.

He proposed on Chuckanut Island, after an especially decadent lunch and sex atop a scratchy wool blanket on a deserted beach. He presented me with a simple gold band in a blue velvet box. His family back in Scotland was very proper, very old-money, from what I could glean. He knew how to do things right.

But I wasn't ready. Not even close. The thought of getting married at twenty-two was terrifying, unreal. I could no more marry Ethan than I could fly to the moon or discover a cure for cancer.

I told him I needed to travel the world, have adventures. I wanted, more than anything, to become a real writer—someone who won awards and inspired rapturous reviews in the *New York Times*. To do that, I thought I had to experience a full, rich, dangerous life. I'd already booked a one-way ticket to Marrakech. After that, I'd see. I had enough saved to wander a bit, hopefully find a job or two along the way to prolong my adventure. I saw myself following in the footsteps of Hemingway, Fitzgerald, Baldwin, and hundreds of other expat writers who'd steeped in the rich broth of other cultures before they put pen to paper. *If you want to write, you've got to have a story to tell.* I was in search of my story.

Now I can't help wondering if I made the right choice.

"You think Ethan will be there?"

Em's dark eyebrows pull together with some emotion I can't quite read. Worry? Impatience? "Please tell me that's not why you agreed to—"

"No," I say, cutting her off. "Of course not."

She relaxes a little. "Sadie's not going to want you

two in the same zip code, let alone the same house. I suspect she's packed him off to Siberia."

I agree. Still, I'll be in his home. I'll see his things. I'll know what his life is like for real, not the tabloid version.

"Sadie still doesn't know he proposed to you first, does she?" Em asks.

"You're the only person I told. Spreading it around just seemed tacky. I didn't want to cheapen their engagement by telling everyone I got there first."

I remember how the whole summer knocked me on my ass. I'd finally gotten what I wanted—or thought I did. Then, when I realized being with Ethan required a massive commitment right away, I couldn't do it. I said no. But Ethan was practical. The clock was ticking. He moved on. I can't blame him, but it does gnaw at me, that little ghost of regret. Sadie chose the path I turned away from, and look where it's taken her.

A deer darts into the road. It bounds across the pavement, all air and lightness, like a bird touching down for a split second before heading once more for the sky. With a sickening thud, the deer glances off our bumper. Then we're speeding past, and it's staggering drunkenly into the trees, swallowed by the forest.

I look at Em. Her face is frozen in shock.

It feels like an omen.

WE MAKE IT to Deception Pass by sunset. The bridge is high and narrow. Em drives with her usual competence, but I can't help gripping the seat as we cross just the same. West of the bridge, the sun sinks into a spray of lacy fog. Tendrils of orange and pink reach across the blue sky. The water is glossy and swirling with eddies, like a Van Gogh. The trees stand sentinel along the island's shore, their trunks dyed terra-cotta in the fading light.

"So you've never seen Sadie and Ethan's place?" I ask.

Em shakes her head. Ani goes on raging from the speakers, asserting that she is not a pretty girl. An osprey swoops low near my window, hunting.

Em's phone starts giving us directions in a bossy British voice. Em takes a series of increasingly smaller roads as we wind around the island. By the time we pull up to a massive wrought-iron gate with a little intercom on the side of the road, my nervousness is so palpable I can taste it. A surveillance camera hovers above the intercom, its robotic eye pivoting to focus on us. Em and I exchange glances as she rolls down her window. Before she can even speak into the intercom, though, the gates swing open slowly. Whoever's on the receiving end of that camera must have spotted us and deemed us worthy.

We follow a winding ribbon of paved road that meanders toward the water. A babbling brook twists and turns to our right. We pass an expansive meadow teaming with wildflowers, edged by pine and cypress. There's an orchard filled with fruit trees, their blossoms just starting to peek out along the branches. Over a crest, we spot a barn where glossy chestnut horses slip in and out of the evening shadows. We take in the view without speaking. I have a feeling Sadie will never use this word, but it's an estate—there's no other way to describe it.

Em shakes her head. "I had no idea."

"I guess this is what an international franchise looks like."

Seventeen years ago, when Sadie was pregnant with Dakota, she got the idea for a middle-grade book: *Dakota's Garden*. Back then she and Ethan were barely scraping by; he had just finished his PhD, and she was twenty-two with an English degree and no discernible skills. Sadie had dabbled in fiction a little in college, but she'd never taken writing all that seriously. I was the one hell-bent on being a serious novelist. She wrote the book in seven weeks, landed a top agent in her first round of queries, and turned it into a multimillion-dollar middle-grade fantasy series. It was quickly snatched up by Universal and became a blockbuster movie franchise.

I've never read the books. When I tried, some restless, hateful part of me kept urging me to throw the beautifully illustrated tome across the room. I had this bitchy Greek chorus of voices in my head scrutinizing every sentence, looking for flaws. When I found descriptions or word choices that struck me as less than perfect, it was gratifying, but then I'd feel dirty for taking such pleasure in Sadie's failings. Much worse were the beautiful passages, the clever dialogue, the ingenious turns of phrase; those filled me with such toxic envy I felt physically sick.

Even without reading them, it's impossible to live in America—or on planet Earth, apparently—without knowing the basic premise. Dakota, a twelve-year-old orphan, crawls through a hole in her evil uncle's hedge and escapes to a lush, Technicolor world where she's schooled in the ancient art of magical botany. Think *Harry Potter*, *The Secret Garden*, *Narnia*, and *Alice in Wonderland*, then mix well into a highly lucrative cocktail of girl-power escapism.

Oh, and Tim Burton directed the first film. So, yeah. There's that.

As we wind down the final stretch of road, the beauty of the property reaches a crescendo. There are flowers everywhere—tangles of nasturtiums, morning glories, clumps of lilies in dark, satiny reds and vivid pinks. As we near the beach, a stretch of driftwood-riddled sand, we curve south. Through the pines, I catch a glimpse of a yurt, round and pale in the twilight. We make our way toward a house a stone's throw from the waterline, a wall of windows looking out on the bay, a brick chimney reaching toward the sky. It's pretty, but not nearly as grand as I would have imagined, given the expansiveness of the property.

"So that's their house?" I'm ashamed of the relief in my voice. I was afraid of what we'd find at the end of this driveway, certain some magical Camelot would emerge from the trees at any moment.

"Maybe, but I thought…" Em sounds doubtful.

We make another turn and catch our breath in unison. There, rising from a shimmering pool, is the *main* house. Three towers connected by walls of windows face us. There's so much glass, wood, and stone, it's hard to take in. It's a modern design, but not one of those streamlined minimalist layouts that look like children's blocks; this is part pagoda, part fortress, part rustic seaside lodge. Everything is pale—the sand-colored decks give way to honey-colored beams and gray siding. The central tower has an upper balcony with a cantilevered roof. Windows line every side of the upper stories, and great walls of glass connect the towers. Forest-green umbrellas pepper the deck, forming seating areas around the deep-turquoise pool that surrounds the base of the central tower. A stone path leads through the water to a pair of pale French doors.

"Mother of God," I say under my breath.

Em lets out a startled laugh. "I guess we're here."

We cruise past the dramatic facade and find ourselves on a circular driveway, passing under a massive stone archway supported by more blond beams. This, I see, is the back part of the central tower. From this angle, it looks like a great floating ship supported by stone, wood, and glass.

I unlatch my seat belt, feeling a little breathless. We park the car by a flower garden surrounding a flagstone deck off the back section of the main tower. In front of us is a shiny new silver Honda.

Em pokes me in the ribs as we sit there in her warm car, staring out the windshield at the deepening twilight. "Remember," she says, "this is supposed to be fun."

I can't help snorting with nervous laughter. It really is too incredible that we're here. When Pete sent me that text, escaping to Fidalgo Island seemed natural, inevitable. Now I see the impulse was harebrained—a decision made on crack. In a surge of panic, I imagine myself turning around and sprinting down the long, curving driveway.

And then, out of nowhere, there she is. Sadie MacTavish. She's wearing wide-legged gossamer-thin pants in a rich shade of indigo. A cream sweater exposes her sharp collarbones. Her dark hair is loose around her shoulders, even glossier and blacker than I remember. She looks older than she did ten years ago, of course, but there is still so much youth and vigor in her body, like she's immune to gravity. She floats toward the car, a relaxed saunter that gives the impression her feet, clad in sandals, barely touch the ground.

I think of the deer, for some reason—the way it seemed to soar into the road before glancing off the bumper and staggering into the woods.

"Relax," Em breathes. "I can feel you tensing up."

"Shut up. You're only making it worse," I say through gritted teeth.

We step out of the car, and Sadie hurries to the driver's side, wrapping Em in a hug. "You made it! Oh my God, thank you so much for coming."

I try to school my features into a serene and friendly expression, though it probably looks more like I've smelled something rank. I wish I'd worn something prettier than my faded jeans and stretched-out Nirvana T-shirt. Next to cool, dewy Sadie I feel scraggly, homeless. I walk around to them, heart pounding. I catch Sadie's eye. She's got Em in her arms, and she's watching me with a curious expression—steely, determined, but also glassy with unshed tears.

When at last she releases Em, I initiate what I hope will be a breezy, impersonal hug. No such luck. I forgot this about Sadie, though it's so much a part of her I can't imagine how it slipped my mind. Sadie is a hugger. No sideways half-hugs or squeamish pelvis-tilting for her. She snakes her skinny arms around my back and pulls me in with decisive force. Before I can do anything to defend myself, I'm locked against her slender frame, my face buried in her voluminous black hair. She smells of violets, just as she always did. Warm, floral, with top notes of freshly baked bread. She holds me in place. Her whole body telegraphs intense concentration, like a psychic trying to intuit a person's illness.

Even after I've escaped her embrace, I don't get far. She seizes my upper arms in her viselike grip and stares into my eyes. Sadie's are green, the color of a sun-dappled creek. I note the merest hint of feathery crow's feet fanning out from the corners of her eyes. Her skin still has that olive-toned, lit-from-within glow, healthier than ever. Her cheekbones are sharp, her Cherokee blood apparent in the dramatic structure it lends to her face. I can't help but wonder what signs of abuse and neglect she's noting in my travel-grimed complexion. I see a flicker of satisfaction and know instantly what she's thinking: even at the game of aging, she's already won.

Regret flares in me like a match. *Why did I come here?*

"So good to see you, June." She nods, agreeing with herself. "I can't tell you what it means to me—and Amy."

I shrug and take half a step back. This is too much, too soon. My brain can't process all this Sadie at once. My leather tote slips from my arm, hits the ground, and random stuff scatters all over the pavement: an energy bar, a tin of mints, my battered wallet, a tampon.

Damn. How soon can I fake appendicitis? Will they airlift me out?

As we're scrambling to gather my belongings, someone bursts through the door. For a second I hold my breath. But no, it's not Ethan. Of course it's not. Instead, stuffing my tampon into my purse, I see a blond girl in her teens. She's wearing a tank top and jeans, butterscotch-colored boots, a surly frown. She's pretty. There's a golden sheen about her, a radiant glamour voluptuous as sunshine.

"Dakota, meet two of my oldest, closest friends, Em and June."

On hearing my name, Dakota's gaze snaps to my face. She has startling navy-blue eyes. Ethan's strong, elegant nose. I can see curiosity in her stare—not general interest, but a specific question, as if she's heard something about me and wants to confirm it. Quickly, the intrigue sinks under a habitual layer of sarcastic disinterest. Resting bitch face.

"We've met," Em says, holding out her hand. "But you won't remember. You were, I don't know…six, maybe?"

"It's been a while." Sadie radiates maternal pride. She tucks a strand of hair behind Dakota's ear; her daughter, predictably, shrugs her off.

Dakota flashes Em the quickest bored glance. Then her eyes seek out mine again, her curiosity making me squirm.

What's she heard about me? From whom?

There's an awkward pause. Nobody seems to know what to say.

Our silence is broken by the sound of a car approaching. We all turn to see a shiny black Porsche tearing up the drive. It slows abruptly and parks behind Em's Fiat. It's hard to make out the driver with the glare on the windshield. Again, my heart slips into my throat, wondering if it's Ethan. Then a tall, well-built guy who looks to be in his early twenties unfolds from the Boxster.

I hear Sadie hiss a breath out through her teeth.

Dakota tilts her chin up, defiant. "Chill, Mom. We're just going to feed the horses and go for a ride."

"Honey." Sadie's smile looks tight enough to snap. "I thought we agreed you'd be here to welcome all of our—"

"We won't be long." Dakota's already hurrying toward the guy, who keeps his distance but offers a polite wave.

As Dakota and her visitor start off toward the stables, Sadie laughs with effort and leads us toward the door. "Seventeen. What are you going to do? Her boyfriend, Ben, is home for the summer."

Em and I make vague, sympathetic noises and follow her inside.

The house is even more of a showpiece than I imagined. Back in college, Sadie showed some flair for interior design. She always liked her spaces, even her dorm room, to look like something straight from the pages of *Dwell*. Now those fantasies have spun themselves into a sprawling modern mansion that's open, airy, and casual by design.

We pass through several rooms, my battered suitcase trailing behind me. One of the wheels must have gotten knocked out of whack; it makes a sullen whining sound now that makes me want to kick it.

What did I imagine when I agreed to come here? That Sadie would be fat and unkempt, her house a hoarder's nightmare? That Ethan would be waiting in the guest room, where he'd whisper ardently how much he's missed me?

"Come on, let me show you to your rooms." Sadie leads us briskly upstairs. Her bare feet move soundlessly. "You've had a long drive. There's plenty of time to settle in. Amy's running errands, and Kimiko won't get here for at least twenty minutes—though who knows with her? Could be midnight."

We round the top of the spiral staircase and head toward the rooms down the hall. The smell of violets and furniture polish mix pleasantly in the air.

"Where's Ethan this weekend?" Em doesn't look at me as she asks. Her tone is elaborately casual.

"Oh, he's staying in the beach house." Sadie casts a glance over her shoulder. "We have a little place on the water."

"Right. We saw that." My voice sounds unnaturally bright.

"He's so sweet. Offered to give us our space for the weekend. Here we are." Sadie leads us into yet another exquisite room. "Em, this will be yours, if that's okay."

It's all dove-gray walls and smoke-colored satin pillows. Beveled mirrors flank either side of the enormous bed, with matching glass lamps and tiny vintage perfume bottles perched on the side tables. Black-and-white framed photos of calla lilies and lighthouses line the walls with gallery-like precision.

"Unacceptable," Em quips.

It's not funny, but we all laugh, hard and shrill. The sound makes my teeth hurt.

"Go ahead and get settled in," Sadie says. "June, yours is down here."

I dutifully follow Sadie down the hall. She leads me to a light, airy room on the west-facing side of the house. It's pure white, like some kind of B and B in heaven. A king-size bed with a Victorian brass frame has been topped with a blinding duvet. Lace hangs from the ceiling in curtains that shield the bed, turning it into a secret retreat. Enormous bay windows look out over Puget Sound. From this height, the water and the islands take on a fairy-tale quality. It's a room for a princess.

"Dakota's old room," Sadie says.

"Wait, this is hers? No, I don't want to—I can stay with Em."

"Don't be silly." Sadie smiles without showing her teeth. "She's got a new room now."

"Oh. Okay."

An awkward pause falls over us. We both break the silence at once.

"I hope—" I begin, just as she says, "I'm so—"

"You go," I say, tipping my palm to her.

She hugs her arms, rocking back on her feet. "I'm just so glad you came, even if it was last minute. I can't even tell you how good it is to see you."

Eager to deflect any heartfelt talks about the ten years of silence between us, I dig around in my bag until I find what I'm looking for. "Listen, I know this is kind of silly, but I have a student who would be so thrilled if you'd sign her copy of *Dakota's Garden*."

"Of course." She looks pleased.

I hand her the book and a pen. "If you could make it out to Sarah with an *h*."

It occurs to me that this is the dynamic that makes Sadie the happiest—when I'm asking favors and she's granting them. I remember how this worked back in the day. She loved it when I had to beg her for something.

She signs the book with a flourish and hands it back to me. "There you go."

I set the book on the bed. "Thanks for making room for me last minute. Your place is gorgeous."

Sadie touches a hanging glass terrarium filled with miniature succulents. It spins gently, catching the light. "We've tried to make it our own."

Her use of the possessive plural seems a little off. Every room I've seen so far is pure Sadie. I've searched for the tiniest shred of Ethan but haven't seen him reflected in anything—at least not the Ethan I used to know. Even here, in Dakota's room, there's none of the sullen girl I saw sloping off to the stables with her boyfriend. The lace and the brass and the white fluffy duvet, the collection of blown glass terrariums dangling in a line—it's all so Sadie. There's no room for a real girl in here; it's a stage set for an idealized princess. It's the perfect room for the character from Sadie's books. Even I could see, in the four seconds interacting with the real deal, that the flesh-and-blood Dakota is nothing like the fictional version. No wonder she insisted on a new room of her own.

Our eyes meet, and for a moment something passes between Sadie and me. Whether it's a pact to be nice or a mutual agreement to hide the knives, I'm not sure. Whatever it is, Sadie seems satisfied. She gives the terrarium one last little spin, admiring the way the sunlight illuminates the tidy fractal patterns of the miniature succulents.

"Let me know if you need anything. Towels in the bathroom down the hall. Make yourself at home."

When her footsteps retreat down the stairs, I let out a sigh and sag onto the bed.

THERE ARE PEOPLE in this world who know how to pack. They neatly fold just the right wrinkle-resistant clothes into a streamlined suitcase; they know exactly where everything is.

I am not one of those people.

Em's always given me grief about it. She calls it my *exploding suitcase problem*. It's true, I'm a chaotic packer. No matter how hard I try to travel light, my baggage inevitably bursts at the seams. I've been known to lay my whole body flat on top of my luggage to force the zipper closed, tooth by jagged tooth, usually while swearing profusely at the cheap-ass undersized suitcase.

Now I heave my heavy bag onto the pristine white bed and force the zipper open. The contents spring forth like a pack of feral cats. A miniature bottle of vodka rolls off the edge and hits the floor with a thunk. I hastily stuff it back in my bag.

My phone vibrates with a text from an unknown number. Hey, June. Ethan here. Hope you don't mind. I poached your number from Sadie's phone.

My heart takes off like a dog chasing a rabbit.

My fingers tremble. I cast a furtive look at the door, which is ajar. It feels suspicious to go close it, so I walk to the windows.

I text back. Hi, Ethan. Long time no see.

The blue dots appear. I will myself to breathe.

Listen, I know this is kind of weird, but I'd really like to see you. You probably can't get away until later.

Would you meet me at midnight tonight? I'll be at the beach house.

"Exploding suitcase: check."

I jump at the sound of Em's voice, stuffing my phone into my back pocket.

"Jesus, Moody. It's just me." She plucks a miniature flashlight from amid my books and clothes, giving me a pointed look. "Were you planning on camping?"

"I come prepared," I say. "You know that."

"You 'prepare' by bringing way more random stuff than you'll ever need. Come on. Let's go check out the view. There's a balcony around here somewhere." She nods toward the door.

I follow her out, grateful for the distraction.

In the rain-scented air, we take in the garden. It's a riot of color: delphiniums, nasturtiums, passionflowers, poppies. Raised beds showcase enough vegetables to feed a small town for a year. Like everything else in Sadie's world, it's just unruly enough to feel organic, just tidy enough to pass as civilized. Twilight deepens the shadows beneath the trellises and stone fountains. A storybook forest stands sentinel on three sides. The glossy water stretches before us, blue and still. The balcony is picture-perfect, sheltered from the wind and rain that sweeps down from Canada and across the sound, battering the houses clinging to the shore.

My gaze falls on a carriage house tucked into the trees a few hundred yards away. It's two stories, dollhouse cute, with oversized French doors both upstairs and down. A neat little balcony adorned with potted herbs completes the effect.

"What's that?" I ask, intrigued. "A guesthouse?"

"I'm pretty sure that's where Amy lives."

I think about what it must be like for Amy, depending on Sadie all these years, living in her shadow. It's painful to imagine how small she must feel in comparison to Sadie's larger-than-life success, but maybe Amy doesn't think of it like that. I suppose Amy isn't as insecure as I am, isn't as prone to measuring her own worth against Sadie's.

"Has Amy always lived with them?" I ask.

Em follows my gaze back to the carriage house. "Mostly. I think she tried renting her own place for a while, but Sadie says it's just easier having her close."

"Easier?" I think I know what she means, but I can't help probing. It's been so long since I've been around the two of them. A lot could have changed since college.

Em shrugs one shoulder. "You know, when things get bad."

This is the type of euphemism we've always employed for Amy's dark days—the long stretches when she won't get out of bed and nobody except Sadie can reach her. I wonder if it's habit, obligation, love, or a combination of all three that inspires Sadie to watch over her cousin, year after year. Does Amy appreciate all that care, or resent it? Probably a little of both.

I look toward the water, my gaze landing on the roof of the beach house. It's gray and weather-beaten, much humbler than the main house. I wonder how often Ethan stays there, and what that says about the state of their marriage.

Em waves a hand at the house. "What do you think of Chez MacTavish?"

"It's so tasteful my eyes hurt. This place is Versailles." I try to sound offhand when I add, "Maybe I should try my hand at kids' books."

Em snorts with laughter.

"What?"

"I think your sensibilities are a little dark for children." Em's smile is rueful. "You'd warp their tiny brains."

It stings a little, thinking about the contrast between Sadie's career trajectory and my own. I'm the one who slaved over every short story in college, my identity rooted in my dream of one day becoming a literary superstar. I really believed that was my fate. The knowledge that Sadie has stumbled on stellar success without much effort irks me.

I change the subject. "Did you pick up on some tension with Dakota's boyfriend?"

"Definitely. I get the sense Mama Bear doesn't approve."

A door slams downstairs. Right below us, on the expansive deck, we hear Amy's voice, as crisp and audible as if she were in the same room. "Sadie? What are you doing back here?"

We widen our eyes at each other. Damn.

Whatever Sadie says in response, it's too low to make out. The door down there opens and closes again, leaving us alone. Maybe.

"Guess we better be careful about where we gossip," I murmur.

Em nods, mortified. "We'll probably get kicked out for bad behavior."

"So what else is new?" I say.

THREE

EM AND I are on our way downstairs when we hear Amy scream. It's a high, piercing note that tears through the silence of the enormous house and sends goose bumps up my arms. We hurry toward the sound.

As we turn the corner into the kitchen, we find Amy and Kimiko in a fierce hug. When Amy spots us over Kimiko's shoulder, she lets out another scream. It's a cry of pleasure, I guess, or surprise. I can't help feeling it's the wrong note, though, more panic than joy.

"Oh my God!" Amy releases Kimiko from her grasp, hurries over to us, and flings her arms around Em, then me. "I can't believe you all showed up. Especially you, June. God, look at us—the Fearless Five. Big-ass bitches in the house!"

I bury my face in Amy's blond hair. She smells fruity, like green apples and ripe pears.

As soon as I step away from Amy, Kimiko and I hug, laughing with pleasure. Her curvy body in my arms brings back so many memories—a montage of sun-bright images playing like a music video inside my brain. I see the five of us cruising downtown Bellingham in Kimiko's old Chevy with the windows down, music blaring; taking turns doing keg stands at some long-ago party; kayaking through Bellingham Bay, the sun warm on our faces, storm clouds gathering in the distance.

"I thought you weren't coming. Last-minute change of heart, huh?" Kimiko asks.

"Something like that."

Kimiko's makeup, as always, is eccentric but impeccable: cat-eye liner, smoky glitter on her lids, nearly purple lipstick that somehow works on her. She's half Japanese, half Italian, with hair that's a wild mass of curls. Right now it's streaked with electric blue, parts of it pulled into tiny Princess Leia buns that come off as fashion-forward instead of goofy. She's wearing a satin slip dress under a leather motorcycle jacket, with the perfect booties to pull the look together. That's the magic of Kimiko; she could take a burlap sack and make it work on the runways of Paris.

Amy screeches again, this time in reaction to something Em's saying. Kimiko and I widen our eyes at each other. The dynamic is so familiar we burst out laughing.

Kimiko turns her attention to Amy. "Bun in the oven's almost done, huh? How's the pregnancy going?"

"Like shit." Amy holds out her arms and stares down at herself. "Obviously. If I survive long enough to pop this kid out, I'll be a blimp."

Amy looks tired, her belly swollen to the size of a large melon. There are dark circles under her eyes. She wears no makeup, and her bright orange dress and bleached-blond hair look slept in. Still, just being in her presence I can feel that old party-girl magic, her enthusiasm infectious as ever.

Sadie sweeps in with a bottle of wine in each hand.

"Amy, you're not a blimp, you're a goddess, so stop saying that."

"Yeah, right." Amy rolls her eyes. "Sadie keeps saying I glow, but really I'm just greasy."

"Now, now," Sadie scolds as she sets wineglasses out on the kitchen island. "On to the important stuff: Pinot Noir or Pinot Grigio?"

"Little of both." Amy laughs at her own joke.

Kimiko takes off her motorcycle jacket. Her strong arms are almost entirely covered in tattoos. She heaves a hemp bag onto the kitchen counter. "I brought supplies."

We all watch as she unpacks a bottle of Bombay Sapphire and two six-packs of tonic from her bag.

Amy whoops in delight. "Kimi's in the house!"

Sadie blinks at Kimiko. "No wine for you?"

"Gives me a headache."

"But gin doesn't?"

"Not until the next day. I prefer my hangovers *after* the party, not during."

Sadie tries to sound gracious, but the strain is evident in her tone. "I thought we'd stick to wine."

Kimiko smirks. "I know how you think, Sades. That's why I decided to BYOB."

There's a shimmer of tension in the air, like heat waves off asphalt. Sadie's always done this. She plans an event with the precision of a general. When somebody dares to question her vision, she freezes.

"It's just..." Sadie casts a sideways glance at Amy, her smile growing thinner by the second. "Amy can't drink, obviously, and she's allergic to wine, so—"

"Gives me hives," Amy interjects. "Remember that

party at the winery in Woodinville? My face looked like a baboon's ass."

Kimiko turns to Amy. "Do you want me to put this stuff back in my car? I totally can."

"Not at all." Amy shakes her head.

"I'll take the Pinot Noir." Em holds her glass out to Sadie.

"Me, too," I say.

Kimiko's already twisting the cap off the gin. She grabs a glass from one of the cabinets. With one deft pour, she fills it half full. There's something practiced and professional about the movement.

"Here, let me get you some ice." Sadie grimaces like she just found a hair in her soup.

Em, who always ran interference between these two, diverts the conversation. "Kimiko, you still tending bar?"

"I've moved on."

"Yeah? To what?"

"Pushing better drugs."

"Crack?" I suggest.

A tense look flits between Amy and Sadie just as a dark shadow passes over Kimiko's face. What's that about? I was kidding, obviously.

"Weed." Kimiko pours tonic into her glass of gin and takes a swig. "Ooh, that's good."

"See? Now everybody's happy." Amy eyes the gin and tonic with longing, but her voice is bright.

"I own a cannabis dispensary in Seattle." Kimiko looks at me with a mixture of pride and defiance. "Best medicinals in the Pacific Northwest."

"Nice," Em says.

"You want Bubba Kush, Dutch Treat, Chemdawg? I'm your girl."

"Bubba Kush," I repeat. "Sounds like a step up from the Mexican ditch weed we used to smoke."

Amy laughs. "The party don't start till Kimi walks in."

Sadie presents a tray of bacon-wrapped figs. "Some nibbles out on the veranda before dinner?"

"Nibbles. Look at us being all fancy." Kimiko's sarcasm is thick.

Sadie's jaw tightens, and a vein pulses at her temple. There's a warning just below the surface. Her smile is honey but her voice is steel. "Let's have a nice evening, okay? We're all here for Amy. Let's keep that in mind."

Amy whoops. It's discordant, jarring.

Kimiko turns on her heel and locks eyes with Amy. "Do you want 'nibbles on the veranda'?"

Amy's gaze darts back and forth between Kimiko and Sadie. She looks like a cornered rabbit. "Uh, sure. Sounds good."

"Okay then. Nibbles it is." Kimiko seizes her drink and strides to the back deck, each footstep like a gunshot on the hardwood floors.

EVERYONE IS STILL wide awake at eleven thirty. I'm beginning to think it's too risky, sneaking off to the beach house. I still haven't even decided if I want to go. Why does Ethan want to see me? My curiosity is strong—okay, yes, it's killing me—but there are other factors at play. Does this mean he still thinks about me? If so, how do I feel about that? I can't deny a slight twinge of pleasure at the idea. Then I think of Em's solemn insistence that I need to get over this "thing" I have with Sadie. If that's my aim, then meeting with her husband at midnight is a huge step in the wrong direction.

Sadie and I spent our entire college career vying for Ethan's attention. He knew we were both crazy about him. He had a knack for keeping us in a state of perpetual yearning and frustration. I suspect he enjoyed the way we competed for his approval. He treated us like a couple of kid sisters, alternately flattering us with flirtation, then dropping off the radar. Now I can't help but feel that old thrill; he wants to see me, not her. Except Sadie's his wife now, and I'm supposed to be her friend—and, anyway, aren't we a little old for such juvenile games?

These are the thoughts hounding me as we sit in the living room, the clock over the fireplace ticking steadily toward midnight. The bright buzz of conversation has barely paused all night.

Kimiko's still drinking gin. She's a little drunk but not wasted. Em and I are both on our third glass of Pinot. Amy's been pounding the sparkling water, watching Kimiko's glass with such yearning I can't help but feel sorry for her. Sadie, of course, is stone-cold sober. She sipped a glass of Grigio with demure restraint at dinner. She's still nursing the same one, if I'm not mistaken.

We're playing Fuck, Marry, Kill. It was our favorite game in college. It's bittersweet—comforting and sad at once. In a way, it's like no time has passed since we last saw each other. Every now and then, though, it feels like we're trying to rekindle our neglected friendships with an old ritual that's lost its sparkle.

It's Amy's turn. She directs her challenge at Kimiko. "Okay, I've got it: the Kims. Kim Kardashian, Kim Jong-un, and Lil' Kim."

Kimiko groans. "Oh, God. Fuck Lil' Kim, marry Kardashian, and kill Jong-un."

"You're going to marry Kim Kardashian?" Em looks scandalized. "She'd be a nightmare to live with."

"You want me to marry Jong-un, though? For real?"

I look around the room, trying to strategize. A haze of wine coats my brain, making it hard to think. All my edges have softened. Am I really going to meet Ethan? I need to leave in the next ten minutes if I expect to make it by midnight.

Ethan remembers the June Moody from years ago. Will he be surprised at the woman I've become? I had no appreciation for my youth, of course, but he probably imagines me succulent, dewy, like most women under thirty. Now my crow's feet have turned from cheerful smile lines to ever-present creases. After Pete's unceremonious dumping, I'm not sure I can handle the inevitable surprise in Ethan's eyes. Will I see the precise moment when he regrets sending that text?

I shouldn't go. I can't go. That's it, then. I won't.

I glance up from my empty wineglass and catch Sadie staring at me. With a hitch of fear, I'm sure she's seen right into my thoughts, piercing my flimsy exterior. Her smile is slow and knowing. Those catlike eyes see all.

"I should go to bed," I hear myself say.

"What? No, you can't," Amy protests loudly.

Em pats my knee. "June's been through a lot lately."

"Really?" Kimiko leans forward. "Do tell."

"Tomorrow, when I'm fresh, you can hear all about my train wreck of a life." I put my wineglass down and stand. "For now, you'll just have to trust I'm a complete mess."

"I'm sure you're not a mess." Sadie pulls a sympathetic face that makes me want to punch her.

"I love stories of other people's disasters." Kimiko stretches, twisting her spine with several audible pops. "Makes me feel like less of a screw-up."

"Anticipation will make it that much sweeter." I head for the stairs, ignoring Amy's calls of protest.

As soon as I get to my room, I slip on my jacket and wrap a scarf around my neck. My body seems to have decided I'm going to see him, even though my brain screams warnings. I apply lipstick—Lady Danger, the color I've worn since college. It looks too vivid on my pale face. My dark-blond hair and blue eyes are washed out, indistinct. With that crazy splash of red at the center, I look like a ghost with a stab wound. I wipe it off, smearing on some lip balm instead. I adjust the waistband of my jeans, trying to view my body the way Ethan will see it. I'm maybe ten pounds heavier than when he knew me. It rounds me out, but not in a bad way.

A fresh wave of guilt washes through me. Here I am, enjoying a delicious buzz off Sadie's wine, my belly still full from her gorgeous three-course meal. I'm standing in her daughter's old room—*their* daughter's old room—getting ready to meet her husband for a secret rendezvous. Shameless.

Regardless of my doubts, my body's determined to go. Is it muscle memory left over from college—Ethan says "jump," I say "how high"? Maybe it's a petty way of getting one over on Sadie, an equally old impulse, ingrained in us after years of competing for his attention. I dither, half of me determined to break the pattern, half of me knowing if I don't go it will haunt me.

A soft knock on my door makes me freeze. *Damn!* I tear off my jacket, shuck off my boots, and dive onto the bed, seizing a book from the pile of my half-unpacked detritus and propping it on my knees. At the last second I remember the scarf and yank it off with such force I almost strangle myself.

"Come in." I try to hit just the right note of sleepy confusion.

I pray it's Em. Of course it's Sadie. Her black wavy hair is as fresh and perfect as ever, her makeup pristine. I will never understand women who glide through the world unsullied, fresh and fragile as blossoms.

"Hey." She leans against the doorframe, blocking the exit.

"Hi." I give her a puzzled look. "Everything okay?"

"Fine, yeah." She looks around. "Wanted to make sure you've got everything you need."

"Oh, yeah, of course. You're a great hostess. Amazing meal, beautiful house—everything's sublime." I'm babbling. The longer she lingers, the more anxious I become. A glance at the ornate clock by the bed confirms I've waited too long already. In three minutes it will be midnight. I can run all the way and I'll still be late.

She goes to a framed photo above the dresser. It's of Dakota and Sadie at the beach. Dakota's maybe seven or eight. She's got one arm slung around Sadie's neck, looking cocky and adorable. Sadie's gazing at the photographer with a look of unadulterated bliss.

"Hard to believe she's seventeen, huh?" There's tenderness in her words. Warmth.

"Guess the clichés are true. They grow up fast."

She lets out a wry laugh. "God, you have no idea."

"No. I don't."

She turns to me, her face tinged with pity. "Do you think…are you planning to have kids?"

The question feels invasive. I learned a long time ago, though, people can be real dicks when it comes to my womb and how I plan to use it.

"No." It's a toneless monosyllable.

"I understand if you don't want to talk about it."

I blink at her. "Good."

She looks taken aback. "June, you seem…"

"What?"

"A little bitter."

I swallow hard. Bitter, cold, barren. These are words thrown at women without children. Like we're a Montana winter. Either we're to be pitied or we're to be blamed, depending on how much choice we had in the matter.

The clock looms in my peripheral vision. I don't dare look at it. If I show the slightest weakness, she'll take a seat on the bed and settle in for a cozy chat. Sadie's always taken pride in her ability to draw people out. In restaurants and bars, she'd ask the servers inappropriate, probing questions about their lives. When she saw a homeless person panhandling, she'd badger them for fifteen minutes about how they'd ended up there.

"I just want you to know, I'm over it." She smooths the bedspread with one hand, though it's already flawless. "Our history, I mean. It's just that. Ancient history."

"Oh. Okay."

She frowns. "Does that come as a surprise?"

I hear Em's voice in my head: *She doesn't dislike you. She won.*

"Not really."

"You sure you're okay? You seem uncomfortable."

"I'm fine. Just tired." If she thinks she can bully me into some heartfelt girl talk, she's mistaken. "See you in the morning?"

Sadie's patronizing smile melts the icy guilt in my stomach. If she treats Ethan like this, no wonder he's arranging a secret rendezvous. The second I think it I feel like a bitch.

"I get it. Hope you wake up in a more receptive mood. Tomorrow, I'm determined to find out what's up with you." Her tone is teasing, but I can still hear the sickly-sweet condescension.

"Tomorrow," I agree.

She closes the door at last.

I force myself to sit there, motionless, for a count of five. Then I pull on my boots and jacket. I reapply Lady Danger.

As I MAKE my way toward the beach house, I can't ignore my sense of foreboding. There's a thin crescent moon hanging over the water. Clouds drift past, moving fast; when they cover the moon, the world goes dark. The trees lining the driveway emit a clean scent. Underneath all that freshness, though, I detect the perfume of decay. I pull my flashlight from my pocket, aiming its ghostly beam at the impenetrable gloom.

This is spookier than I'd imagined. Of course, my

nerves are already shot after my narrow escape from Sadieville. I recall her superior smile, the maternal condescension as she interrogated me about kids. Could she really be that clueless? Why in God's name would I confide in her about something so personal? It reminds me how much I despise her calculating sweetness. That cloying, angelic smile. The impeccable black gloss of her hair. The way she lulls her victims into a trance with her high-end world where nothing is ever anything but perfect. Her blithe assumption that you'll spring open like a jack-in-the-box the second she cranks your handle. She doesn't disarm people; she manipulates them. It's another testimony to her insensitivity that she doesn't see the difference.

My anger propels me down the dark road. I follow the sound of lapping surf, the blacktop springy under my boots. A creature scurries through the underbrush, making me flinch. I point my flashlight at the woods. It's full of darting shadows and eerie shapes.

A sound to my right spins me around. Movement in the trees. This time it's way too loud for a raccoon or a possum. I freeze, turning off my flashlight. Even standing perfectly still in the dark, I feel exposed on the road. The dense forest could hide anything—or anyone. The little hairs on my arms rise. I swear I can feel someone watching me.

A twig snaps. Are those footsteps?

Heart pounding, I turn on my flashlight again and point it in the direction of the sound. I sweep the forest for several seconds before the beam catches on legs. I jerk the light up and illuminate a man's face just as he winces away from the harsh beam.

I scream—one short, sharp yelp of panic.

The figure emerges from the trees, a looming silhouette in the pale moonlight.

"Sorry. Didn't mean to startle you."

It's been years since I've heard Ethan's voice, but there's no trace of his Scottish brogue in this one. Not Ethan, then.

"You scared the crap out of me." It's too dark, and I'm too disoriented for politeness. "This is private property, you know."

He breathes out, sounding annoyed. "Yeah, I realize that. I live here."

"Oh, I didn't—" I break off, not sure how to finish. "I thought only the MacTavishes and Amy—I didn't realize."

His tone softens a little. "I'm the landscaper. I live in the yurt." He gestures over his shoulder at the trees.

I remember the round building I caught a glimpse of on our way in. "Got it. Okay."

"My name's Leo." He takes a step closer. In the moonlight, I catch the amused curve of his lips. He's about my age, I think, though it's hard to tell without training my flashlight on his face again.

After an awkward pause, he adds, "And you are? That is, if you don't mind me asking."

"Oh God, sorry. I'm June. Moody."

"June Moody." He ponders this like it's a Zen koan. "Glad to meet you."

I pull my scarf tighter. The breeze coming out of the west is crisp and cold as a glacier. "I'm just out for a walk."

"Okay." He doesn't challenge me on it. "Well, have a good night, then."

"You too."

I catch one last glimmer of his dark eyes in the moonlight. Then he turns toward the trees and melts back into the shadows like a mirage.

I stand there, wondering what this means. Am I going to get ratted out by Leo the gardener? Will he see me walking down the road to the beach house and put two and two together? I try to imagine what he'd say to Sadie.

That's paranoid. Leo doesn't give a damn where I'm going or who I'm sneaking off to meet. He's the landscaper. It's above his pay grade to spy on the guests and report back to his queen bee. At least, I hope it is.

I make my way down the road, trying to shrug off the encounter. As I walk the last few yards down the driveway and hang a sharp left toward the beach house, I spot Ethan. He's standing on the front porch, illuminated by the golden light spilling out from the wall of west-facing windows. It's hard to make out any details, but I recognize him, even though he's barely more than a dark smudge against the stars. I climb the weather-beaten stairs.

"You're late." I can hear the smile in his voice. His Scottish brogue has mellowed some, but it's still there.

He doesn't move to hug me, nor does he even face me. Cool as always. I stand next to him, mirroring his posture. I look out at the water stretching before us like we're a couple of theatergoers waiting for the curtain to rise. The dark outline of the Canadian mountains looms in the distance. The bay ripples beneath the slender yellow moon.

"I almost didn't make it." I try to sound as calm and unruffled as him, but fail. There's a breathlessness there that has nothing to do with my walk.

He glances at me, then fixes his gaze on the water again. "What's the matter, June? Didn't you want to see me?"

I breathe out a nervous laugh. "I'm here, aren't I?"

"You're here."

We listen to the lapping of waves. Bullfrogs add their plaintive croaks to the symphony of crickets.

"Why am I here?" I ask.

He turns to face me. "I wanted to see you. Is that a crime?"

"I got that part, but why?"

His low chuckle makes me smile. I can't turn toward him. My eyes stay locked on the moon.

"You still plunge right into the hard questions, just like you did in freshman English." He sounds amused. He shakes his head, his tone shifting. "We haven't talked properly since you left for Marrakech."

"I saw you at Kimiko's wedding."

"Sadie was attached to me like a conjoined twin that day." The bitterness in his voice makes me wince.

"Is there something you want to tell me?"

He sighs. "I've always regretted not getting a chance to explain."

"What's there to explain? You needed to marry someone. I said no, so you moved on to the next likely candidate."

"That's not—hey, you know it was more complicated

than that." His voice is low and husky. "I was crazy about you. When you turned me down, I was crushed."

"Mistakes were made." I try to sound flippant, but it's not convincing. "Things seem to have worked out for you."

"Did you meet Dakota?" There's a note of reverence in his voice.

"I did. She's lovely."

His face is full of bemused affection, like a man who can't quite believe his luck. "She'll be the death of me."

"Your life looks pretty good, from where I'm standing."

"Some liars are so expert they deceive themselves," he quotes.

I try to remember where I've heard that. "Shakespeare?"

"Austin O'Malley. Poor bastard was poisoned by his pretty young wife, so he should know." He shoots me an apologetic smile. "Sorry. I pepper the conversation with pretentious bon mots when I'm nervous."

"Bon mots," I echo. "I think *that's* more pretentious than anything you've said so far."

"Touché."

"Are you happy?" I have no patience for Ethan's usual flirty banter. I took a risk, coming here. I deserve to know why he summoned me.

He sighs. "Not really. You?"

"Doubt I'd be here if I were." Unable to resist, I turn to face him.

He's wearing a dark wool pea coat, the same style he wore back in college. His face is etched with lines, but not many. He's cut his hair short, a little spiky, the auburn now threaded with a few strands of gray at the temples. Those pale blue eyes drink me in, dancing with humor.

"I've missed you." He brushes my hand with his, a touch so light it could be the wind. Then he stuffs both hands into his pockets.

"Could have fooled me," I say.

"What do you mean?" He looks unsure.

I shrug. "It's been—what? Seventeen years? Pretty long silence for a guy who's pining."

"That goes both ways."

"Except you're the one married with a kid." I flash him a rueful grin. "So not really."

"Double touché." He turns back to face the view. So do I. We say nothing.

"How are things with Sadie?"

"Oh, you know." He runs a hand through his hair. "Wretched."

"Didn't get that impression from her."

He looks at me. "You two talked?"

"I could hardly walk into her house and give her the silent treatment."

"About us, I mean?"

"She cornered me for a cozy chat. Though I think she wanted to focus on my failings, not hers. That's why I'm late." I shake my head, feeling another trickle of resentment at the memory of her imperious smile.

"It's all about appearances with Sadie." The bitterness in Ethan's voice is unmistakable. "The important thing is keeping up the illusion."

"Is that true for you, too?" I don't know why I keep probing. He's given me his answer. The whole situation suddenly strikes me as unseemly—meeting him here in secret, asking him pointed questions about the death of his marriage. I'm a vulture, great black wings outstretched, hooked beak ready to tear into gore. It's not a version of myself I cherish.

"It's not really about keeping up appearances for me. I love Dakota more than anything in the world." The sadness in his eyes seems to illuminate his whole face. "Leaving Sadie would mean leaving her."

"There's this thing? It's called joint custody. You should look into it."

He breathes out, his cheeks puffing with air. "Sadie and Dakota are a bad combination. I've always been the buffer between them." He searches the sky. "Dakota's had her share of issues. The last thing I want to do is add to those."

I consider this. "She's seventeen, right? When she goes away to college or moves out…"

"She's off to college in the fall, actually. She's very bright." There's warm paternal pride in his voice. The subtext isn't lost on me, either. If Dakota's off on her own, his reasons for staying with Sadie dissipate.

I hold his gaze, feeling light-headed. "So that changes things?"

He nods.

"Are you saying you're leaving her?" It's blunt, to the point, but I see no reason to be coy.

"I am." He faces me.

I turn away.

The wind picks up again, combing through the high branches with a soft sigh.

"You remember our picnics on Chuckanut Island?" The smile's back in his voice.

I laugh. "How could I forget?"

"You were so nervous." Almost to himself, Ethan adds, "I loved that about you."

"You loved how nervous I was?" I knock my elbow against his. "Or you loved how intimidated I was by you?"

"Both."

I groan. "The sophisticated graduate student, wielding his power over the fidgety little undergrad."

He lowers his voice. "Sadie and I were never going to make each other happy. You and I always could, without even trying."

It's a scene I've fantasized about for years. Yet, now that it's happening, a part of me sits in the audience, watching the actors say their lines, analyzing the blocking. I can't tell if this is a defense mechanism or my intuition warning me to beware.

The warmth in Ethan's eyes turns to questions. He reaches to touch my face. His fingers trace the line of my jaw. The breeze combs through our hair, a cold sigh.

My mind's churning. God knows I've never felt deep, visceral joy with any man but Ethan. Nobody's ever slashed that joy to ribbons the way he did, either. When I turned down his proposal and he started seeing Sadie, it knocked the wind out of me. I left for Marrakech days after they got engaged, feeling raw and disillusioned. I watched from afar as Sadie and Ethan's life together blossomed into a rare, exotic flower.

"I guess you traveled the world, just like you

planned." I can't read his tone; is it accusatory, or is that my imagination? "Where all did you go?"

"I was gone three years. Spent about a month in Morocco, then up to Spain and Portugal. I got a job in Ireland, saved enough to spend a summer in Romania. Eventually I made my way over to Asia—Japan, mostly, teaching English."

"Sounds like quite an adventure."

"It was." I'm wary, unsure where this is going.

"Did you find what you were looking for?"

I sigh. "I went there to become a writer, so…maybe not. Still waiting to produce the Great American Novel."

"Are you still writing?"

"I am." I shrug. "Maybe I'm just not that good."

"We both know talent and commercial success aren't the same thing."

I wonder if this is meant as a dig at Sadie.

I change the subject. "Why are you staying down here?"

"It's a girls weekend." He shrugs. "I'd just be in the way. Besides, Sadie and I don't live together very well. I stay here most of the time. Pretty much all the time, unless she has guests who need to see her marriage is as perfect as everything else." He lowers his voice. "Will you come inside?"

I hesitate. I don't know what Ethan has in mind here—a weekend fling while his wife sleeps just up the road? The idea is gross, flattering, and insulting at the same time.

"I don't think that's a good idea," I murmur.

Our eyes lock. My body still responds to him, but in a muted way. He speaks to that eighteen-year-old part of me, and old habits die hard. My younger self feels the old thrill, the triumph of having won his approval, his desire. After Pete's rejection, being wanted by anyone is a welcome balm to my bruised ego. But the truth is, I don't know this man anymore. I'm not here to rekindle my old feelings for Ethan. What I need to do is put all that behind me.

"I'd like to make peace with Sadie." I surprise myself with the simple clarity of this.

"Do what you have to do," he says. "That's the June Moody way, right?"

I don't know what this means. I study his face, trying to figure him out. I know if I linger, though, he'll kiss me, and I'm not sure I want to risk that. Not when I'm this vulnerable, this hungry for validation. It's too dangerous. I turn and start to walk away.

"June?"

I turn back to face him. "Yes?"

"It's good to see you again."

"Good to see you, too," I say, knowing it's at least in part a lie. *Confusing* would be a much more accurate description.

I pull out my flashlight and begin the walk back to Sadie's.

FOUR

THE NEXT MORNING, Sadie gives us a full tour of the house. We traipse through the indoor basketball court, the wine cellar, the screening room, the indoor lap pool, the five guest rooms, the spalike bathrooms, the state-of-the-art kitchen, the ceramics studio, writing studio, yoga studio, and meditation studio. By the end, I'm sweating with jealousy. I wish I could find something tacky about it, something off, but everything is so exquisitely curated it's impossible to roll my eyes at anything.

As we walk, Sadie discusses the many charities she's formed, from meditation classes for inner-city youth to the self-sustaining organic farms she founded in Bangladesh. I feel like a money-grubbing lowlife by comparison. My charitable donations begin and end with Girl Scout cookies, and that's only because I'm addicted.

At last we reach the pinnacle of the tour, the pièce de résistance: Sadie's shoe room. It's a wonderland of Louboutin, Alexander Wang, Jimmy Choo. The colors stretch along the shelves, a candy store of shiny temptation. The lighting is impeccable. I never want to leave.

"My God," Kimiko breathes. "I could live here."

"It's just a shoe room." Sadie's effort to deflect comes

off a little insincere. She acts like all of this is silly, like her money and everything it buys isn't worth discussing.

"Isn't it hard to decide, with all these choices?" Em, whose fashion sense has always been decidedly functional, looks bewildered.

Sadie shrugs. "I thrive on options."

"Too bad we don't wear the same size." Amy plops down on a velvet settee, out of breath. "I'd be rolling in hand-me-downs."

"What's this?" Em's wandered into the walk-in closet. It's filled mostly with Sadie's clothes, though there's a small section for Ethan. Em's pointing at a safe on the wall with a combination lock.

"Oh, that's Ethan's gun safe." Sadie rolls her eyes. "He grew up hunting, so it seems normal to him. I hate even having that thing in the house, but at least this keeps it secure."

"What kind of gun?" Kimiko looks intrigued.

Sadie waves a hand in the air, dismissive. "Who knows? Some kind of handgun, I think. A Smith and Wesson, maybe?"

We all stare at the safe.

"Anyway." Sadie claps her hands together. "We should get going. I have a very special day planned, and it doesn't take place in my closet."

"What's on the agenda, captain?" Kimiko's fixated on a particularly gorgeous leather jacket, one hand caressing the buttery suede.

Sadie beams like a game show hostess revealing the big prize. "First, we kayak around Deception Pass, over to the other side of the island."

"Kayaking?" I've explored the sound a little by boat,

but that was years ago, in college. As I recall, kayaking can be pretty strenuous. The five of us went a few times, and even at twenty it left my muscles aching. I glance at Amy, still slumped on the settee. "I've heard the tides are pretty intense around Deception Pass."

Sadie dismisses my concern with a wave of her hand. "Don't worry. You'll love it."

Amy looks slightly sick.

I try again. "Sounds a bit grueling, and I don't know if Amy should be—"

"Exercise is the best thing for her. Of course, we could take the *Dakota*, but—"

"The *Dakota*?" Em echoes. "What's that?"

"Our boat."

Behind her, Amy mouths the word *yacht*.

I suppress a grin. Of course they have a yacht. Why am I surprised?

Sadie continues, oblivious to our wide-eyed awe. "Kayaks are so nimble, you can see a lot more wildlife, and they're quiet—it's just you and the tides. We spend most of our time in the water—surfing, kiteboarding, kayaking—we're always out there doing something. It's a way of life around here."

The four of us are silent. I can't help thinking it's probably not a way of life for the poor schmucks who have to drag their asses to work every day.

Amy still looks queasy. "I don't know, Sadie, I'll have to pee every five minutes, and—"

"This is your weekend, sweetie." Sadie wraps an arm around her. "We can't abandon our guest of honor."

Amy's expression is easy enough to read: *If it's my weekend, why am I being forced to kayak?* She swallows hard, though, nodding her acquiescence like a scolded child.

"Maybe Amy has a point," I say, glancing around at the others.

"Come on, ladies. Face your fears!" Sadie cries, her tone a little brittle.

It used to be our battle cry, back in the day. Before we did something crazy, like launching into a keg stand or leaping from a too-high ledge into a freezing lake, we'd yell, "Face your fears!" Sadie invokes it now to shame us into going along with her plans.

Sadie catches my eye, and I recognize the look from our college days. It's a dare, a challenge.

"Kayaking it is." I lift my chin, ready for anything.

AN HOUR LATER, we're dragging three top-of-the-line kayaks to the water's edge.

"You okay?" Em studies me from behind her aviators.

"Didn't sleep much," I mumble.

"Poor thing." Sadie's closing in fast on my left. I can see her in my peripheral vision, her black hair pristine in the early-morning light. "Was Dakota's old bed uncomfortable? We can move you if you want."

The truth is, I spent hours tossing and turning, thinking about Ethan. Am I being presumptuous, assuming he wanted to sleep with me? I still can't decide if it's the ultimate in sleazy or just *mostly* sleazy peppered with specks of romance. Am I weak to feel flattered? Is it disgusting that I thought about going back down there to find out what I've been missing all these years?

It's not something I'm proud of. It's just the truth.

"It was perfect. Thanks." I stride toward the water. I can imagine the *what's up with her?* look Sadie's flashing Em, but I don't glance over my shoulder to confirm.

Sadie announces who will share kayaks with brisk efficiency, like a camp counselor assigning us to our bunks. I'm paired with Amy, Em with Dakota, and Sadie with Kimiko.

As I survey the water, my bravado from earlier starts to fade. I'll be responsible for the safety of a heavily pregnant woman, and I haven't been in a kayak since college. I recall the water under the bridge we crossed yesterday. The tides looked muscular and turbulent, even from a distance.

"Are you sure about this, Sadie?" I glance at Amy, who looks unhappy.

"It's fine. I kayaked when I was pregnant all the time."

I spot Leo coming out of his yurt, a mug of coffee in one hand.

Sadie follows my gaze. "Oh, that's Leo. My landscaper."

I give her a look of polite interest, pretending this is news to me. Then I change the subject back to the kayaking question. "I'm just not sure I feel comfortable—"

"Seriously, June. I won't let anything happen to you."

"I'm not worried about myself," I say, defensive. "It's more about Amy."

Sadie's smile is a weird blend of benevolence and warning. "You think I'd let something happen to Amy?"

"No, of course not. It's just—"

"Not to put too fine a point on it, June, but I've been watching out for Amy most of my life." Sadie raises her eyebrows, that patronizing smirk still in place. "I think I know what she can handle."

Her blithe confidence makes me second-guess my fears. Kayaking can be a cake walk in calm water, so maybe I'm being a baby. I can't stop thinking about the texture of the water under the bridge, though. It looked dangerous.

"So the tide's not too—" I begin, but she cuts me off.

"I know these waters inside and out, okay? The current's no big deal this time of day."

Amy's expression has gone from uneasy to mutinous. "I'll still have to pee the whole time."

Sadie smiles tightly. "We're not going far. Honestly, ladies, where's your spirit of adventure? It'll be like old times. Remember how much fun we used to have?"

I want to suggest that Sadie should ride with Amy. I'd feel less nervous if I wasn't responsible for her safety. It would sound rude, though, like Amy's a burden. This is supposed to be Amy's weekend. The last thing I want to do is make her feel like a liability.

Sadie punches the air. "Face your fears."

I nod, defeated. "Okay then. You're the boss."

AMY AND I fall behind immediately. We trail in their wake, the distance between us and the others growing with every stroke. Amy's barely paddling.

"You mind if I just—?" She turns around in her seat and sits backward, resting her calves on the space between her seat and mine, her legs sprawled. She squirms around, trying to get comfortable. "I have to stretch out."

"No problem."

Amy turns her face to the sun, resting her head on

the curve of the hull. "Great idea, going on an epic kayak adventure. Never mind that I'm profoundly uncomfortable back here."

"Preaching to the choir," I say. My biceps already burn, but I'll be damned if we're going to fall any farther behind. This will not go down in history as the day June and Amy had to be rescued by the Coast Guard.

"You and Em have the right idea, skipping the whole kid thing." This seems like a non sequitur, but maybe it's not. I suppose, with that belly, motherhood is on a constant loop in her brain. "Kimiko's son is a holy terror. Have you met him?"

I shake my head no.

"Twelve years old with a mouth on him like Lil Wayne." She shakes her head. "I can't believe I got knocked up a few years shy of forty. Leave it to me."

"Is it too rude to ask about the dad?"

She flashes a wry smile. "One-night stand with some kid in his twenties. I think his name was Derek, but it might have been Darren. Met him at a bar in Walla Walla."

Same old Amy—a belligerent nonconformist. She used to brag about her white-trash background. Apparently, her mom was the black sheep of the family. Sadie's mom was the successful one. When Amy's parents died and she moved in with Sadie's family, she went from a double-wide in Tacoma to a stately colonial in a posh suburb of Seattle. Maybe it's a defense mechanism, but shocking people has always been Amy's favorite pastime. Her rebellious streak seemed less awkward in college. Now I can't decide if it's brave or sad.

She closes her eyes again, tipping her face back to

soak up the weak sunlight reaching through the clouds. "Any second now, all hell's going to break loose."

"How so?"

"Sleep deprivation, postpartum, the whole nine yards." She sighs. "And we both know Sadie's going to colonize my offspring."

I snort with laughter. A fine mist hangs on the water. We drift into a patch of it. Though there's sweat trickling between my breasts and down my spine, I shiver in the sudden cold.

Amy flexes her bare toes. "You know it's true. I'm not going to have any say in how this kid is raised. Sadie's planted a flag in my womb."

"It's your kid." I don't know why I'm saying this. Amy's dependent on Sadie in every way. If she wants to go on living rent-free as Sadie's loyal sidekick, she's right—Sadie will micromanage her child's upbringing.

It sucks, but what are her options? Amy's got no degree, no work experience. Her last semester in college, her depression got so bad she barely got out of bed for over a week. Her roommate decided she was suicidal, so she called 911. Amy ended up in a psych ward. She never graduated.

Amy runs a hand over her belly. "Dakota's got one foot out the door. Now Sadie's transferring all her perfect-mommy zeal to a new victim."

"That doesn't sound healthy."

Amy puffs out a breath. "Welcome to Sadiesota. It's a police state, but it's a pretty one."

It's hard to gauge how serious Amy's being. Maybe she's just going for maximum shock value, playing up the drama. I paddle along the shore, around the bend.

We fall into silence, just the lapping of the water against the boat and the gentle swish of my oars for company. A flock of pelicans fly overhead in a V formation. One plunges into the water with a splash, emerging triumphant with a fish wriggling in its beak. A cold wind pushes offshore, bringing with it a damp smell of moss and pine, a clean perfume that revives me as it caresses my sweaty limbs.

We come around another bend and I see it: Deception Pass. The other kayaks are small dots in the distance now. The bridges are even more impressive from this angle. They stretch in two curving, luxurious arcs, intersected by a tiny wooded island in the middle. The late-morning sunlight paints the water gold. Swirls and eddies rush through, forming small waves here and there. They look powerful, dangerous, but also beautiful.

I peer up at the tiny figures standing at the railing, gazing down into the dark water. What would it be like to fall from that high? For a second I can feel it, the wind against my face, the flat black water getting closer and closer every second.

"God. That's gorgeous," I breathe.

Amy casts a quick look over her shoulder. "It's a bridge. Don't know why everyone's always losing their mind over it."

A dark shape passes under our kayak. I think of the orcas out here, the dolphins and humpback whales. It was probably just a seal, but I paddle a little faster just the same.

"How was it seeing Ethan again?" Amy doesn't look

at me when she says it. She keeps her eyes closed, head lolling back like she's planning to nap.

Whoa. Where did that come from? "I—why would you—?"

"Come on. Of course you'd want to see him. He asked you to marry him, after all. A girl doesn't forget that, even after fifteen years."

"How did you know—?"

"Don't be naïve. I'm woven into the fibers of this family. For better or worse. I know things." Her eyes stay closed, like all of this is no big deal, but I hear the tension behind her words. "I saw you walking down to his place last night."

I hesitate too long to make a denial plausible. I sigh. "He asked me to meet him."

"So what's going on with you two?" Her voice is tight with disappointment.

"Nothing happened. I was too curious not to go, that's all."

"Did you satisfy your curiosity?" There's a sarcastic edge to her question I don't appreciate.

"It was weird, if you want to know the truth. Whatever happened between us is in the past." I try to give my words a *case closed* finality. I can't deal with navigating the current and fending off her barbed questions all at once.

Amy must get the message, because she throws a lazy glance over her shoulder and changes the subject. "So, there's a place up here you've got to watch for."

"Yeah?" My stomach clenches with nerves as the current picks up speed.

We're moving much faster all of a sudden. The others have already disappeared around the bend. Screw Sadie and her assurances. *Face your fears.* Easy for her to say, when she's got an able-bodied copilot.

Amy shows no sign of picking up a paddle.

The current is no longer gently tugging us forward. It grabs us by the bow and yanks us toward the pass with startling power. Up ahead, swirls and eddies beckon. We're approaching them more quickly than ever, the kayak tipping dangerously as the tides grow more turbulent.

"See that part over there?" Amy jerks her chin toward the cliffs to our right. They're covered in barnacles. Dark strands of seaweed cling to their jagged shapes. "Kayakers call that the Room of Doom."

"Good to know," I mumble.

Amy finally sits up straight and turns around to face the rough water ahead. She still doesn't put her paddle in the water, though. She's calm, resigned. I wonder about her meds. Em mentioned they had to adjust them to keep the baby safe. Right now she has the laconic ease of someone on tranquilizers, observing the dangerous water like it has nothing to do with her.

Next thing I know, we're swirling, caught in a whirlpool. We list so far to the right I'm sure we'll tip over. Without warning, we're spit out of the whirlpool and shot toward the rocks. Heart hammering, I paddle hard, trying to steer us away from their sharp edges. My muscles burn with effort. I hear a scraping sound as the hull drags along stone.

Just as suddenly, we're released. We've passed under the bridge and we're floating in a tranquil, glossy stream.

"Fuck," I breathe, blinking.

Amy goes back to lounging, a serene smile playing on her lips. "Good work, Moody. Way to keep us alive."

I bark out a laugh and keep paddling.

IN THE AFTERNOON, we go to a spa by the water. It's a soothing, elegant place—lavender scented, with gorgeous views. I run into Sadie in the waiting room. She must be between appointments. Since I've finished my one treatment, I have some time to kill. I'm still pissed at her about this morning's kayaking adventure. Nobody else seems weird about it, but I can't stop thinking about how she put Amy and me in danger. It takes a special kind of hubris to endanger your friends without even realizing you've done it.

I try to avoid Sadie as I navigate the plump linen couches. A dozen women dressed in fluffy white robes read magazines and sip cucumber water. Sadie calls my name, making it impossible to ignore her. Reluctantly, I make my way to her. She pats the spot on the couch beside her. I sit.

"How was your massage?" she asks, her eyes bright.

"Great. I was just heading for the steam room," I say, trying to stand.

She grabs my hand and pulls me back down. "June, sweetie, I can tell you're upset. What's going on?"

I sigh. Okay, looks like we're doing this. I glance around at the nearly full waiting room. Tranquil spa music piped through invisible speakers plays at a restful volume. I keep my voice low, feeling self-conscious. "If you want to know the truth, I'm a little irked about this morning."

"This morning?" Sadie looks puzzled. "Why, what happened?"

Her cluelessness only intensifies my frustration. "Amy and I almost capsized under the bridge. It was sketchy. You didn't even hang back to coach us."

"Oh." Her eyes widen, all innocent surprise. "I'm sorry. You used to be pretty athletic. I figured you could handle it."

"I did handle it. I just don't think it's cool that you'd put us both at risk like that." My voice rises, in spite of my effort to stay calm. "Even if you don't give a shit about us, maybe you could spare a thought for the baby."

Several women glance up from their magazines, their mouths puckered in distaste.

Am I overreacting? Maybe. At this point, though, it feels good to call her on it. Still, I need to chill; my breathing is shallow, my face is hot.

Her eyes go cold and still. "That's one of the worst things anyone's ever said to me."

"Somehow I doubt that."

Sadie leans in closer and hisses into my ear. "You think that was hard? Did you have to paddle once or twice? Were you worried about Amy? Well, imagine doing it for thirty years, June. Alone. Without help from any of you."

So it *was* intentional. I think back to Em's theory that this weekend is Sadie's version of a cry for help. I wish she'd just come out and ask for that help, not play games with our lives to make her point. This is pure Sadie, though—a passive-aggressive attempt to prove that life with Amy is harder than it looks.

I stand. I'm not having this conversation. Not here. I

walk away from her, wishing—even as I do—that she hadn't gotten the last word.

I TAKE REFUGE in the steam room. The steam is so thick it's hard to see if anyone else is in here. I hesitate as the door closes behind me, trying to get oriented.

Is it my imagination, or can I feel another presence here? My skin crawls with the feeling of eyes on me. I clutch my towel, blinking against the clouds of steam. I think about leaving, but I'm still too riled from my conversation with Sadie. I need to relax before I face the others again.

As my eyes adjust, a face emerges from the mist, navy-blue eyes fixed on me. I let out a little gasp of surprise.

"Hi. I couldn't see you at first," I murmur, embarrassed.

"Hey." Dakota's tucked away in the far corner, on the top bench, where the steam is thickest.

Sipping my cucumber water, I take a seat in the middle of the same bench, not wanting to invade her space, but also not wanting to seem antisocial. The spa music sounds too loud, Asian flutes meant to be relaxing; to me they sound menacing and dissonant.

I sneak a sideways glance at Dakota. She stretches out her long legs. They're slender and surprisingly tanned for a girl who lives in Western Washington. I wonder if her bronzed skin comes from tanning booths or a recent tropical vacation.

"So, I hear you're off to college next year. Where are you going?"

She runs a hand through her hair. "We're kind of in a standoff on that."

"What do you mean?"

"I've decided on UCLA." She says it with a stubborn edge, her jaw tightening with determination. "That's where my boyfriend goes."

"Oh, cool. The guy you hung out with yesterday?"

"Uh-huh. He's in med school." There's a note of pride in her voice.

"An older man, then."

"Not much. He's twenty-two," Dakota says. "I work at a summer camp on Orcas Island. We met there."

I do the math. Five years between them. Not much in the big picture, but a world of difference at their age.

"Mom thinks Ben's too old for me. Never mind that she and Dad are six years apart." Her face becomes a mask of indifference. "She wants me to go to Yale."

"Great school. Can't argue with that."

Her eyes narrow. "It's my life."

"Right, of course, but you can't blame her for—"

"She refuses to pay for UCLA, and because of her income, I don't qualify for scholarships. It's BS."

"That does sound frustrating," I say, trying to be diplomatic.

"It's so unfair. Every time I try to talk to her about it, she gets all salty." Her voice rises enough to echo off the glass walls.

"I'm sure you guys will work it out." I say this softly, trying to soothe her. I nudge the conversation in a different direction. "What will you study?"

"I haven't decided yet. I'm debating between screen-writing and acting."

She's got so much star quality, I can see her making a name for herself. She has just the right cocktail of fragility and swagger.

"I got my MFA at UCLA," I say.

"Shut up." She bugs her eyes at me.

"True story. It's a great school. You're going to love it."

She gazes at me with something like respect. "That was a long time ago, huh?"

"I guess." I can't help but register the sting. A pang of self-consciousness makes me look down. My clean, makeup-free face feels too exposed. I fold my arms over my bare breasts, not as perky as they once were. The steam has no doubt turned my naturally pinkish complexion the attractive shade of a stewed tomato.

"The professors you studied with probably aren't around anymore." Dakota looks apologetic.

"It wasn't *that* long ago." I change the subject, embarrassed by the defensive edge in my voice. "How does Ben like it?"

"He loves it." She stretches her arms up, totally at ease in her body. "If I can just get my mom to let go of her Ivy League obsession, everything will be perfect."

I think of Sadie cornering me just now in the waiting room, the ugly glint of determination and anger in her eyes. I can see a similar stubborn streak in her daughter. They're stuck in a battle of wills. I can't help but wonder if Sadie MacTavish has finally met her match.

FIVE

I WALK DOWN the road toward the beach house before
dinner, just as sunset starts staining the rain clouds a
fiery orange. I need to clear my head.

Before I get to Ethan's house, I step off the paved
driveway into the forest of cedar and pine. I'm not ready
to turn back, but I don't want to run into Ethan either.
My encounter with him last night left me uneasy, especially now that I know Amy saw me. Did she tell Sadie?
I don't think she would, but the idea makes me nervous.

There's still some light left in the sky, but in the
woods it's much darker. I pull out my flashlight and
find a deer path through the trees. Whispery cobwebs
slither against my skin. Occasionally a bramble reaches
out and snags on my jeans, forcing me to stop and dis-
entangle myself. After a few more minutes of walking,
I spot the landscaper's yurt through the trees. Its curved
canvas walls glow a warm gold. The skylight sits at the
apex of the circular roof like a lozenge of amber. I stand
there motionless a moment, listening. I can make out
thin strains of music, something mellow and acoustic.

I've almost decided to turn around when the door of
the yurt flies open. I fumble to turn my flashlight off,
hoping I won't be seen.

Sadie tears out onto the small porch, her whole body
tense. "Fine! Stay miserable. That seems to be what

you want." She pauses a moment, as if waiting for a response. When she doesn't get one, she charges down the stairs. I catch a glimpse of her face in the dim light. Every muscle is rigid with anger, her mouth clamped tight, her dark hair blown back by a breeze.

She heads straight for me. Though I've got nothing to feel guilty about, for some reason my brain starts spitting out excuses for why I'm here. I stand there, frozen in place, holding my breath. At the last second Sadie veers right and plunges into the forest, surefooted as a cat in the darkness.

I exhale, relieved. The moment I just witnessed felt too private, too loaded. It seemed a lot more complicated than a meeting between employer and employee. I look back toward the yurt and see Leo standing on his porch, his brow furrowed. He watches Sadie's silhouette as it slips deeper into the shadows. Then he turns and stares right at me.

"Hey." I raise a hand lamely, stepping into the light so he can see me better.

"June Moody." He says it slowly, without a trace of surprise, like my arrival was expected.

"Just out for a walk." Again, lame, but I feel obligated to justify my presence.

He smiles. "Is that your only line?"

For a second, I have no idea what he's talking about. Then I recall our conversation last night, the amused curve of his lips when I babbled my excuses for traipsing around the estate at midnight. He must think I'm a real piece of work.

"You want to come in?" He shivers in his T-shirt. "It's cold out here."

I take a step closer, intrigued in spite of myself. "You don't mind?"

"I wouldn't ask if I did."

As I cross the lawn and climb the stairs, I glance back at the forest. Sadie's long gone. Either that, or she's watching from the woods. For some reason this thought makes my heart spin inside me like a weather vane. I hate the idea of her tracking my movements with those stormy eyes.

"You want a cup of tea?" he asks. Once the door's shut, the warmth of the round room encircles us. "Or a drink? All I have is whiskey."

"Whiskey, please." My nerves are on edge, and I need something to slow my racing pulse.

He pours out a few fingers of Maker's and hands me the glass. The room is simple yet cozy, lit by the faint amber glow of the floor lamp. A Persian rug dominates the space. There's a primitive kitchen to my right, a bed and a couple armchairs to my left. I take in the color scheme, sapphire blues and ocean greens, with accents of brass and gold. It's the only place on the whole estate that doesn't look curated by Sadie. I breathe a sigh of relief, comforted by its slightly shabby simplicity.

"Is Sadie okay?" I hope it comes out light rather than nosy.

He sips his whiskey, sitting in a beat-up leather chair near the potbelly stove. He gestures toward the seat opposite, an olive-green velvet wing chair that hugs me when I sit in it.

"She seemed upset," I add unnecessarily.

"You guys are pretty close?"

"We've known each other a long time," I hedge.

"But are you close?"

"Not especially." With one hand, I lift the whiskey to my lips and take another drink. "We never really got along."

"Yet you're here." Leo leans forward. His shoulder muscles move beneath his threadbare T-shirt. It's distracting.

"I wanted to support Amy."

He sips his drink, eyes on the ceiling. "I've known you all of five minutes, but I call bullshit on that."

I laugh, surprised. "Okay, fine. I was supposed to go camping with my boyfriend, but he left me for a twentysomething hottie in Amsterdam. I couldn't face wallowing in my apartment alone." I'm baffled by how easily the admission slips from my lips.

"Now that," he says, raising his glass, "sounds like the truth."

We clink glasses and drink.

"So what's your deal?" There's something about this man that invites questions. He seems displaced somehow, a shipwreck survivor washed up on a foreign shore. "How did you end up here?"

He looks down, sadness passing over his face. I take the opportunity to study him more closely. His dark hair is a little unruly, with strands that fall forward, brushing his forehead. I marvel at his dramatic bone structure—it's made for this light. The hollows beneath his cheekbones give him a lean, hungry look. The soft glow of the floor lamp turns his brown eyes to honey as he looks up.

"That's a sad story I don't want to tell right now."

"So I have to bare my soul, but you get to remain coy?"

"I do. It's my yurt."

"Can't argue with that." I look around, drinking in the watery colors again, the beams of the yurt exposed like ribs. "It's cozy in here."

He follows my gaze. "It's a refuge."

"You like working for Sadie?"

His eyebrows arch. "Why do you ask?"

"Another question that's off-limits?"

"No. Sorry. The answer is yes and no." He leans back in his chair, running one hand over the armrest. "I love what I do here—the plants, the flowers, the vegetables. I love this place. I don't love the drama."

"What sort of drama?" I lean back in my chair, too, trying to signal casual interest rather than burning curiosity.

He studies me. "How long were you out there?"

"Just now? Not long. Why?"

"These walls are pretty thin." He looks around. "You can hear pretty much everything."

"I showed up right when Sadie stormed out. I swear."

Leo's gaze falls to his drink. "She likes me because I'm discreet. My job depends on it." He breathes out a self-deprecating laugh. "The reality is, I'm too self-absorbed to care about her problems. I just want to grow things and keep to myself."

"Yet you invited me in. Why?"

He looks right at me. "Two reasons: one, I wanted to find out what you overheard."

"And the other?" It comes out barely more than a whisper.

"Keeping to myself gets lonely."

I'm annoyed at the heat I feel creeping from my neck to my hairline. Blushing is not an option. I'm a modern woman. I used to navigate Tinder dates with the confident precision of a CEO running a board meeting. Why am I turning bright red just because this guy says the word *lonely*?

He watches me, his gaze merciless. "You okay?"

"Yeah." I clear my throat. My instinct is to deflect, change the subject to something mundane and safe. At the same time, this unexpected honesty is like a drug. I want more. "So, I'm not allowed to ask about your sad story."

"We've established that." He grins. I notice his dimples; the right one is deeper than the left. There's something sad about his face, even when he's smiling.

"What if I limit myself to basic geographic trajectories? Are you from Washington?"

He shakes his head. For a second I think he's rejecting this question too, but then he answers. "I moved here from New York. I was born in California."

"What brought you here?" I ask.

A shadow crosses his face again, a melancholy so palpable I feel it settle over the room like a storm front. I lean toward him instinctively. Something tells me I have to tread carefully. "That's the part you don't want to talk about."

His gaze locks with mine. "Good guess, June Moody."

BACK AT THE HOUSE, everyone gathers in the kitchen to help with dinner. Sadie's making seared scallops, wild-mushroom ragout, and a roasted beet salad with goat cheese. Kimiko mixes gin and tonics for Em, herself, and me, earning a little huff of annoyance from Sadie, who pours herself a single glass of white wine and nurses it throughout the meal. The three of us have worked our way through most of the remaining Bombay Sapphire by the time we've finished dinner.

Kimiko pulls me outside when the others start on the dishes. I keep her company while she gets stoned, though I don't smoke. The gin's already making me a little sloppy, and I haven't smoked weed in years. Kimiko's wearing a slinky sequined top the color of a mermaid's tail. It shimmers in the yellow light cast by the tasteful garden lanterns. She's always been beautiful, but now there's a new edge to her face, a world-weary exhaustion that makes her simultaneously hard and gorgeous. It's a seasoned face, one marked by disappointment— maybe even tragedy.

I remember how we used to braid each other's hair back in college. She taught me how to do cornrows. Her hair's so thick and kinky, she used to say it was the only way to "tame the beast." It took me ages to get it right. It became a ritual; every Thursday night we'd watch CSI and I'd do her hair. Sometimes she'd do mine too. I loved the feel of the tiny braids lining my head. It was always so calming, feeling the rhythmic tugging at my scalp, though I had to keep reminding her not to pull too tight.

I feel a pang of remorse for all the years I've been out of touch with her. "So, you seeing anyone?" I ask.

She arches her eyebrows. "Not lately. I dated this dude from Tacoma for a few months, but he was a drama queen. Who's got time for that?"

"I hear you."

She grins. "Remember the Moody-Ray?"

I giggle at the memory. Kimiko used to say I had an extra-sensitive BS detector; she called it the Moody-Ray. She claimed I could train it on anyone and see their true nature, an x-ray vision that could get past what they wanted people to see and access their essence.

Kimiko smiles at the sky. "You're the one who figured out that guy Mike was a douchebag."

"Didn't he end up joining a cult?"

"Some kind of survivalist commune in Idaho." Kimiko laughs. I've missed that laugh.

"Should we head back in?" I shiver as a gust of wind pushes through the yard.

"I'm going to chill out here a minute." Kimiko's mouth twists in a wry smile. She lifts the lighter to her pipe and coaxes it to life again. "There's only so much Sadie I can take in one day."

I study her, trying to read her expression. "Is something going on with you guys?"

"No. Not really." She says it too quickly, though, her eyes guarded.

"Oh-kay..." My tone makes it clear I'm not convinced. I wait another beat, but when she doesn't volunteer an explanation, I decide to leave it. "Don't get too cold out here, stoner."

"You'll find me frozen, clutching my pipe and lighter."

Heading back inside, I pause at the glass doors framing the kitchen. Only Em and Sadie remain. Sadie's leaning in close to Em, her face rigid. She's saying something quickly. Through the thick glass, I can't make out her words, but Em leans against the counter, listening. I can see her only in profile, but I can tell she's tense. A muscle in Em's jaw flutters like a trapped butterfly. Whatever Sadie's telling her, it can't be good.

Em leaves the room just as I enter. Sadie frowns when our eyes meet. Concerned, I follow Em.

I catch the door of the guest room before Em can shut herself in. "Hey. What was that about?"

She ignores my question, which is unlike her.

I try again. "Em? What's up?"

"I'm fine," she forces through gritted teeth. "Just getting out of these clothes."

"You're not fine. I can tell."

"Remind me why we came here?" She puffs out a bitter laugh, sagging onto the bed.

I'm trying to work out what Sadie could have said that would make Em so tense. I always thought Em had a remarkably uncomplicated relationship with Sadie. Amy, Kimiko, and I respond to Sadie's moods like puppets dancing around on strings. Only Em is stubborn and grounded enough to weather her manipulations without budging an inch.

"What did she say to you?"

Em stands and starts pulling off her blouse. "She's working on a book."

"Okay…" I rack my brain for how this could possibly upset Em. Sadie's a writer. Working on books is what she does. "And…?"

"It's about me." Em jerks an old T-shirt over her head.

I stare at her, wide-eyed. "About you?"

"She's trying to rebrand herself for an older audience.

She wants to leave fantasy behind. Now she's all about gritty and real." She grimaces. "I guess she doesn't have enough 'gritty, real' material from her own life, so she's decided to borrow mine."

"Oh." This comes as a surprise. Em grew up on Orcas Island with a single mom. She doesn't talk a lot about her past, but I got the impression her childhood on that remote San Juan island was pretty idyllic. "When you say it's about you, do you mean—?"

"Something that happened to me in high school." Em yanks her pants off and stands there. In her stark-white underwear, she looks exposed and vulnerable. She blinks hard. I can see she's fighting tears. "Something that needs to stay buried."

I'm confused. How can there be something major in Em's past that I don't know about? Worse, why would Sadie know about it and not me? I try to push the thought away. It's not useful, dragging my own jealousy into this.

Em seizes a pair of sweat pants and pulls them on. Her every move is impatient, like she can't wait to escape from this conversation. I try not to feel hurt. She's upset with Sadie, not me.

When she's dressed, she turns to me, her eyes fierce with outrage. "I don't want to even *think* about any of that, and now she's dredging it up for the entire planet to examine."

I don't know what to say. I'm so wrong-footed in this conversation.

"She has no right." Em stares at me, her eyes bright. There's a dangerous glimmer there, a savage fear I've never seen before. "I'll sue her if I have to."

"Sue her?" I'm startled. Em's not a litigious person. I can't imagine what would inspire this train of thought.

Em massages her neck, staring at the floor. "No. That would only make it worse."

It's like she's having this conversation with herself. "I can't offer advice if I don't know what you're talking about."

"I never asked for advice." Her voice goes hard.

I hold up my hands. "Okay. My bad. I'll leave you alone." I start for the door, wounded.

Em reaches out and grabs my arm. "Sorry, I didn't mean—"

"No, you're right, I shouldn't have cornered you."

"Shut up." She laughs, breaking the tension. "You were only trying to help. I'm being a bitch. I just..."

"You just what?"

She sighs. "It's such a betrayal."

"Maybe you should be flattered. She hasn't shown any interest in writing about my life."

"It's not flattering," she insists, her tone going flat and hard again. "It's a total breach of trust. Plus it's bringing it all back, you know? I thought I'd put it behind me, dealt with it, but this makes it impossible to move on."

Her eyes beg me to understand. I just wish I knew what the hell she's talking about.

"I have a right to my secrets." Em's jaw tightens. There's determination there, something I'm used to seeing in Em. There's also anger—more than anger, barely contained rage that is completely foreign in her normally calm, reasonable face.

I hold her gaze. "I can't make you tell me if you

don't want to. You know I'm here for you, though, if you change your mind."

She nods, her expression softening. "Thanks."

We make our way back down the stairs. The mood isn't that of a celebratory gathering among old friends. Instead, it feels like we're arming ourselves for battle.

"Screw it," Em says as we head for the kitchen. "I'm sick of this. Let's do some shots."

We've already had a few G&Ts, but I squeeze her hand in solidarity. "That's the spirit."

THE REST OF the night is a series of blurred snapshots: The feel of someone's warm lips closing over mine. Hands in my hair. Golden light all around us.

There are large black patches where everything goes dark.

I can see myself sitting on a beach. The stars pulse with clear, silver joy; I can feel their happiness coursing through my body. There's cold sand between my toes. Somebody is braiding my hair.

A scream, high and sharp, full of panic; my throat aches as I realize it's coming from me.

These are the fragments I'm left with—shards of sensation, broken and scattered. I'm aware only of the gaps, the dark places where my memories crouch, unwilling to be coaxed into the light.

SIX

SUNLIGHT STABS AT my eyes. I squeeze them shut, rolling myself across the bed in search of darkness.

My arm lands on flesh. Both eyes fly open, surprise whipping me into consciousness. I blink. Em lies beside me, her face slack with sleep. She has a long, vivid streak of pink frosting across her cheekbone. She's wearing at least seven necklaces. Bracelets cover her arms. Absently, I rub the frosting off her cheek with my thumb. My head is pounding.

Things must have gotten crazy last night.

I close my eyes, waiting for the evening to come into focus. There's nothing but a blank screen. I wait, figuring alcohol and dehydration have thrust my brain into an underwater torpor.

Bright laughter as gems sparkle in my hands.

A candy-land of shoes—patent leather, suede, satin.

Em wading through a sea of silks and cashmeres.

Then, nothing.

I don't black out. Ever. Sure, I've gotten drunk enough for the memories to go a little thin in places, but I've never forgotten an entire evening. Staring at the blank screen inside my mind, alarm bells scream.

I'm wearing pajamas I don't recognize. They're an exquisite dark-blue silk with cream polka dots. Though I try with all my might, I don't remember putting them on.

Em blinks, opens her eyes with a groan. "Are there tire tracks running up my body?"

"No. Why?"

"I'm pretty sure I got run over by a truck." She sits up, rubbing the sleep from her eyes. "Water. I need water."

"Me, too." I decide to push aside my lack of memory for now, focus on getting hydrated. No need to panic.

Em stumbles out of bed. "God, I've got to pee like a race horse."

"You pee," I say. "I'll get us water." My tongue feels like sandpaper inside my mouth.

"And Advil. For the love of God, unsafe quantities of Advil." She stumbles down the hall toward the bathroom.

It takes me longer than it should to reach the stairs. My balance is off, my head feels like it's exploding, and I can't seem to walk in a straight line. Maybe I'm still drunk. I have to stop every few seconds to lean against something. Steeling myself for the long walk downstairs, I visualize the ceramic water dispenser in the kitchen. That gives me the motivation to keep moving.

But as I make my way toward the stairs, it becomes apparent my legs aren't quite up to the task. They feel shaky, weak. My knees creak; I feel a hundred years old. What kind of hangover is this, anyway? Did we pass out for several decades and wake up senior citizens?

That's when I see it. The dark splatter on the wall at the top of the stairs. I stare at it, entranced.

"Em?" My voice sounds distant, hard to hear over the roar in my ears.

The toilet flushes, and I listen as Em retraces her

steps down the hallway. "Don't wake every—" She stops midword. "What the hell?"

A sick wave of dread sloshes through me as I force my shaky legs to carry me the rest of the way to the wall. It's an undeniable splatter pattern, the color of rust. Somebody's tried, halfheartedly, to scrub it away, but the sinister shape remains, delicate as a cobweb.

"Oh my God." I hug myself. Fear starts to claw at my chest. "Is that—?"

"Blood? I think so." Em searches the wall, her eyes analyzing every inch. "What the hell happened last night?"

My head is throbbing like a snail packed into a too-tight shell. Somebody's cell is blaring an insidious ring tone that sounds suspiciously like "Single Ladies." I want to run back to Dakota's fluffy white bed and erase all of this.

"What's going on?" Kimiko appears downstairs in the foyer, at the bottom of the spiral staircase. She rubs her eyes and stretches. Her nose is badly bruised, and crusted blood forms a crescent around her nostrils.

Amy waddles in her wake, her belly swathed in a filmy yellow nightgown. Her blond hair stands up all over her head like an electroshock patient.

"Jesus, Kimi, what happened to you?" I ask, startled by the sight of her battered face.

She looks baffled. "What do you mean?"

"Your nose. It's all—bloody," Amy says, getting up on her tippy-toes to get a better look.

"God, I don't know." Kimiko touches her nose gingerly, frowns when her fingers come away tinged with blood.

"There's blood up here on the wall," I blurt.

Kimiko's gaze swivels from me to the wall and back again. "What?"

"Come up here, you guys. It looks like blood."

Amy's eyes roam around the foyer and up the stairs, finally landing on us. "What do you mean, blood?"

I groan. "How many times do I have to say it?"

Kimiko and Amy scamper up the stairs and join me at the top. Together, we examine the stain.

Kimiko looks at me. Up close, her injured nose is even more grisly than I thought. "How did it get here?"

"I have no idea," I say.

Amy chews on her lip so hard I'm afraid she'll break the skin. She darts a look down the hallway. "Where's Sadie?"

We all look around.

"Maybe she's still asleep," Em suggests.

Amy shakes her head. "She never sleeps in. She's always up by dawn."

I hurry down the hall and throw open the door to the master bedroom. It's a crazy mess, clothes and shoes everywhere. A memory tugs at me—something about those shoes—but I'm too groggy to make sense of it. Beneath the tangle of clothes, Sadie's bed is still made up, no sign of anyone having slept in it.

With wobbly steps, I return to the top of the staircase. They all stare at me, waiting.

"It's a mess in there. The bed's still made, though. Maybe she crashed out in another room?" Even as I say this, I can hear the tentative upturn at the end, rendering it more question than statement. "Maybe she—"

"No." Amy's adamant. "She's addicted to that bed. It cost like eight grand. She'd never sleep anywhere else."

"What about Dakota?" I search their faces. "Has anyone seen her?"

"I'm sure she's not up," Amy says. "She always sleeps late."

"Go look," I say. "Just to be sure."

Amy obliges, moving down the long hallway, then easing the door to Dakota's room open quietly, peeking in, and shutting it again. She nods as she heads back to us. "Passed out."

"Is Sadie's car here?" I ask, directing my question at nobody in particular.

Em hurries down the stairs and goes to the garage. We wait in silence, each of us trying not to assume the worst. Em returns, breathless, her face flushed. "It's gone."

"Okay, so maybe she went out." Kimiko looks hopeful. "To get groceries or something."

Em's expression is dark as she holds up a phone. "I found this."

Amy sucks in a breath. "There's no way she'd leave without that."

"Where'd you find it?" Kimiko demands.

"On the floor of the garage." Em swallows hard.

We take this in, the silence ominous.

"Okay, let's split up and look around," I say, my heart pounding in my chest. "She's probably hungover. God knows I am. Maybe she dropped her phone last night and Ethan took her car out this morning."

"Something's wrong." Amy's face scrunches up like she's on the verge of tears. "Nothing about this is normal."

Em ignores Amy's mounting distress. "June's right. We should look around. I'll take the east wing."

"I'll take the upper floor," Amy offers.

Kimiko nods. "I can do downstairs."

"I guess that leaves me with the grounds." Secretly, I'm glad for the chance to go outside. The walls feel like they're closing in. Fresh air sounds like heaven.

I hurry back to my room to change out of the foreign pajamas. Though the fabric is softer than anything I've ever owned, something about their whispery texture is creeping me out. I try to picture myself putting them on, but that only agitates me more. The abyss where my memories should be is a bottomless pit. What does this sudden amnesia mean?

I toss them on the bed and pull on jeans, a T-shirt, and my wool sweater.

It takes me a moment after stepping onto the patio to realize it's late morning. The sun is high in the east, casting beams through thick clouds. I breathe in, tasting the morning dew in the back of my throat. I need this—a moment to clear my pounding head, to slow my racing pulse. I walk across the slate deck. There's a wilderness of bushes where the deck ends. I navigate their edges, brushing away damp spider webs.

I make my way toward Ethan's beach house. He must know where Sadie is. There's got to be a logical explanation. We're probably overreacting. Maybe that dark stain on the wall was wine. Sadie's in her yoga studio, or taking an important international call about her clothing collective in Bhutan. It's understandable she'd have things to do. It was Amy's panic that got me worked up.

I traipse up the steps and knock on Ethan's door. It's

glass paneled. When he appears in the foyer, he's wearing only plaid boxers. I blink, trying not to feel weird about seeing him in his underwear. He looks good; I'll give him that. Fit and trim, with the long, ropy muscles of a swimmer.

He swings the door open with a smile. There's a pillow crease along one cheek. "June. I was wondering if I'd get to see you again."

"Sadie's missing." I know it's an awkward non sequitur, but I'm too hungover for small talk. The cool morning air helped sweep the cobwebs from my brain, but now my headache rushes back with eye-watering intensity. Behind Ethan, I catch sight of a sunlit room and pale, overstuffed furniture. It's as tasteful as everything else on this compound.

Ethan's brow furrows in confusion. "What do you mean, missing?"

"Her car's gone, and Em found her phone on the garage floor. There was—" I break off, unsure if I should finish. "Anyway, she wasn't there."

"There was what?" He scratches the back of his head, blinking.

I lick my lips, decide he has a right to know. "Blood. On the wall."

The color drains from his face.

"Or it could be wine," I backpedal. "We're not sure."

He turns and walks away from me, stumbling into the sunlit living room.

I follow Ethan into the house.

He perches absently on the couch, his forehead creased in thought. "Where was it?"

"What, her phone?"

"No." He looks sick. "The blood."

"At the top of the stairs."

He shakes his head, studying the floor, one hand stroking his chin. "And nobody's seen her?"

"We're looking for her now. That's why I'm here. You haven't heard from her?"

His gaze drifts back to my face. "We haven't talked since before you guys got here—Wednesday morning, I think."

"No sign of her, even from a distance?"

"I noticed everyone taking the kayaks out yesterday." He squints at the ceiling. "That's the last time I saw her. I was trying to give you guys space."

"It's probably nothing," I say. "She might be doing yoga or something. Or maybe she went to the store and dropped her phone without realizing."

He looks skeptical. "That's not her style—not with guests in the house. She'd be in the kitchen making everyone breakfast first thing."

Fear trickles through me, cold as seawater. "Amy said it was weird."

"More than weird." Ethan looks haunted. For the first time I notice dark circles under his eyes the color of bruises. Stubble covers his jaw. "It's unheard of. Sadie loves to play hostess. She lives for it."

We say nothing for a moment, only the distant cry of seagulls filtering into the room.

"What about Dakota? Is she okay?" His eyebrows pull together.

I nod. "She's fine—still asleep when I left."

He frowns, but his shoulders relax a little.

"Where do you think Sadie might be?"

His hand goes to his hair again, rubbing the back of his head as if he's trying to jump-start his brain. "I've got no idea."

"Well, maybe someone's found her by now." I take a step toward the door. "I'm going to keep checking the property."

He gets to his feet. "I'll go with you."

"You search the beach," I say. "We've all split up. It'll be faster that way."

"Okay." He nods, still blinking, bleary-eyed.

"It'll be okay," I tell him, though the sick churning in my stomach hints otherwise. "We'll find her."

He offers a weak smile as I head back out the door.

I SPEND TEN minutes trying to track down Leo. He doesn't answer when I knock on the door of his yurt. His truck is missing. I search the woods and the gardens, but there's no sign of him. Up the road, there's a barn and stables. I poke my head inside the barn, the warm scent of hay hanging in the air. I can't find a light switch as I grope at the wall, though, and the shadowy interior is too intimidating to venture into without a flashlight, which I didn't think to bring during the day.

"Sadie?" My voice gets swallowed by the darkness. I try again, louder. "Sadie? You in here?" Only a small scurrying sound at the far end of the barn answers me. A mouse? Suddenly I feel ridiculous; why would Sadie be hiding in a pitch-black barn? I close the door and resume my search.

Three horses stare at me with great liquid eyes as I walk past the stables. I stroke one's long brown face. "Hey there, pretty girl," I whisper, trying to sound friendly. The animal shies away from me, making me flinch.

I call Sadie's name a couple of times, but I only hear the horses' hooves clicking against the stable floor, their tails switching, the buzz of flies. I move on.

Behind the barn is a large workshop, with saws and tables and stacks of lumber. There's another area filled with ceramic pots and great wooden bins. Some of them are full of wood chips, others soil. The scent of sawdust and dirt fills my head, an earthy perfume. A worktable in the corner is partly covered in tiny pots sprouting seedlings. I find myself crossing to it, drawn by its tidy rows. They're arranged close to the window, the green shoots reaching for the glowing panes of light. I study them. There's something hopeful and vulnerable about them that makes me think of Leo. I see him poking the seeds into dark pockets of soil, his strong hands tucking them in like secrets.

There's nobody here, I tell myself. *Keep moving.*

When I walk past the forest that leads back down to the yurt, I stop. A memory's trying to surface. I remember my mouth opening around a scream. I venture off the curving drive into the veil of shade, the moist scent of the woods rising up to meet me—mushrooms and earth and pine needles. I was here last night. Why? I can see my own bare feet, feel the cold mud and the tickle of velvety moss between my toes. I was screaming. Why was I screaming?

The memory of that kiss comes back to me, too. Lust blossoms inside me, hot and low. It's a visceral memory, tongue against tongue, a moan deep in my throat, hands reaching up to grasp hair—but whose? I don't even know if it was a man or a woman. The panic from earlier this morning swirls inside me like a whirlpool. How can I have these memories with nothing to attach them to?

I leave the woods and follow the road to the main house. Maybe someone's found Sadie by now. The clouds have thickened during my search; they're the purplish gray of a fresh bruise. I walk as fast as I can.

"WE NEED TO call 911." Em removes her fingers from the bloodstain and rakes a hand through her hair, brow furrowed.

We're standing on the bridgelike landing of the stairs, with a flight leading up and another curling around below us, leading to the front entryway. Sadie's still missing.

During her search, Em discovered more signs of violence—a hastily scrubbed dark red stain on the wood floor of the landing separating the upper part of the staircase from the lower. A rug that wasn't there before had been used to cover it up. Now the four of us gather on the landing. It's a dramatic space; the walls made of roughly hewn stones curve around the spiral stairs. The effect is reminiscent of a medieval tower, though the blond wood and metal rails give off an industrial vibe.

Amy hovers on the steps, staring at the dark amoeba. "I have a really bad feeling about this."

Em straightens and looks around at us. "Did anyone find any sign of her at all? Any clues about where she could be?"

"No." Kimiko winces. "We kind of trashed this place

last night, though. It looks like a hurricane hit downstairs."

"Are we sure this is blood?" I squat down to look at the stain myself. "Could it be wine or food?"

"I doubt it. Somebody tried to cover it up." Em lets this hang in the air.

"That doesn't mean—somebody might do that for any spill." But my voice is tinged with mounting hysteria. I try again to find some memory of last night, my brain swiveling like a searchlight in every direction, desperate to land on a snapshot, a fragment of conversation—anything. I've got nothing. My heart doubles its tempo. "Does anybody remember spilling or—anything?"

Silence. I wonder if their memories are as scattered and confusing as my own.

"Has anyone seen my phone? I'm calling the cops." Em looks around.

"What's wrong?" A voice at the top of the stairs makes us all jerk around in unison. We must look guilty as sin.

"Dakota. Sweetie." Amy pastes on a sickly smile.

Dakota looks about ten years old, fragile and afraid. "What's happened?"

I surprise myself by hurrying up the staircase toward her. I fix my gaze on her frightened face. "We're not sure. We can't find your mom. Have you seen her?"

She shakes her head. Her hair stands up in staticky strands like a little girl's. Her voice is hoarse with sleep. "I just woke up."

"Who has a phone?" Em heads down the stairs. "I can't find mine."

Dakota looks at Em, her brow furrowing in confusion. "Why are you wearing Mom's jewelry?"

Em looks down at herself with a startled flinch, like she's suddenly realized there are snakes wrapped around her neck and arms. She's still wearing the layers of expensive-looking jewelry—pearls, sapphires, jade. "Jesus, I don't know." She takes it all off, piling it on the hallway table.

"Nine-one-one. Now," Amy orders.

Kimiko shakes her head. "Wait a minute. Let's not call anyone until we get our bearings."

"What do you mean, wait a minute?" Amy's apoplectic. "Sadie's missing. We have to report it."

Kimiko's still wearing her outfit from last night—black jeans and that sequined top. She's at least six or seven inches taller than Amy and she uses it to full advantage, looking down at her. Her wild hair bursts in all directions like a lion's mane. "Adults aren't even considered missing for twenty-four hours."

My eye falls again on the blood splatter at the top of the stairs, just above Dakota's head. It forms a rust-colored constellation. My stomach roils, and for a terrible second I think I might be sick. All the while, there's a high, panicky voice screaming at the back of my brain: *She's dead. She's dead. She's dead.*

Dakota pulls away slowly, looking dazed. She turns to follow my gaze. When she sees the bloodstain, her face turns white.

"She's probably fine," Kimiko says. "Maybe she just needed a moment to herself."

Dakota bursts into ragged sobs. I want to get her away from the bloody wall, so I steer her down the hall toward her old bedroom, the one Em and I woke up in. I wrap an arm around her shoulders, just in case her knees give out. I feel her resisting for a second, but then she goes pliable and allows me to walk her into the room. I guide her toward the bed, pushing aside the lace canopy. She sits, still crying, her face bloodless, almost gray. I kneel before her on the floor.

"Why don't you lie down for a minute?" I notice there's an empty bottle of Jack Daniels in the center of the fluffy duvet. Jesus, what happened last night? I grope again for shards of memory but find nothing new. I seize the bottle and drop it in the trash. Whiskey always gives me the nastiest hangovers, and my head's pounding in that telltale Jack Daniels way, but I have no memory of drinking anything but the glass of whiskey at Leo's and the gin and tonics Kimiko kept pouring. Oh, right, and then there were shots after dinner. Tequila, I think. God, what were we thinking?

Dakota's looking up at me, her face distorted by tears. She's perched on the edge of the bed like she doesn't trust it to bear her weight.

"I'm cold." She's wearing a tiny white camisole and boy shorts. Her arms and legs have broken out in goose-flesh. She shivers.

"Climb under the covers, okay?" I stand and pull the duvet back. Just in time, I notice my black lace bra sticking out from under a pillow, the one I save for nights when I expect to get lucky. I toss it at my suitcase. God, I don't even remember wearing that. "You're in shock."

"Wh-what happened?" Her teeth start to chatter. She climbs into bed, curling into a fetal position.

I cover her with the comforter, pulling it all the way

up to her chin. I rub her back, trying to warm her. "We don't know. We woke up and she was gone. Her car's missing, too. She probably just went to run an errand."

We listen to the argument raging downstairs. Amy and Em want to call the cops, but Kimiko insists they wait. Dakota goes on shivering beneath the duvet, crying into the pillow.

"Just rest for a few minutes, okay? Try to think of something relaxing." Even as I'm saying it, I realize this is the stupidest, most useless piece of advice I've ever offered anyone.

Dakota's shiny hair is splayed out on the pillow. "Where do you think she went?"

"I don't know."

She lets out a muffled whimper, her mouth pressed against the pillow.

"Shhh." I stroke her hair, wincing as my head pounds with fresh urgency. The tangled web of voices coming from downstairs only makes it worse. "It's going to be okay."

She glances up at me with a lost expression that makes her look much younger than seventeen. "It's not going to be okay. Something's wrong. I just know it."

I'm not sure what to say to this. "Try to rest for now. We'll figure this out."

She doesn't answer, just curls tighter into a ball. I sit with her for a long time, listening to the sounds of chaos downstairs, hearing Dakota's words circle inside my head.

SEVEN

THE BLOODSTAINS ARE still there on my way back, looking as ghastly as ever. It occurs to me there's a statue missing, too. There used to be a stone figurine sitting on a table near the top of the staircase, tucked into a decorative alcove. I barely noticed it, but now the empty spot is obvious. I think it was one of those tall skinny Buddhas. I try to remember, but it feels like wading through mud.

Making my way downstairs, my legs ache with fatigue. I hold tight to the banister. When I get to the bottom, Em and Kimiko are still arguing.

"I don't care. We need to call 911," Em's saying. Her voice carries the strained patience of someone who has repeated the same thing so many times she's starting to lose it.

Amy's hyperventilating, leaning on the banister. I go to her. "It's okay, Amy. Breathe."

She gasps for air, her face a mottled red, her eyes glassy.

"You guys, I think Amy's having a panic attack."

Kimiko and Em both look over, startled.

"Go get her a paper bag," Em orders.

I run to the kitchen and tear open the drawers and cupboards. It seems to take forever. I can hear Amy gasping. I picture the baby inside her, convulsing from lack of oxygen. Do people die of panic attacks? Do they miscarry? That's all we need.

I yank one of the drawers open so hard it comes all the way out and clatters to the floor, spilling linen napkins and silver napkin holders. In the final cupboard, I find some lunch sacks. I grab one and sprint back to the foyer, holding out the bag.

Em shakes it open and hands it to Amy. "Breathe into this. It'll help."

Amy obeys, filling the little sack like someone blowing up a balloon. When she inhales, the bag flattens, sticking to itself. As her breathing slows, her face loses its disturbing, beet-red hue.

"There you go. Good. You keep breathing, I'll call 911." Em picks up Sadie's phone from the hallway table.

"I'm serious, Em, don't call yet. She's probably fine." Kimiko's voice is dangerous, low.

"She's missing. There's blood. We need to report it." Em starts to dial.

Kimiko seizes the phone with a vicious yank. In one swift movement, she flings it hard against the wall, where it shatters.

We stare at Kimiko, shocked.

"Nobody's calling anyone until we talk this through." Her nostrils flare, defiant.

"Keep it down." I gesture upstairs, as if I'm saying this for Dakota's sake, but the truth is my head pounds every time someone talks above a whisper.

I go to the shattered phone and pick it up. "This is Sadie's, right?"

"Yeah," Amy confirms. "Could be full of clues. Except Kimiko just destroyed it."

I study the phone, but it's dead. The glass screen is a spider's web. Why this is the thing that sets me off, I don't know, but it does. My stomach heaves.

I barely make it to the bathroom before I throw up. I flush the toilet and splash cold water onto my face. My mouth finds the steady, clear stream and I drink in greedy slurps, spitting half of it into the sink, trying to erase the taste of vomit. With one shaky hand I grope for a washcloth folded neatly over a brass bar. I run it under cold water, press its coolness against the back of my neck.

I feel a little better after throwing up. Was that hangover induced or fear? Maybe a little of both. Down the hall, their voices continue to fling accusations, blurring together.

"If she were a kid, this would be different." Kimiko turns to me as I join them again, trying to get me on her side. "But she's not. She's an adult—a celebrity, in fact."

Amy removes the bag from her mouth to give Kimi a scathing look. "What difference does that—?"

"If word gets out she's missing, we'll have the media crawling all over this place. That will only complicate things."

"That's irrelevant," Em says. "The cops are professionals. They'll know how to find—"

"I've been dealing with cops for the past year," Kimiko says, her lip curling with disgust. "Believe me. They only make everything a thousand times worse—"

"If your son's dealing crack," Amy snipes. "But this is different. We're not criminals."

Whoa. Kimiko's son was selling drugs?

Kimiko throws Amy a hateful glare. "That's low,

Amy. Even for you." She storms down the hall and out the kitchen doors to the patio.

I follow in Kimiko's wake, calling her name. By the time I catch up to her, she's sitting by the pool on a lawn chair, head in her hands.

I sit in the chair beside her. "You need to calm down, Kimi."

She takes a deep breath as if searching for patience. "We have to consider how this looks. We were all here last night. Now Sadie's missing, and it seems like something really bad might have happened."

"Okay, yes, I hear you, but—"

Kimiko interrupts. "If they find Sadie someplace injured—or worse—we're the main suspects. Forget that. *I'm* the main suspect."

"What?" I stare at her, dumbfounded. "Why you?"

"Sadie lent me cash to start my dispensary. A lot of cash." Kimiko looks past me, regret darkening her eyes. "It was stupid. I shouldn't have taken it."

"I don't see why that would make you a—"

"We've been fighting about it. A lot. Mostly via text."

"Is that why you smashed her phone just now?" A cold feeling rushes through me.

"That just happened. I wasn't thinking." She winces. "Poor impulse control."

I'm not sure I believe her. It's a terrible feeling. Here she is, one of my oldest friends, and I can't even tell if she's lying.

"Friends fight," I say. "It happens. That doesn't make you a suspect. And anyway, we don't even know where she is. She might be fine."

"She wanted her money, June." Kimiko looks scared.

"She was going to force me to sell the whole thing if I didn't pay her back. That's my livelihood. It's also a really strong motive."

We both turn at the sound of the sliding-glass doors opening. Em and Amy join us, perching on nearby chairs. Kimiko shoots them wary glances but keeps on talking.

"And here's the thing. I don't know if I drank too much or what, but my memories of last night are spotty. There are some crazy messes downstairs. I have no idea how any of that went down."

I let my breath out in a rush. Thank God I'm not the only one with missing time. "I keep trying to picture what happened last night, and almost nothing is coming to me."

Kimiko and I turn to the others.

After a moment, Em nods. "Same here."

Amy stares at the cloudy sky, concentrating. "God, you're right." She looks down at her nightgown, mystified. "When did I put this on?"

"Those pajamas I woke up in weren't even mine," I say.

Amy jerks around to face me. "Those were Sadie's. I was wondering why you had them on."

"Focus, people," Em barks. "We still need to call the cops."

Kimiko shakes her head. "Not yet."

Amy continues scrutinizing me. Her voice goes quiet with menace. "Why *were* you wearing Sadie's pajamas?"

"Hell if I know, Amy," I blurt, my nerves frayed. "That's the whole point. We don't remember."

Em tries to come to my rescue. "The pajamas don't mean anything, okay? Let it—"

"And you were wearing her jewelry." Amy transfers her accusing glare to Em. "Where did you get all that?"

Kimiko groans. "This is what I'm saying. We've got shit to figure out."

"And what the hell happened to your nose?" Amy leans closer to Kimiko. "It looks broken."

Kimiko touches her bruised, swollen nose and winces. "Mother of God, that hurts."

I'm relieved it's not just me with a black hole where my memories should be. Still, a voice in my mind whispers, *What if one of us is lying?*

Amy's eyes light up with fresh panic, an idea taking root. "If we were all—I don't know, drugged—then somebody might have come in here and drugged us, right? Maybe somebody dosed us and kidnapped Sadie."

"Right." Kimiko folds her arms. "So we call the cops, tell them we woke up, found bloodstains, a demolished house, and our friend missing. We've got a collective case of amnesia, but we're pretty sure some random stranger broke into a gated compound, drugged us, and kidnapped Sadie. That sounds really fucking plausible."

When she puts it like that, I see her point.

"What are you suggesting?" Amy's face is red and mottled. "We just pretend nothing happened? Meanwhile, Sadie could be bleeding to death in someone's basement?"

"Jesus, Amy." I cover my mouth, horrified. The nausea bubbles up again, but I take a deep breath, willing myself not to be sick.

"I'm suggesting," Kimiko says, her voice dropping lower as she looks at each of us in turn, "we don't call anyone until we figure this out."

TWENTY MINUTES LATER, we're in the kitchen, still debating. There's a large chocolate cake slathered in pink frosting sitting on the kitchen island with about a third of it missing. It looks like somebody dug into it with their hands, just grabbed enormous hunks rather than slicing it with a knife. I remember the smear of pink frosting on Em's cheek this morning. There's also batter flung in Jackson Pollock patterns along one wall.

Our panic level has dialed down a little. It's gone from code red to code yellow. I think it's mostly the shock. Also, the debilitating hangover we're all tortured by. It's impossible to maintain a high level of hysteria when your head's in a vise.

I pick up the drawer I flung to the floor in my panic and wrestle it back into place.

"I'm not saying I have the answer," Kimiko says, holding a bag of frozen peas to her nose. "But we have to focus on what we know, and how it will look to the cops. Sadie's missing. We can't change that. But how we handle it from here will make all the difference."

Em leans against the kitchen island, staring out the wall of windows. I recognize the distant look on her face. She's gone into computer mode, analyzing the possibilities. Half of her is here in the room with us; the other half is burrowing into algorithms, twisting round and round to find a solution.

Amy stares into her coffee. She's gone from panicky to petulant.

"Did you notice the statue?" My voice is barely above a whisper.

They all turn to me and stare like I'm speaking Swahili.

"What statue?" Em asks.

"At the top of the stairs. The white stone figure. Some kind of Buddha, I think."

"Kwan Yin?" Amy says.

"I guess. Yeah."

Kimiko looks confused. "What about it?"

"It's gone." My voice shakes. The words taste sour in my mouth. Or maybe that's the aftertaste of vomit. I have a sudden burning desire to brush my teeth.

"Jesus," Em whispers.

Amy begins to cry. The tears run down her face, silent but prolific, forming long black streaks down her cheeks, darkened by the dregs of last night's mascara.

Kimiko starts to pace, removing the peas from her face. "Okay, that's good."

Every head in the room swivels toward her.

"Not *good*." She holds out a hand. "What I mean is, the more we know about how this happened, the better. Since none of us remember what actually went down, we have to use the evidence to piece together a picture."

"We're all *saying* we don't remember." My guts churn with queasy fear at the thought taking shape. "That doesn't mean it's true. If one of us drugged everyone, then that person's lying to the rest of us."

Kimiko stops pacing and looks at me. "Good point."

"I mean, is that what we think?" I look around the room. In spite of all the Advil I've consumed, the movement still makes my head throb. "We were drugged?"

Amy hasn't bothered to wipe away her tears. "If one

of us drugged everyone, and it wasn't an outsider, that's all the more reason to call 911."

"Hey, if you're ready to face the cops, be my guest." Kimiko lifts her chin in a challenge.

Amy snorts in disbelief. "When we tried, you shattered the damn phone."

Kimiko closes her eyes and opens them again. "I know this is harsh, but we've got to face it: one of us is probably responsible for whatever happened to Sadie. We might not remember it—either we were blackout drunk or drugged or whatever—but this place is pretty protected. It was most likely an inside job."

We all make sounds of protest.

Kimiko silences us with a look. "I get how crazy that sounds, but frankly, anything else sounds even crazier."

We sit there, taking this in.

"It could have been an intruder," Amy insists, her voice small and childlike.

Kimiko ignores this. "One of us or Ethan. I don't remember seeing him, but he's on the property, right?"

"I went to his place this morning."

They all turn to me. "What did he say?"

"He's as mystified as we are." I clear my throat, avoiding looking at Amy. "At least, that's what he said. I told him to search the beach."

"He'll come up here when he's done, and we can get more answers." Kimiko looks at Amy. "Is there anyone else who lives on the property?"

"Just Leo."

Kimiko looks baffled. "Who the hell is Leo?"

"The landscaper," Amy says, defensive.

What do I tell them about Leo? *I couldn't find him.*

He wasn't in his yurt. Which doesn't mean anything—he could be working someplace on the property, or in town. *Or burying Sadie's body*, a sinister voice whispers at the back of my mind.

"The guy who lives in the yurt, right?" I've got no idea why I'm pretending I haven't talked to Leo a couple of times now. Somehow it seems safer, less complicated, and there's no time to second-guess myself. "I knocked on his door. There was no answer."

I remember Sadie bursting out of there like a woman on a mission; I can still see her charging through the forest, mad as hell. What did he say to piss her off like that? I recall her angry words. *Fine. Stay miserable. That seems to be what you want.* Why didn't I ask more questions? I consider sharing this with the others, but it feels like lobbing a Molotov cocktail into a building already alive with flames.

"Did anyone see Ethan or Leo in the main house last night?" Em perks up.

This would be the perfect time to tell them about the argument I caught the tail end of yesterday evening. That's not what Em asked, though. I'm splitting hairs and I know it. If I tell them about Sadie storming out of Leo's yurt, they might assume he's guilty before they even meet him. Leo's the closest thing to a stranger we've got on the property. It would be natural for everyone to turn on him. It might send us on a wild-goose chase when we need to focus on what actually happened. I don't know Leo well, but my instincts tell me he's not a violent man. Instead of speaking up, I find myself gnawing the inside of my cheek so hard I taste blood.

Nobody answers Em.

Kimiko breaks the silence. "Just because none of us saw them, that doesn't mean they weren't here. If we all blacked out, there's no way to know for sure."

Em looks at me, her face putty colored. "What about Dakota? Does she remember what happened?"

"I don't think so."

"You're not sure, though?" Em pins me with her gaze. "She might remember something?"

I shrug. "She woke up to bloodstains and her mom missing. I wasn't going to make it worse by interrogating her."

"Does anyone have some Valium or lorazepam or something?" Kimiko looks around at our confused expressions. "For Dakota, I mean. She's in shock. It might help."

Amy's face contorts with contempt. She scoffs. "Typical."

"What? I'm just saying—"

"Drugs are your solution to everything." Amy glares at her.

Kimiko's eyes go wide at the accusation. She presses the frozen peas against her nose again, winces, and removes them.

"I still say we need to call the cops—I mean, they're the professionals." Amy sounds desperate. "They'll find her. She could be in trouble, and we're wasting time."

Kimiko takes a step toward Amy. "You trust the cops around here? Really? The same ones who dragged you to the psych ward? Are those your knights in shining armor?"

Amy jerks her head back like Kimiko has just hit her.

"I'm not trying to be cruel, but do you really trust them to find the truth in this whole mess? Because I, for one, do not. As a person of color—"

"Wait," Amy asks, "I don't understand."

Kimiko puts a hand up. "I'm just saying."

"What are you saying exactly?" Amy demands.

"They'll find the most convenient scapegoat—one of us—and pin it on us. End of story. And, given the choices, I'm going to look mighty tempting."

"Japanese-Italian-Americans aren't exactly filling up the *Most Wanted* list." Amy's words drip with sarcasm.

"In this neck of the woods, I'm 'exotic.'" Kimiko uses air quotes. "That's enough to make them look twice."

I see Kimiko's point. We don't know what kind of conclusions the cops will jump to. This is northwestern Washington, an overwhelmingly white area. I don't want to assume Kimiko will come off as more suspicious because she looks different but I also don't think her fears are completely paranoid. I have my own reasons for thinking I might look sketchy—waking in Sadie's pajamas, meeting with Ethan in secret, having no memories of last night. The thought of facing cops with so little information to offer them scares me, too.

A sniffling sound in the doorway makes us turn. Dakota hovers there, her brow furrowed. She's thrown a huge sweater over her boy shorts. Gossamer strands of her blond hair stand up in a staticky halo. Her eyes are red and puffy from crying. She sniffles, her shoulders slumped.

"Oh, sweetie." Amy stands and goes to her.

Dakota walks into Amy's arms, collapsing against her.

We exchange uneasy glances. I wonder how long she's been standing within earshot. God, the poor girl. This must be a nightmare for her. It's a nightmare for all of us, but most of all her.

"How do you feel?" I ask, my tone tentative.

Dakota pulls away from Amy and looks at me. "How do you think I feel? I'm freaking out."

"Of course."

"I can't believe she's just gone." She swipes at her cheeks with her palms. The gesture is so childlike, it breaks my heart. "What did the cops say?"

A guilty silence. Amy opens her mouth to answer, but Kimiko cuts her off. "We're trying to figure some stuff out before we—"

"Wait, what?" Dakota's eyes go wide. "You haven't even *called* them yet?"

"We're going to," Kimiko assures her. "We just—"

"What the hell are you waiting for?" I recoil at Dakota's accusing tone, but Kimiko holds her ground.

"For one thing, we wanted to find out what you remember." I can tell it takes effort for Kimiko to keep her tone even.

"What *I* remember?" Dakota treats the room at large to a scathing look.

Kimiko continues, undeterred. "We think we might have been drugged. None of us remembers much from last night."

"Drugged," Dakota repeats, her voice flat with disbelief.

"Yeah." Kimiko takes a deep breath and soldiers on. "You might be the only person here who remembers anything clearly. What happened?"

Dakota grabs a Kleenex from a box on the counter and wipes her eyes. She stares at the ceiling with a look of intense concentration. "I came into the living room around eleven. You guys were wasted."

"What were we talking about?" Even asking the question fills me with prickly dread.

Dakota shakes her head. "Honestly? I don't even know. You were all really animated, but none of it made much sense."

"What happened after that?" I ask.

Dakota's expression goes sheepish. "I sort of…snuck one tiny gin and tonic. After that I don't remember anything."

Amy squints at her. "Nothing?"

"It's like…totally blank." She gapes at us. "Oh my God, do you think I was drugged, too?"

"What if we were roofied?" Em grips the counter top, leaning forward.

We all look at her.

"Like in *The Hangover*?" Amy asks.

"Yeah, exactly," Em says. "Rohypnol, or maybe GHB. That's the one most people get dosed with these days." She spots her purse across the room, goes to it, and digs until she finds her phone.

Kimiko tenses.

"Relax," Em tells her. "I just want to look it up." She starts tapping and swiping, her fingers working fast. "This girl I know got dosed at a bar and forgot the whole night. There's a few different date-rape drugs out there. They make some people euphoric; others get really sleepy. Most people don't remember what happened later, even though they seemed fully conscious at the time."

Kimiko nods. "My friend Quinn had that happen once. He went out on a date with some dude he met online; woke up ten hours later in a random apartment, no idea how he got there. Someone saw him dancing at a club, but he's got no memory of it."

Em scowls at her phone. I can tell by the change in her expression she's seen something she doesn't like.

"What?" I ask.

Em glances at Dakota, her expression cagey.

Dakota huffs. "I'm not a little kid. Just say it."

"One of the possible side effects is violent behavior."

We all stare at the floor. I'm sure we're all picturing that missing stone statue smashing into the back of Sadie's head. Her body tumbling down the stairs, legs and arms akimbo. Can we see our fingers grasping that statue? Is there some faint trace of muscle memory left?

I look around the room. We all had our grudges against Sadie, God knows—some more serious than others. With only a jumble of crazy memories, even I have to question what I'm capable of.

Then something occurs to me. Contrary to movie logic, most people don't dose their friends just for kicks. Whoever drugged us must have intended to get rid of Sadie. Maybe they wanted to put us in this position— unreliable witnesses who suspect everyone, even themselves.

Amy stands, her hands cupped over her belly. She looks slightly green. "I can't believe she's out there somewhere and we're just sitting here talking. I mean, what the hell? We have to do something."

Kimiko takes a step toward her. "We have to think this through. They won't even start a search for twenty-four hours."

Em looks skeptical. "Are you sure that's true?"

I study the hard, determined lines of Kimiko's face. She's so adamant about not calling the cops. I understand her fear of being singled out as the only minority, but is there something else going on here? She was the one mixing G&Ts. She even brought her own gin. I recall her pulling the bottle of Bombay Sapphire from a bag, her tone light and teasing. *I decided to BYOB.*

"What's there to think about, anyway? None of us remembers anything." Amy's voice goes shrill again. "Sadie could be slowly bleeding out in some—"

"Hey," I interrupt, casting a pointed look at Dakota.

Amy gets the message and makes an effort to soften her tone. "So what if they won't launch a full-on search right away? We still need to report her missing."

"We're going to call them." Kimiko puts up a hand, placating. "But let's talk to Ethan and this gardener guy first, okay? Find out what they remember. When it comes to cops, knowledge is power."

None of us states the obvious, though I can feel the thought pushing through the room like a dark tide. Who's to say Ethan and Leo will tell the truth? Who's to say any of us will?

TEN MINUTES LATER, Ethan strides into the living room. His hair is damp and he shucks off his pea coat, which is soaked. It's his house, of course, but it feels like he's the guest. We're gathered around the gas fire as rain hammers on the roof. Dakota went outside to take a call from her boyfriend, but the rest of us are all here. Every face pivots toward Ethan like a flower searching for the sun.

"You haven't found her?" Ethan's face is somber.

We shake our heads.

Kimiko speaks up. "We've looked all over."

"I searched up and down the beach. She's not there." His crow's feet fan out from the corners of his eyes. His forehead puckers with concern. "Where's Dakota?"

As if on cue, Dakota hurries into the room and rushes into his arms. Everyone backs away as father and daughter embrace. Ethan's hand reaches up and cups the back of her head, pulling her closer. I have to look away. A hush falls over the room, thick as snow. The air sizzles with the sound of the gas fire. The moment stretches on.

Amy avoids the sight of them, too. Her eyes search her lap. She folds the fabric of her nightgown into tiny pleats. Her fingers work like she's doing origami.

I wonder what she feels for Ethan. What has it been like living in his backyard all these years?

But then Amy was always immune to Ethan's charms. I remember when she first met him. We ran into him on our way to class, pausing in Red Square, our messenger bags strapped across our chests. I introduced them, trying hard not to show how thrilled I was to see him, forcing a casual cadence into my voice. Until then, Amy knew him only as the grad student TA Sadie and I had been obsessing over for weeks. As he walked away, she rolled her eyes.

"What?" I asked, puzzled.

"That guy's too slick; he's working that accent and those eyes."

"He can't help it if he's sexy."

"Nothing good comes of guys like that. They've got the world by the balls, and they know it."

Amy still hasn't looked up from her fastidious night-gown pleating. She's giving it the concentration of an artist perfecting her work. I wonder if she's avoiding him because she's ashamed we haven't called the cops. Or maybe they're always this way—orbiting one another in carefully prescribed paths that refuse to intersect.

"So nobody's seen any sign of her?" Ethan's brogue is thicker than usual as he pulls away from Dakota. It always gets more pronounced when he's drunk or emotional.

"Nothing except her phone. You?" Em asks.

He shakes his head, a mournful cast to his eyes. "Not even footprints on the beach. She's just gone."

We sit in silence, itching with all the unsaid possibilities.

"Have you called the cops?" he asks, his eyebrows arching.

Kimiko speaks up. "We wanted to talk to you first, see if you know anything."

Ethan throws a questioning glance my way. "June must have told you. I haven't seen her in days. I've got nothing to add."

"You sure about that?" Amy's question comes out sharp, jagged.

Nobody says anything for a long moment, the atmosphere in the room suddenly thick and oppressive.

I speak up, not sure what I'll say until I hear myself saying it. "Ethan's not the villain here. We have to stick together and figure out where Sadie is."

"I'm sure detectives will be more adept at that than us." Amy's tone is tart.

Kimiko throws up her hands. "Not necessarily."

"God, are we back to that again?" Amy mimics Kimiko's husky voice. "'As a person of color, I'm a suspect.' Please, Kimi. You need to get over yourself."

"Just because it's not a reality for you doesn't mean it's not a reality," she shoots back.

"Kimiko's right." I don't think we should discount her fears. "Cops have biases, like anyone. It's something to consider."

"What are you talking about?" Ethan looks bewildered. He runs a hand over his face. "We have to call the cops. They need to know she's missing."

"I agree." Em picks up her phone. "I'll call them right now."

"Hold on." Kimiko puts a hand over Em's phone. "I thought we agreed we'd talk to this gardener guy first."

"We need to call them right now." Amy's voice goes shrill again.

Kimiko looks to Ethan for support. "But maybe Leo knows where she is. We can avoid the whole media circus, get her back here safe and sound."

I'm cynical about Kimiko's sudden flash of optimism. Surely she knows it won't be that simple. Still, I have to admit talking to Leo is a good idea.

An explosive crack at the window makes us all jump.

"What was that?" Em gasps.

"A bird." Ethan hasn't moved. "They fly into the

glass all the time. The reflection makes it look like the sky."

Without warning, Ethan cups his face in his hands and starts to cry.

I go to the kitchen and make a pot of coffee. It's too excruciating watching Ethan come undone.

I could feel Amy looking at me when I left the room, gauging my reaction. She knows I went to meet him the other night, that I snuck off to his place after midnight. It's one thing keeping my secret from Sadie, which I hope and pray she did. It's something else keeping it from the cops.

If she lets that slip to them, how's it going to look? Rocky marriage, old girlfriend shows up, sneaks off for a secret rendezvous with the husband? Then the wife goes missing, leaving signs of violence in her wake, and the girlfriend's memory is conveniently blank? Not good.

That's the problem with secrets. They buzz around inside the keeper like a hive of bees. Before long, somebody pokes it and the secrets swarm out, vexed and ready to sting.

"You need some help?"

I'm in the process of scooping ground beans into the coffeemaker when a voice behind me makes me jump. I toss the grounds into the air, dusting the counter.

Kimiko goes to the sink, grabs a sponge, and hands it to me. "Didn't mean to startle you."

"Guess we're all a little high strung."

"This can't be easy for you."

I concentrate on wiping up the coffee grounds, avoiding her gaze. "None of this is easy for any of us."

"I swear," I whisper, adamant. "I'd tell you if I remembered."

That kiss. The intimacy, the warmth, the searing intensity of it. Was the person's mouth familiar? Could it have been Ethan I kissed? The answer feels just out of reach, a wispy shape beyond my grasp.

"If he doesn't have a solid alibi, this could get bad for him," she murmurs.

"Why do you say that?"

She darts a quick look over her shoulder at the door. "Their marriage was in trouble. I know that much. He had good reason to want her out of the picture."

"What do you mean?" I lean closer, listening all the while for footsteps.

"Sadie told me if he ever left her she'd make his life hell. Her lawyers would ensure he had nothing—worse than nothing. Crippling debt."

"Could she really do that?"

She shrugs. "Sadie thought so. He probably did too. Ethan was always hopeless with money. Sadie ran the show."

"But still—"

The sound of someone coming forces us apart. No doubt the guilty expressions linger on our faces.

Ethan appears in the doorway. His eyes are a little red, his hair spiky, as if he's just raked a hand through it. "I thought I smelled coffee."

"You want a cup?" I busy myself pulling mugs from the cupboards, grateful for an excuse to hide my face.

"Sure," Ethan says, his eyes burning into the back of my head. "I could use some caffeine."

"None for me," Kimiko says, her tone light. "I'll see if anyone else wants some, though."

As she leaves the room, I pour coffee into two mugs. For some reason my hand is shaking. "Cream? Sugar?"

"Black is fine."

I hand him his cup. Our eyes meet. There's a pleading look on his face as he takes the mug from me. I wonder what he wants.

"You okay?" I ask, my voice soft.

"Not great." The raw huskiness in his tone tells me what an understatement this is. "You?"

"Same."

He glances over his shoulder, just as Kimiko did moments earlier. It's painful how cagey we all are, keeping secrets from each other, speaking in whispers. "Maybe it's best if I tell the cops about seeing you the other night. If we try to cover it up, we'll only look more suspicious."

My stomach twists, but I recognize the truth of this. "You're probably right. Will you tell them everything?"

"Our history, you mean?"

I nod.

"I plan to be honest, but not garrulous." He blows wisps of steam from his coffee but doesn't drink. "We can't afford to look like we're sneaking about."

I watch him, trying to gauge his state of mind. "Where were you last night?"

He rubs his face with one hand. "Down at my place."

"Is there anyone who can back you up on that?"

For a second, he hesitates. I can't read his expression.

"Amy and Em want coffee," Kimiko says as she bustles back into the room. "I'll get it."

Ethan and I step apart instinctively. I can't help noticing we push away from each other just as Kimiko and I
did minutes earlier. When she's fetched the coffee and
hurried back out, I look up and find him staring at me.

I raise my eyebrows in a question.

"You're asking if I have an alibi." Ethan sits on a
stool, his expression somber.

"Yeah. That's what I'm asking." I hurry to soften
it. "I mean, hopefully she's fine and none of this will
matter, but..."

"If she's not, it looks bad."

I bite my lip. "It could."

"To answer your question, no, nobody can confirm I
was at the beach house last night." He stares into space,
considering. "But you guys were here with her, and you
know I never laid eyes on Sadie all night."

Something in my face must alarm him.

"Obviously, I've stayed away, you all know—"

"That's the thing," I interrupt. "None of us remember much of last night. We have patchy memories here
and there, but for some reason, that's all we've got."

He stares at me. "How can that be? Were you wasted?"

"We drank, but I don't think it was enough to—" I
break off, frustrated. "It's possible we were drugged.
We don't know."

"Drugged," Ethan echoes, fear in his eyes.

"It's possible." Then, even though it makes my guts
churn to say it out loud, I force myself to ask, "Did I...
see you last night? Were we together at any point?"

His eyebrows pull together. "No."

A great wave of relief breaks over me.

His puzzled scowl deepens. "Did you think we—?"

"I didn't know. It's scary, having all this missing time."

"Well, you're safe on that score."

I change the subject. "Any idea where Leo is? Kimiko's got it in her head we need to talk to him before we call the cops."

"No idea." He studies me. "You've met Leo?"

"Oh. Yeah. I've seen him around." My voice sounds overly casual. I concern myself with the counters again, wiping up the smeared cake.

"You think he knows something?"

"Not necessarily, but he does live here. Maybe he saw her."

He pulls out his phone. "I'll text him. But I'm not waiting on his response. We should have called the cops already."

"Kimiko thinks we should hold off, find out whatever we—"

"Kimiko's not in charge here," he cuts in, his volume rising. "Why you're all following her lead is beyond me. Not sure if you noticed, but she's a guest in this house. She can stop acting like she runs the place."

I hold out my hands, not wanting to defend Kimiko, but not thrilled by his tone, either. He's gone all alpha male on me. "Fine. You should tell her, though, not me."

"I will." His mouth tightens into a hard line as he stalks toward the living room.

I watch him go, cold dread spreading out in the pit of my stomach. I hate watching us all fracture like this, everyone questioning and suspecting one another. Where the hell is Sadie? Like Amy said, she could be out there somewhere alive. But if nothing bad has happened to her, why is there so much blood in the stairwell?

EIGHT

A FEW MINUTES LATER, I hear a commotion in the living room. Rushing to the doorway, I see Ethan facing off with Kimiko. The rain slashes hard at the windows as they glare at one another.

"This is ridiculous." Ethan's almost shouting. His face is red, his shoulders tense. "My wife is missing, and you're dithering over petty details."

"We just want to get all the facts." Kimiko's tone is equally hostile.

"Why? Because you think it looks suspicious?" Ethan throws up his hands. "Well, you're right. It looks bloody suspicious, and this whole 'we were drugged' story sounds daft. Do you know what happened to Sadie, or don't you?"

Em steps in front of Kimiko, protective. "Of course we don't. Just call them already."

Ethan pulls his phone from his pocket and stabs at the keys. "You should have called them the second you noticed she was gone." He pauses, listening, then stalks out of the room, saying, "Yes, hello? I'd like to report a missing person."

An awkward silence falls over us as his voice trails down the hall and up the stairs.

Dakota, who was standing at her father's side during his tirade, glowers at us. "He's right, you know. I've only been awake for like an hour, but you guys knew she was missing way before that. Why didn't you just call the police?"

Kimiko groans in frustration. "You know why. We told you."

"Because you're afraid they'll find out the truth?" Dakota narrows her eyes at Kimiko. "What are you trying to hide?"

This is going nowhere. I distract Dakota with a question. "Did Leo answer Ethan's text?"

Dakota nods. "He's in Port Townsend. Won't be back for hours."

"Ethan asked if he knew where Sadie is?"

"Obviously." Dakota gives me a withering look. "He knows nothing. At least, that's what he says."

Kimiko blinks at Dakota, cheeks sucked in like she's trying hard not to slap her. "I still say dragging the cops into this is premature."

Dakota winces in disgust, turns on her heel, and leaves the room, one hand stretched over her forehead like she can't bear to witness the egregious mess we've made of everything.

Now that I know the cops will be here soon, I find myself scrambling to figure out what we should tell them. In that sense, Kimi's right—we have to consider how this whole shit show will look to them. The blackout thing is problematic, especially since we have no evidence we were drugged. Maybe we should think up a story to take the place of our collective missing memories. It doesn't have to be complicated. In fact, the simpler the better. If the cops come and we share a bunch of disjointed, dreamlike fragments with no explanation, that will only deepen their suspicions.

Is it wrong that Sadie might be out there suffering and I'm more worried about looking bad in front of the cops?

If it is, I know I'm not alone in my fear. I can see the same looks on Em, Kimiko, and Amy. We're thinking about our position in all this. Yes, we're worried about Sadie, but that's dwarfed by our darkest fears. We have no memory of last night, and our friend is missing. The bloodstains loom large in our minds, treacherous maps of possibility. If Sadie's dead, we're implicated.

"When the cops get here, we should say we all fell asleep by midnight." I try to sound firm in spite of the wobble in my belly. It feels like vertigo—like standing on a cliff's edge looking straight down. "Whatever happened to Sadie happened while we slept."

"So…even if we have memories, we shouldn't share them?" Amy asks.

"We don't want to confuse them," I say. "The whole blackout thing is distracting, and the end result is the same. We don't remember. End of story."

"You're suggesting we lie?" Amy's forehead crinkles with worry.

"Edit." I try to sound convincing. It's sketchy, I know, but so is bringing collective amnesia into this already convoluted situation. "Say you were asleep. It might as well be true."

Three doubtful faces study me.

"June's right," Em says after a moment with a decisive nod. "It's simpler that way."

"But it's not *true*." Amy looks tortured.

Em waves a hand like she's erasing a chalkboard. "It might as well be. We're useless at piecing together what happened. If you remember something important, tell us right now. Otherwise, when the cops get here, keep it to yourself."

A silence falls over us as we consider this.

"Yeah, okay." Kimiko leans one hip against the back of the couch. "I guess it's better than the alternative."

Amy still looks unconvinced. "What if someone remembers something important later on? We can hardly say, 'Hey, Officer? I know I said I was dead asleep, but I just recovered this memory that conveniently explains everything.'"

"If we remember something later," I fight to keep my voice calm, "we'll find a way to let them know."

"Find a way?" There's a faintly manic note to her words. "What, send them an anonymous note?"

Em puts a hand on Amy's arm. "It's not a perfect plan, but the truth is too convoluted."

After a long, airless moment, Amy sags into the nearest chair, nodding. "Okay. Fine. It's pretty lame, but it will have to do."

There's no guarantee, of course, that Ethan and Dakota will follow our lead, especially now that they seem to be siding against us. If they challenge us, though, it will be our word against theirs—four against two. We'll just have to tough it out and hope for the best.

As Amy says, it's pretty lame, but with the cops coming any minute now, it's all we've got.

WHEN OFFICER FISHER is seated in the living room, Em offers him coffee or tea, but he doesn't take her up on it. We're all here. Ethan hovers, moving from perch to perch, not quite able to sit down. Watching him pace the room is making me crazy. I wish he'd just settle.

Fisher looks about forty, maybe a little older. He's got short, boyish hair that's dishwater blond on top, then fades into silvery stubble where it's buzzed on the sides. He takes us all in with watery gray eyes.

"When did you first realize Mrs. MacTavish was missing?" He addresses Ethan, but lets his gaze wander to the rest of us. I think he's trying to figure out what this is, how we all fit here; is this a party, a harem, a cult?

"We called as soon as we'd checked the property," Ethan says.

"We heard an adult's not officially missing for twenty-four hours," I add, "but we were worried."

Fisher barely glances at me. "Common misconception. Always best to call us right away. The sooner the better."

"Okay, good. So we did the right thing." I'm careful not to look at anyone but him.

"Absolutely. Though these cases usually resolve themselves in a day or two."

"Really?" Em looks hopeful.

Fisher nods. "Sometimes people just need a little space."

Ethan clears his throat. "There's a rather worrying stain in the stairwell. A couple of them, actually. We're not sure, but it looks like blood."

"I'll need to look at that." Fisher's tone is brisk and efficient, more housing inspector than police officer who just realized his missing-person case might actually be homicide. "I noticed a security camera at the front gate. Has anyone looked at the footage from last night?"

"Oh, that doesn't record anything." Ethan's tone is apologetic. "It's just a live feed."

Fisher glances at us, then turns his gaze back to Ethan. "So, who lives here? All of you?"

"No. My wife was hosting a girls weekend," Ethan says. "These are her guests." He gestures at Kimiko, Em, and me.

Fisher nods at Dakota without quite looking at her. "This is your daughter?"

Ethan nods.

"And I live here. On the property, I mean." Amy shoots a quick, resentful look at Ethan.

Fisher gets our full names and writes them all down, spelling each one carefully. He takes our phone numbers as well.

"So this is everyone?" Fisher's question seems directed at me.

For a second, I just gape at him, unsure of what he's asking.

"You're here for the weekend," he clarifies, noting my confusion. "Is this everyone, or are there more guests?"

"Oh, right." I lick my lips, feeling parched. "This is it."

Fisher squints at Ethan like he's trying to understand a complex equation. "Were you here last night? I think you mentioned on the phone you weren't in the house when your wife went missing."

"I've been staying at the beach house. It's down by

the water." He waves a hand at the floor-to-ceiling windows facing west. When nobody says anything, he adds, "I wanted to give the girls their space."

"Was anyone else on the property?"

"There's a landscaper who lives by the water," Ethan offers. "He went to Port Townsend this morning to run some errands."

Fisher perks up. "Have you asked him if he's seen Mrs. MacTavish?"

"He hasn't."

Fisher sighs. "So it was just the ladies in the house last night? Was anyone else present?"

"Not that we know of." I figure it's best to hedge my bets.

Fisher doesn't like this. "What do you mean, 'that you know of'?"

"Well, we drank a fair bit. Maybe too much. We all passed out." I look around; Kimiko and Em both keep their eyes on the floor. Amy watches me like a startled deer. Dakota wears a blank expression I can't read. Ethan's mouth puckers like he's working hard not to interject. "I suppose it's possible somebody could have come in without us knowing. It's a big house."

Fisher eyes Amy's pregnant belly. "You all drank so much you passed out?"

Amy shakes her head, her eyes frightened.

I try to clarify. "I don't mean we literally passed out. We were tired from kayaking all day. We had some drinks—not Amy, but the rest of us—and then we went to bed. I'm just saying we can't be positive someone didn't enter the house without us realizing."

"Do you generally lock the house at night?" Fisher asks Ethan.

Again, Ethan's tone is apologetic. "Not really. We're pretty lax, to be honest. We're so far from any neighbors, and I suppose the gate gives us a false sense of security."

Out of nowhere, a rapid-fire reel of memories flips through my brain like a film montage: that kiss, the sea of silks and cashmeres, the woods, the beach, the scream.

Fisher studies his notes and looks back at Ethan. "I believe you told the dispatcher her car's missing?"

"Yes," Ethan says. "It was parked in the garage last night. Now it's gone."

"So it's possible she's just out? Running errands or something?" He sounds hopeful again.

"But her phone was on the garage floor." Amy tries to emphasize how dire this is. "She'd never leave her phone."

"And her purse?" Fisher asks.

"We haven't found it," Amy tells him. "It's not in any of the usual places."

Kimiko sits on the arm of the couch, a combative gleam in her eye. "What will you do, exactly, now that you know she's missing?"

Officer Fisher looks Kimiko over. "What do you mean?"

"What's the procedure?"

He scribbles something in his notebook. I'm dying to know what he wrote.

"We'll file a report, see if anything turns up." Fisher jabs his ballpoint pen with his thumb, the tip appearing and disappearing with audible clicks. I wish he wouldn't. It's getting on my nerves. "You said her phone's still here?"

We all nod. He scribbles.

"It's broken though." I say this in a decisive tone meant to ward off further questions.

Fisher doesn't hesitate. "How did it break?"

"I broke it," Kimi blurts, her chin jutting out in defiance.

An awkward pause as Fisher studies her, curious. "Why?"

"I didn't mean to." Kimiko's eyes dart to meet mine, then back to Fisher. "It was an accident."

Another dangerous pause.

Fisher leans forward. "An accident?"

"Okay, I threw it against the wall." Kimiko tilts her face down this time, not meeting his eyes. "I didn't want anyone calling the cops."

Kimiko's always been a train wreck around authority figures, but seriously? Good God, what is she doing?

Fisher glances at Ethan, then fixes his stare on Kimi again. "Why's that?"

Her spine straightens, a regal arch of the brows. "I was afraid you would see us as suspects."

"We can't assume a crime's even been committed." Fisher keeps his voice low. "Why would you be suspects?"

Kimi shrugs. Her answer is inaudible.

"What's that?" He leans closer, his voice too loud in the high-ceilinged room.

Kimiko looks him in the eye. "I was afraid I might be a suspect because I'm a minority."

Fisher tilts his head. "You assumed we'd be racially biased?"

"Frankly, yes." Her hands shoot out to her sides. "I've had bad experiences. What can I say?"

He gives her a tired look and changes the subject. "So the phone's broken. I'll take it, put our guys on it. You'd be surprised at the magic they can perform on a dead phone."

I can feel the question shooting through the room like a shot of adrenaline: *What does Sadie's phone reveal about me?*

"Any arguments since you've been here?" Fisher looks at me.

I'm torn between my two guiding principles: stick as close to the truth as possible, and keep your answers minimal. "Maybe some tension."

As if summoned by my words, a fresh layer of tension falls over us, an invisible net draping itself over the room, pulling tight.

"What sort of tension?"

"You know how it is when you get together with old friends." I make my tone light and search his face for signs of empathy. He just blinks at me, impassive as a cow. "I think we were all a little nervous, wanted to impress each other. The usual reunion weekend stuff." I glance around. "Some of us haven't seen each other in years."

Fisher turns his gaze back to Kimiko. "What happened to your nose?"

Kimiko bleats out a nervous laugh. "Got really drunk. Walked right into a glass door. Feel totally stupid about it."

He scribbles something, then looks up again. He addresses the room at large. "So no arguments?"

"No arguments," I confirm.

Dakota speaks for the first time, her tone sardonic. "Just really animated conversation."

"What does that mean?" Fisher's eyebrows arch.

"It's a girls weekend," I say, willing myself not to shoot Dakota a dirty look. "Things get lively."

Fisher looks like he might ask more about this, but apparently decides not to. Instead, he directs his next question at Ethan. "Do you have any recent photos of Mrs. MacTavish?"

Ethan nods. "Yes, of course."

Dakota is scrolling through her phone. "I have some."

"A hard copy would be better," Fisher says on a sigh.

Dakota gets up, pulls a photo album from one of the built-in bookshelves. She flips through the pages a moment, her back to us. She pulls a picture from one of the pages and hands it to Fisher.

"Have you noticed anything missing?" Fisher surveys us, but his question is directed at Ethan.

I think of the statue. We all do, I can tell. Maybe Kimiko was right; we should have discussed in more detail what to tell the police and what to keep to ourselves. I open my mouth to speak, but Ethan's already talking.

"Just her car and her purse so far, but we'll keep looking."

"Um, actually," I interject, "there's something else."

Everyone looks at me.

"There was a statue, at the top of the stairs, about this tall." I hold my hands a foot apart. "It was there yesterday, I think, but now it's missing."

Fisher looks at Ethan. "Don't suppose you have any pictures of that?"

Ethan looks blank. I guess we never told him about the statue. "That Asian thing?"

"Kwan Yin," Amy corrects him, her tone sour.

Fisher looks at her. "Kwan who?"

"The Chinese goddess of compassion," Amy explains.

"Good to know. Does anyone have a picture of it?" Fisher asks again.

We all shake our heads. Ethan's neck is red and splotchy. I can tell he's angry but trying hard not to show it.

"Okay, well, if you find one, let me know. I'll take a look at the stairs now, if that's okay." Fisher tucks his notebook into his pocket and stands, casting his eyes toward Ethan again. "You can show me where the statue was."

"Of course."

"What happens now?" Kimiko butts in, her tone querulous. "Will you start looking for her?"

"We'll put out an APB right away, then see what we can glean from her phone. Rest assured, we'll do everything we can to find her."

Em pipes up, a worried furrow between her brows. "June and I were hoping to head home soon—tomorrow, ideally. We're worried about her, obviously, but I have work on Monday, and it's a long drive back to California."

"That should be fine." Fisher looks unfazed. "We'll keep you updated."

"Thank you, Officer." Ethan starts to lead him toward the stairs.

"Sadie MacTavish." When Fisher passes a framed print of the *Dakota's Garden* movie poster, he smacks his forehead. "I knew that sounded familiar. The author, right?"

We nod. I wondered how long it would take for that shoe to drop.

"My eight-year-old loves those movies—the books, too." Fisher's eyes widen as he takes in Dakota with new interest. "You're Dakota! The girl in the books."

Dakota's expression is exasperated. "Except I'm an actual person, and she's a character."

That's it, then. Everything's changed. This missing person isn't just anyone. Of course, the second Officer Fisher saw the estate and the expensive sheen of everything in Sadie's world, he knew he was dealing with somebody wealthy. Now, though, she's a bona fide celebrity. He's got to know if she stays missing, it'll be big news. His every move will be scrutinized. It's something I've avoided dwelling on too much.

Detail is the enemy. Scrutiny is the enemy.

Everyone is the enemy.

AFTER FISHER LEAVES with a blood sample, I wander into the kitchen with Dakota and Amy. Ethan marches in and scowls at me, his face livid. "Why didn't you tell me about the statue?"

"I wasn't trying to keep it from you." I look at the others, thrown by his fury. "It's been a crazy morning. I guess we just…forgot."

"Forgot," he echoes, incredulous.

"God, Ethan, just relax," Amy chides. "It's not a conspiracy."

Ethan turns to Dakota. "Did they tell you?"

She nods, shooting a disdainful look my way. "I figured they would have told you, too."

Ethan turns back to me, his eyes narrowed to slits. "And what was that about 'passing out'? Why didn't you tell him the same crazy story you told me about being drugged?"

"That was June's idea." Amy puts her hands up, distancing herself.

"We don't know if we were drugged." I can't help the edge of defensiveness in my voice. "It's just a theory. It's too confusing."

"Don't you mean suspicious?" Ethan's nostrils flare as he scrutinizes me.

I recoil. Ethan's never talked to me this way. Why is he turning on me? It's unnerving. "Okay, yes. It sounds suspicious. What would you like us to do, stencil *Suspect* in big block letters on our foreheads?" I will myself to stay calm, but exhaustion keeps creeping over me, and my patience is wearing thin.

He gives me a look of pure disgust and stalks out of the room.

Dakota picks up the interrogation where her father left off. "Keeping things from the cops is only making things worse."

"We're not keeping things from them," I snap.

"You totally are. And now you're lying to us, too." It's clear who the *us* is. She and her father are now a unit. The rest of us are inconvenient intruders.

"I notice you didn't mention anything about sneaking gin and blacking out. If you're so committed to the truth, why didn't you tell them that?" I know I should leave it—she's just a kid—but I can't help myself. She's pissing me off.

She huffs and leaves the room.

I watch as Amy throws the strange, misshapen cake in the garbage. That's when I notice the scratches on her arms. They're long, angry wounds, dark red, the kind you might get if someone clawed you with her fingernails.

Amy catches me staring and pushes the sleeves of her sweater down, looking away.

"Where did you get those scratches?" I take hold of her arms, pushing up her sleeves and examining them more closely.

Amy jerks her arms away. "I don't know."

"You know something."

She won't look at me.

"Come on, Amy." I soften my tone. "Tell me the truth."

"It's nothing."

"If it's nothing, then why are you getting so weird?" I demand.

"You don't think I had something to do with—?" She stops, unable to finish.

Em and Kimiko come into the kitchen. They're deep in conversation, but I need to get Amy someplace private. She's way more likely to tell me about the scratches without an audience.

"Let's go to your place," I suggest. "You've looked for Sadie there, right?"

"Just long enough to make sure she wasn't there."

"Let's check it out. Maybe there are clues."

Her face retains the sullen pout she's displayed all

morning, but she nods. Together we go outside and scamper from the veranda to her house as a soft rain starts to fall. She pushes open the front door.

I'm surprised at the pristine beauty of her small living room and kitchen. It's got a dollhouse charm, with upscale farmhouse styling. It's a far cry from the grubby apartment she rented as a student. I don't remember the details, but a general impression of dark, hastily applied paint, horror-movie posters, and vinyl beanbags comes to mind. Amy must see me do a double take, because she scoffs.

"Nice, right? It's all Sadie. Believe me. Everything you see is totally her." She wipes her feet on the entryway rug, which is made of thick bristly sisal and says *Welcome* inside a big green heart.

"How do you keep everything so clean?"

"I don't. Sadie has a cleaner who comes every Tuesday."

I wipe my own feet when she's done. Everything is so white and pristine, it seems criminal to track mud inside. "Must be hard."

"What?" I can tell by her sideways glance she's trying to decide if I'm being sarcastic.

I hesitate, unsure of exactly how to phrase it. "Just, you know, letting someone else make those choices. How to furnish your house, that sort of thing."

"God, June, you don't even know." She sounds tired.

She makes a beeline for the stairs, and I follow. At the top, there's a bathroom to one side, and on the other is her bedroom. The wood floors and white furnishings give it a cozy, boatlike vibe. Amy stands in the doorway to her bedroom, looking around.

"Nothing seems to be missing." She goes inside, scanning the walls, the bed, the white linen chair.

As she stares out the French doors, her gaze loses focus. "Man, this is crazy."

I follow her into the bedroom. "How *did* you get those scratches?"

"Seriously?" She spins around. "Kimi's got a broken nose. You're not grilling her."

"I'm not grilling you. I'm just saying, it might be important. Do you remember how you got them?"

She sinks onto her bed, closes her eyes. "There's something. A memory. But I don't know what it means."

"I have a few of those, too," I admit. "What do you remember?"

"I wanted to bake a cake. I have no idea why." She looks out over the garden again, lost in recollection.

I wait for her to say more, but she just goes on staring out the French doors, her gaze distant. The rain taps out an intricate rhythm on the roof.

"You got the scratches baking a cake?" I don't even try to hide how unlikely this sounds.

Amy shakes her head, still not meeting my gaze. "Sadie tried to stop me. I can picture her face. She was angry. She had those little lines between her eyebrows that only break through the Botox when she's really pissed. She was trying to wrestle the electric mixer from my hands. Batter flew everywhere."

"Why would she try to stop you from baking a cake?" I ask, confused.

Amy blows a breath out, filling her cheeks. "When Sadie has guests, she cooks normal meals, but usually it's all kale smoothies and wheatgrass juice around here.

Sadie makes a cake exactly once a year, on Dakota's birthday. Other than that, it's verboten." Amy's smile is sad. "Dakota's birthday isn't until August, but Sadie's a planner. This will be her eighteenth, her last one living at home. She even ordered special baking chocolate from France."

"And that's what you used?"

Tears sparkle in her eyes. She nods.

"That's when she scratched you?"

Amy shakes her head like someone waking from a dream. "I don't know. Maybe. Seems as likely as anything else."

"You did bake it, though. She didn't stop you."

Her chin wobbles. "You think I did something to her, don't you?"

"No. Of course not." The truth is, I don't know what to believe. I hate that I'm questioning her with the same accusatory tone Ethan and Dakota just used on me, but these aren't just mild scratches; they're wounds. And her explanation is way too vague to provide much comfort.

Amy starts to cry. I sit beside her on the bed, wrap an arm around her. She says something into my shoulder so garbled I can't make it out.

"What's that?" I ask.

Her blue eyes search my face. "What if I've done something terrible? God knows I hated her sometimes."

I feel my stomach drop. Is she confessing? "Do you remember doing something terrible?"

"I don't remember much of anything. None of us do. How can we know?"

It's a good point. If we were drugged, though, one of us deliberately chose to put everyone in this position—

not knowing what happened, or what role we played in it. That implies whatever happened to Sadie was premeditated.

But who would do that? Why would they choose to act now, with a house filled with potential witnesses? Maybe this person figured if they abducted or killed her with all of us here, it would muddy the waters. Add drugs and booze to the mix, and the cops would have plenty of suspects, arrows pointing in so many directions they might never close the case.

Who had a strong enough motive? God knows we all held grudges against Sadie, but are any of them powerful enough to warrant doing her real harm? Those bloodstains could have come from a fight that got out of hand—especially if everyone was drugged to the gills. Which assumes the drugs were a separate event, though—not part of a larger plan to get rid of Sadie but a prank, some kind of sick attempt to make our weekend more exciting. I can't imagine anyone thinking that was a good idea. Not even Kimiko—with her playful love of altered states—would do that. We're almost forty, for God's sake, not eighteen.

I will my brain to work faster, but the hangover lingers, making me sluggish and muddled. Did one of us kill Sadie and dispose of her body? It seems so surreal. My premeditated-dosing theory doesn't jive with the bloodstains. Those stains point to a spontaneous attack; they imply an act of passion, not planning. Surely if this person had it all mapped out, including rendering us insensible with date-rape drugs, they'd get rid of her without leaving such damning evidence behind.

Amy, I realize, is still waiting for a response. I choose

my words carefully. "There's a pretty good chance that, if we were drugged, whoever dosed us also did—whatever they did—to Sadie. Don't you think?"

I can see her turning this over. Then a fresh thought occurs to her, and her eyes go wide with horror. She looks down at her swollen belly like she's just now noticed it. "Oh my God! What if I *was* drugged? The baby—I didn't even think—why didn't I think about that until now?"

"Have you felt it kicking?" I ask.

"What's wrong with me? Why didn't it occur to me to worry?" She runs her hands over her bump like she can ascertain the baby's health through her fingertips.

"Have you felt it kicking?" I repeat, slower and more deliberately this time.

She blinks, looking blank. "Actually, yeah. A lot. Does that mean—?"

"That's a good sign." The truth is, I know precious little about it, but Amy needs reassurance. "We should call your doctor, though, get you checked out."

"Who would do that to me? To my baby?" Amy looks at the ceiling, fear and fury mixing in her expression.

"Did you drink anything last night?" If we were drugged, it makes sense someone put it into our booze.

Amy's cheeks turn bright red. "One G&T. That's it. I swear."

I sigh, running a hand through my hair. It's tangled from last night. I feel a sudden desperate desire to take a shower, to wash last night from my skin, turn the water so hot it will scald the fragments of memory from my compromised brain.

Amy's eyes narrow to slits. "Kimiko's the one who brought the gin. She mixed everyone's drinks."

The same thought occurred to me, so I can't exactly shoot it down. Still, I don't like the knowing tone she's using, as if this proves something. "The bottle was out in the open. Anyone could have put something in it."

"She made a big deal about bringing it, though. Remember? Sadie wanted us to stick to wine, and she was like, 'I know you, Sades. That's why I brought my—'"

"It doesn't mean she drugged us," I insist. "If anything, she would have been more subtle about bringing her own gin if she planned to dose us with it, right?"

Amy ignores me. She's picking up speed, talking faster, a growing sense of conviction giving her words momentum. "You have to admit she's been acting like a freak. All that stuff about not calling the cops? And the way she *destroyed* Sadie's phone? Who does that?"

"She doesn't like cops." I keep my tone neutral.

"I'm just saying, if anyone drugged us, it's her."

I turn my theory over in my head again, looking at it from different angles. Maybe I'm too quick to assume none of us would drug everyone for fun—that it must be connected to Sadie's disappearance. I recall a night Kimiko fed the four of us pot brownies and didn't tell us until we were all good and high. Sadie was so pissed, she could barely speak. Still, that was ages ago. Kimiko's not an impish kid anymore. And besides, that was weed, not whatever the hell we might have taken this time.

We still don't even know for sure that drugs were involved. Maybe what I told the cops was true; we were all wiped out from the exercise and fresh air. We drank too much and passed out. So what if none of us remembers going to bed? It doesn't mean we were drugged.

I wish I was firing on all cylinders.

Amy flops back on her bed. Tears well up in her eyes again, spilling down the sides of her face, running toward her ears. "This whole thing is so crazy."

I recall what Kimiko told me in the kitchen about Ethan. Though I hate how we're all speculating behind each other's backs, accusing one another in whispers, I want to know Amy's take. "Is it true Ethan and Sadie were breaking up?"

She turns over onto her side. With a huff, she sits up, grabs a pillow, and squishes it under her head. She lies down again, trying to get comfortable, one hand over her belly. "Why do you ask?"

"Ethan said something about it."

"Well, then. Why would you doubt it?" There's something hard and guarded in her voice.

I shrug. "Nothing happened between us, but he made it pretty clear he's open to that. Sometimes guys exaggerate their marital problems. You know, the whole 'My wife doesn't understand me' cliché. Doesn't mean they were actually going to split up."

"Ethan's not like that." Half defensive, half raw.

I study Amy. She stares right back, tears gone now, an angry petulance to her lips. I sense I'm pushing my luck, pursuing this line of questions, but Ethan is the only one with an obvious motive. Though that only holds up if what Kimiko told me is true.

"If they did break up, would Sadie really get everything? Did they have a prenup or something?"

"Who told you that?" she snaps.

I consider refusing to answer but decide she'll figure it out anyway. "Kimiko."

Amy sits up, her spine ramrod straight. "She's just trying to throw suspicion onto him. God! She's really pissing me off."

I refuse to be distracted by this. "So it's not true about Sadie threatening to leave Ethan with nothing?"

Her gaze shifts away from me, sliding to the corner of the room. "I don't—I mean no, probably not."

"You're not sure?" I can't help the skeptical note that creeps into my voice. She said it herself: she knows plenty about the MacTavish household. How did she put it? Something about being woven into the fibers of this family, for better or worse.

"Sadie never told me that in so many words." She glances at me, looks away again. "I mean, once in a while I'd hear them arguing. Like most couples, money's something they bickered about. Doesn't mean she'd leave him penniless."

There's something she's not saying. I let the silence stretch out between us, the rain syncopating a quick rhythm on the roof.

Amy sighs, the rigid indignation seeping from her posture. "Sadie's worked hard for what she's got. This is all hers." She gestures at the room.

"So it is true."

"I'm not saying that. But if Ethan left her for someone else and she was pissed off about it?" She gives me a pointed look. "Sure, she'd probably screw him in the divorce. She has enough lawyers. Wouldn't you?"

A sick feeling washes through me; cold tingles run

down the front of my body. "You didn't see Ethan in the house last night, though, did you?"

Her eyes widen. "No. Definitely not."

"I'm not saying he did anything." I raise my hands, palms out. "I'm just trying to figure out what happened."

"Honestly, if I were you, I wouldn't pursue this line of thought."

"What do you mean?" I ask, wary.

"If this turns out to be—God forbid—murder, and the cops think Ethan did it?" She waits until I meet her gaze. There's something cold and impassive in her face, a warning. "You're not in the clear either."

I watch her, not daring to look away. "Meaning?"

"Come on, Moody. You snuck off to meet him at least once in the middle of the night." She raises an eyebrow. "That's not going to look good."

Is Amy threatening to tell the cops about that? I gape at her stupidly, unsure of how to react. Ethan already said he's planning to tell them about it, but the idea that Amy would make me look bad intentionally sends a jolt of fear through me, and I don't appreciate the snide tone or the implied threat.

She must read some of this in my face, because she scoffs. "I'm not planning to say anything. I'm just letting you know, you're not as stealthy as you think. If I saw you go down there, God knows who else did. We've got plenty of potential witnesses here."

Her use of the term *witnesses* feels like a knife at my throat. "I'm not trying to be stealthy. I've got nothing to hide. Ethan said he's going to tell them, if it comes to that. I will, too. We figure it's better to come clean, especially since nothing happened." There's a flicker of prim righteousness in my voice.

Amy snorts. Resentment swells inside me.

I stand, suddenly done with this conversation. "I'm going back to the house. You coming?"

Her gaze lingers, studying me with a calculating frown. "No. I'm going to call my doctor, let her know the situation, see if I need to go in."

"You should." I soften a little. "You want me to stay while you do that?"

"No." Amy pulls out her phone. "I'm fine. Thanks."

I let myself out, feeling nauseous and uneasy. Walking slowly through the thickening rain, I don't even care that I'm getting soaked. It feels good, being out in the brisk, ocean-scented air. I pray it will clear the last of my hangover, sharpen my senses. I need to get my head in the game, stop bumbling around like a drunk sorority girl at a frat party.

Amy's made it clear she's not an ally. Ethan and Dakota are sticking to each other like glue—family with family, outsiders be damned. Kimiko's all over the place, with her crazy, phone-smashing impulses and her certainty that the cops are out to get her. Even Em, the person I trust the most, has become mysterious, stewing over this new book Sadie was writing, refusing to tell me her secret.

I can't afford to trust anyone.

More than ever, I need to find out what really happened last night.

I WANDER THE HOUSE, looking for the others. There's a restless density to the air, a menacing bite to the silence.

I find myself drawn to a room at the end of a long hallway. This wasn't one of the rooms on Sadie's tour. It's at the far end of the second floor. As soon as I push open the door, I can feel Ethan everywhere.

There's a smell in here that's different from every other room. It's so masculine, so Ethan. I take a deep breath, filling my lungs. It's the rich perfume of leather and musty old books, the faint whiff of his citrusy cologne.

The peacock-green walls, the old-fashioned rolltop desk, the mustard-yellow couch and the brown leather chair beneath a brass gooseneck lamp—it's all vintage Ethan. More than anything, though, the floor-to-ceiling bookshelves packed with neatly arranged titles makes me think of him. There's even a wooden ladder that slides along the rails like the kind in old-fashioned bookstores. I can see him standing before our freshman English class in his fisherman sweater, plucking the novels he loved one by one from a teetering tower and waxing poetic about them as we sat riveted.

Going to the bookshelves, I run my fingers over the spines, my eyes skimming over the authors: Hardy, Milton, Conan Doyle, Dickens, Tolstoy, Nabokov. There's a special section for his modern Scottish favorites: Galloway, Kelman, Gray, Welsh. I smile at the corner dedicated to his secret guilty pleasure, trashy dime-store horror from the 1950s. Even their spines are lurid, with dripping bloody knives and devil faces crowding around titles like *Satan's Child* and *Beyond the Curtain of Dark*.

"What are you looking for?" Dakota's voice startles me.

I spin around so fast I knock a copy of *Satan's Child* to the floor. "You scared me."

"Sorry." She doesn't sound apologetic. She stands in the doorway, watching me. The light slanting through the windows shows the gemstone complexity of her eyes. There are layers in there—flecks of gold, veins of violet, fairy rings of copper.

I back away from her and sink into the brown leather chair, another wave of exhaustion hitting me.

She folds her skinny arms over her chest and leans against the wall. "Well? You didn't answer my question."

"I'm not looking for anything," I say. "I just didn't see this room before. It's very Ethan."

She doesn't answer.

"I wasn't trying to invade his space. It's just a cool office." I try to strike a balance between apologetic and unashamed. Just because I don't live here and she does, that doesn't give her the right to treat me like an intruder.

Dakota changes the subject. "Did you notice the mess in the kitchen?"

"What mess? The cake?"

"Something brown got splattered on the walls. At first, I thought it was blood—" She stops, her face going slack.

"What?" I study her, trying to read her eyes.

She blinks at me. "I just remembered something. Amy and Mom fighting."

"Yeah?"

"Amy wanted to bake a cake, but Mom wouldn't let her."

I nod. "Amy mentioned that."

Dakota comes over and sits on the couch, tucking her bare feet under her. "She and Mom fight. A lot."

"Over what?"

"Everything." She grabs a tissue from the side table and blows her nose. Her eyes are still bloodshot. I think she's been crying again. "You name it. For the last seven months, it's been all about the baby."

"What about it?"

She looks at me with a hint of pity. "Amy thinks Mom's going to highjack her kid and raise it herself."

I try to act surprised. "You think she'd do that?"

The look of pity deepens. "Have you met my mom? She's a total control freak. Babies are her favorite, because they have no will of their own."

She keeps her voice down, as if Sadie might barge in here any second. Lowering her voice to a whisper, she leans closer. "What if Amy finally lost it and hurt Mom, then tried to cover it up?"

"Amy wanted to go to the police right away," I point out. "She was adamant about it. You think she'd push for that if she'd done something wrong?"

"She's bipolar. Even if she didn't do anything, I'm scared they'll think she did. I mean, she's had some pretty gnarly episodes. That's not going to look good."

"No, it won't," I agree.

Dakota sighs, tears glistening in her eyes. "She might even be in Mom's will. I don't know for sure. That could look like a motive."

"Sadie had a will?"

"I think so. Wouldn't she?" Dakota gestures vaguely. "She's got lawyers and stuff. She's famous. I'm sure they'd push her to make one, right?"

"I guess that makes sense."

My phone buzzes with a text. I pull it from my back pocket. It's from Em. Where are you? We need to talk. I stuff the phone back into my pocket. When I look up, Dakota's staring hard, like she can see right through me.

"Everything okay?" She tries to sound concerned, but it's easy to detect the note of suspicion there.

"It's nothing. Just Em wondering where I am."

"You really think it was smart, lying to the cops?" she asks.

I'm not eager to revisit this topic—what's done is done—but I can't think of a way to shut it down, so I keep it simple. "I wasn't lying, exactly. I just didn't know what to say about all those missing hours."

She looks at the ceiling. "I mean, I see what you're saying. The whole 'we were drugged' thing sounds sketchy, but don't you think it might backfire, leaving that out?"

"Honestly? I'm not sure."

"Do you remember anything?" she asks.

"Just snippets. Nothing that makes much sense."

"I guess we're all wondering…" Her tone is musing, her eyes still on the ceiling.

"Wondering what?"

She looks at me. "If we did something. Something we don't remember."

Her question leaves me blinking. "None of us want to believe we're capable of…whatever this is."

The insanity of our situation hits me with fresh force. I let my head slump back against the leather chair, dizzy with stress.

Dakota lies down on the couch, resting her head on a

velvet pillow. I see the effort she makes not to cry—the muscles in her jaw tense, her brow tightens—but tears slide down her face anyway. For a second, I consider going to sit by her, stroking her hair, trying to provide comfort; it seems too intimate, though, invasive.

Instead, I prop my elbows on my knees and wait until she looks my way. "This has to be so hard on you."

She lets out a choked sound that's half laugh, half sob. "I just really want to know where she is, you know?"

"Of course."

"I'm worried about my dad, too. They weren't getting along. If something happened to Mom—" She stops herself.

I think of the way Dakota and Ethan clung to one another earlier, his hand cupping her head. The warmth between Dakota and her dad is the opposite of the coolness she emanated in her mother's presence. It must be confusing, having Sadie's frosty perfection on one side, Ethan's heat and humor on the other.

"He was alone at the beach house. That's not an alibi. If Mom doesn't show up, and they arrest Dad, I'll basically be an orphan." Her voice breaks. "Just like the girl in Mom's books."

Something inside me collapses like a house of cards. What she doesn't know is that it's even worse: he secretly met with me the night before. That makes him more suspect, and—as Amy so helpfully pointed out— it also implicates me.

"You used to be into him, huh? Back in college?" Dakota's blue eyes are trained on me, as if she's reading my thoughts. One thing Ethan has always been is preternaturally perceptive. I can tell she inherited this trait.

I lick my lips, my mouth suddenly dry. "I was, yeah."

"Are you still?" Her eyes never leave my face.

I'm still bent forward, resting on my knees. I want to hide, pull away, but I resist the urge. "We haven't spent much time together in years. We don't really know each other anymore."

"He told me about you once." She's so quiet now I can barely make out the words.

I'm dying to press for more details, but I just sit there, holding her gaze. I think about Amy casually blindsiding me yesterday with her knowledge that Ethan asked me to marry him—something I thought I'd done an admirable job keeping mostly secret. Sure, I told Em about it, but I trusted her not to tell anyone. I still do. Until now, I'd assumed only Ethan, Em, and I knew about it. Why would he tell anyone, let alone his wife, her cousin, or his daughter?

Em appears in the doorway, shattering the moment. "There you are." She looks at Dakota. "Sorry to interrupt, but I need to borrow June for a moment."

"What is it?" Dakota sits up, avid interest lighting up her face. "Did they find her?"

"No. I just need to talk to June about—our travel plans." Her effort to conceal the urgency is obvious.

I can tell Dakota doesn't buy it, but what can she say? I stand, giving Dakota's shoulder a quick pat on my way out. "We'll talk more later."

As we leave, I can feel her eyes following us.

I've got to watch myself with her.

NINE

EM AND I stand in Sadie's bedroom. It looks like a bomb went off in here. When I just glanced in here this morning, I was too distracted to take it in, but now I see that clothes, shoes, and jewelry cover every surface. It's beautiful, in a chaotic way; the festive mélange of colors and textures forms a haphazard collage, a pastiche of cashmere, silk, linen, and leather.

A fresh memory surfaces: Em and me tiptoeing into Sadie's shoe closet, staring at the wonderland of colors and textures. Playing dress-up in Sadie's room, trying on all her things. Em holds out her arm, covered from elbow to wrist in shiny bracelets. We're giggling like little girls. I can feel my face going hot.

"Holy Jesus," I whisper, surveying the mess. "Did we do this?"

"Right? That's what I thought." Em's face is tense with worry. She rubs her cheeks and sits on the floor amid the wreckage.

I go to Sadie's shoe closet. All the orderly, custom-made shelves filled with Jimmy Choo and Louboutin are now empty, the shoes lying in disarray all over the floor. "But why?"

"I keep asking myself the same thing." Em crawls to the entrance of the closet, wading through a tangle of sweaters. "What do you remember?"

I concentrate, clearing a space amid the shoes to sit down. "I have this image of gems in my hands, sparkly colors. You and me surrounded by piles of clothes. We kept getting the giggles. I think we were trying on makeup at one point."

Em nods. "I put on dark-red lipstick, and you told me I looked like Winona Ryder."

"What the hell, Em?" I stare at her. "It seems so unlike us."

She shrugs. "If we were dosed with roofies or GHB, those lower your inhibitions. Maybe, when Sadie showed us all this, we had a burning desire to explore, play dress-up."

"So we came back high as kites and ransacked the place?" I can't help taking this to a darker place inside my head. "Looks like we wanted to do more than just 'explore.' Maybe we wanted to mess it up."

Em's brow furrows. "I don't think we broke anything."

"This place was a shrine to perfection yesterday. Now it looks like a war zone."

"What are you saying?" She sounds impatient.

My gut tells me I was driven not by a childish desire to play princess but a need to violate. My decades-long obsession with Sadie's beauty and magnetism, her ability to do everything just a little better than everyone else—maybe it erupted in a destructive urge to inhabit and destroy, the need to dismember and consume every part of Sadie's shiny, candy-colored life.

Out loud, I can't quite bring myself to voice all of this. Instead, I murmur, "I'm just not sure it was so innocent."

"Well, I'm not the one who was obsessed with Sadie." Her impatience turns to defensiveness. "I didn't want her life. I've got my own."

"Oh, and I don't have a life?" Her comment stings. Is this what Em thinks of me—that I'm pathetic, neurotic, maybe even pathological?

"That's not what I'm—"

"Okay, fine," I say, squaring off to face her. "You were just playing in here, being a little girl, because you've got zero issues. I'm the one with the jealousy problem. I get it. If anyone wanted to mess this place up, it was me, not you."

"You're putting words in my mouth." She sounds exhausted. "That's not what I meant."

"Let's not talk about this, okay?"

Em's the one person on the planet I trust more than anyone, but I'm not in the mood to dissect this shameful part of myself. Even she would find it repellant. My jealousy of Sadie is a malignant tumor. It's grown over the years, fed by her *Vanity Fair* articles, her Facebook posts, her Instagram feed. Even when I unplugged from Sadie's media stream, I could feel her out there, a glaring sun trying to break through my shuttered blinds. The gorgeous, voluptuous curves of her life made my own existence look malnourished and scraggly.

If this room is any indication, last night that tumor started running the show. It doesn't take a huge leap to connect my violence toward her belongings to violence against Sadie herself.

Em massages her temples. "It's so maddening, all this missing time."

"I know."

My eyes fall on a beautiful oxblood boot lying on its side, the heel tangled with a canary-yellow belt. I don't want to think about the storyline the cops will piece together. As Amy said, I'm not going to come out of it looking blameless. Anyone can tell them how Sadie and I spent college locked in mortal combat, competing not just for Ethan's attention but for everything else worth having. When they learn I met with Ethan in secret my first night here, then came in here and demolished Sadie's inner sanctum, there's no way that's going to look anything but suspicious.

If I suspect myself, why wouldn't they?

"Do you think Fisher saw this?" Em's voice sounds choked.

I shake my head. "He just looked at the stairwell. He didn't search the whole house. I think they need a warrant for that."

"Do we admit we kind of remember being in here, or is that just asking for trouble?"

I sigh, reaching out to stroke an impossibly soft cashmere scarf. "Maybe telling them we crashed out wasn't such a good idea. Now if we admit to fragments of memory, we'll contradict ourselves."

"But if we flat out deny any memory of it, all they have to do is look for prints. We'll be all over this place." She stares at the empty shelves of the walk-in closet, her eyes wide with fear.

I look around, imagining all the damning bits of DNA we've left behind—strands of hair, skin cells, our fingerprints as distinct and pristine as bull's-eyes.

"June?"

Something in her voice makes me look at her, my heart beating faster. "Yeah?"

"I'm scared." She hugs her knees, lowers her voice to a breathy whisper. "Do you think she's dead?"

I close my eyes, trying to find an answer that's true. It's the stark reality we've all been skirting around. At the same time, we've been preparing ourselves for it, bracing for the possibility, even as we actively deny it. "I don't know. Maybe."

"I have to tell you something."

My senses go on high alert. I'm not sure I want to hear her confession. I force myself to say, "What is it?"

"I've been looking for her manuscript."

"Her manuscript?"

"Her work in progress." She breathes out a sad sigh. "The one I told you about last night."

With a chill, I recall how infuriated Em was, the hurt and betrayal in her eyes when she told me about Sadie's new book. Something she said comes floating back to me now, through the sluggish brain fog of my hangover. *I have a right to my secrets.*

Em looks contrite. She chews on a fingernail, an old habit I thought she'd kicked back in college. "I tried to get into her computer a little while ago, but it was password protected. I even looked in her drawers, but then Ethan came in, and I had to make up some excuse."

"What exactly were you trying to—?"

"I told you," she snaps. "She has no right to tell my story. Everyone I grew up with will know it's about me. My mom will be—God, I can't even think about it. She'll be so irate. I can't have the whole world pawing through my private…"

"Your private what?"

"Shame." The second it's out of her mouth, she looks like she wants to take it back.

I study her, confused. What the hell is going on here? Em's my best friend in the world. How can she be carrying something this heavy without me having the slightest inkling about it?

"Look, I know you said you don't want to talk about it, but…" I can't keep the frustration from my voice.

She considers me for a long moment. "You know how I told you I lost my virginity on prom night?"

"Yeah."

"I lied." Her hands fly to her face. She won't look at me. "I lost it when I was sixteen. With my mom's boyfriend."

"Em, oh my God." I move toward her, but she flinches away from me. "Why didn't you tell me?"

She jerks her hands away from her eyes, staring at me with a hostility that looks totally out of place on her. "I told you, I don't want to talk about it. I didn't want to talk about it then and I don't now."

"It can't be healthy, though, keeping it a secret."

She stands, her hands balled into fists. "What is wrong with you people? It's *my* secret, and I have a right to keep it that way. Nobody else gets to decide."

"Okay, yes." I try to placate her. "I see that. But—"

"No! There are no buts here. It's my decision. End of story. If I wanted to shout it from the rooftops in some kind of 'me too' frenzy, then fine, that's my right. If I want to keep it to myself, that's also *my goddamn right*." Her shoulders rise with tension. "Sadie has some crazy notion that it will be empowering. Like if she tells my story it will help me heal, help other people heal—blah, blah, blah. So patronizing. The bottom line is, she doesn't get to make that call. This book will destroy my relationship with my mom, okay? I never even told Reggie—I never told anyone."

"Except Sadie."

Em's face is rigid with anger, her face splotchy and red. She doesn't respond.

"Why her?" It comes out sounding petty, childish.

Em grimaces. "Really, June? Are you going to make *even this* a competition between you and the Great Sadie MacTavish?"

"No—I mean…" I take a deep breath, defensiveness colliding with the realization that she's right. This isn't about me. "I'm sorry, I just wondered, that's all. You're my best friend. I didn't realize you and Sadie were that close."

She sighs, sinking back onto the floor. "The summer you and Ethan were together, after graduation? Sadie and I went to a music festival. He was there. Johan. He's a drummer in some stupid band. Sadie saw how upset I was after talking to him, and it just—I don't know. It all came out. She's the only person I ever told. It felt kind of good at the time—cathartic, I guess. Now I wish I'd kept my mouth shut."

I'm not sure what to say. It feels like every conversational alley has a great big roadblock in front of it. I can't ask any details about Johan the mysterious drummer, obviously. She's made her feelings on that abundantly clear.

Em glares at the floor. "Sadie was dead set on keeping it one hundred percent real. Remember how obsessed she was with Truman Capote's *In Cold Blood*? This is like her version. Orcas Island is so small, and the details she planned to include would make it obvious to anyone from there that it's about me. She wasn't even going to change our first names."

"Why would she do that?" I'm mystified.

"Because she could, I guess." After a long, tense silence, Em runs her hands through her hair and lowers her voice to a whisper. "All I remember about last night is how angry I was at Sadie. How badly I wanted to stop her from doing this—from dragging all this out of the past and into the present."

"What are you saying?" The little hairs on the back of my neck stand at attention.

She hugs her knees tighter, gnawing on her lip. "I've never been that pissed at anyone in my life. I felt so betrayed. So hurt."

For the second time today, I wonder if I'm about to hear a confession. When I thought Amy might be about to spill, that was bad enough. If it's Em, I don't think I can handle it.

Is Em capable of attacking Sadie in a blind rage? Maybe it was more calculated than that. Maybe she knew she had to keep Sadie from publishing this book and violence was the only path open to her. I remember her saying last night that she'd sue her. That was so out of character. As soon as she'd said it, though, she must have realized legal means were out of the question. You can't sue somebody for writing a novel based on something you consider to be "your secret." Even if she tried, Sadie has way more lawyers and resources than Em. That battle was lost before it even began.

I hear her voice in my head, raw yet determined. *Screw it, let's do some shots.* After that, everything goes black.

I study Em's profile, wondering how far she'd go to keep this from coming out.

I can't endure the suspense. I steel myself to ask her, flat out. "Are you saying you know what happened to Sadie? That you had something to do with it?"

Her eyes go wide. "No. Of course not."

I try to gauge her sincerity. I'm so used to trusting what Em tells me without question. Now, though, I'm forced to admit I never knew her as well as I assumed.

She massages her neck. "But that's the problem, right? All this missing time. I don't know for sure what I did or didn't do. None of us do."

"That's the problem," I agree.

Em looks around, her eyebrows raised in question. "Do you think we should clean up in here? Is that tampering with evidence?"

I ponder this, trying to imagine how the cops will view it. If we clean up and wipe everything down, at least we don't have to worry about them finding traces of us all over her beautiful things.

"Fisher didn't tell us not to…" I can hear the note of doubt in my voice.

Em stands. "I say we do it. If he asks, we'll say we didn't want her coming home to a mess."

I get to my feet, glad for something to do. Going into the bathroom, I grab two washcloths and hand one to Em.

She looks at it. "What's this for?"

"Wiping prints."

I see her throat move in a hard swallow, but she doesn't argue.

We get to work.

WE'RE STILL CLEANING the bedroom when Kimiko finds us. She looks around at the remaining mess, her dark eyes taking it in. "What the hell happened in here?"

Em and I exchange a quick glance. We haven't talked about what to tell the others. I make an executive decision.

"We don't know. If Sadie sees it like this, though, she'll freak. We thought we'd tidy up."

Kimiko eyes the washcloth in my hand, one brow arching. Her lips fold in like she's holding back whatever she's tempted to say.

"Where's everyone else?" I ask, changing the subject.

"Out looking for Sadie."

Em looks up from the silk blouses she's arranging in the closet. "Where?"

"Anywhere they can think of, I guess. The places she goes—grocery stores and cafés, that kind of thing." Kimiko picks up a floppy hat from the floor and tries it on. "It would be so random if they found her pushing a cart through Safeway like nothing's wrong."

I can't help thinking she's being a little cavalier. Her eyes are bloodshot. I wonder if she's stoned.

I've just finished arranging a row of stilettos, wiping each one with meticulous care, when something occurs to me. If the cops do dust for prints and they find everything conspicuously print-free, will that trigger even louder alarm bells than finding our grubby smudges everywhere? I woke up in Sadie's pajamas. Em was wearing Sadie's jewelry. If Amy or Kimiko bring this up it won't take much detective work to deduce that we wiped the place down. Surely they'll wonder what we're hiding.

It's like a Russian nesting doll of danger. Each time we do something to cover our tracks, a new problem emerges.

Kimiko sits on the bed, watching us. "What's with the washcloths?"

The shoe room is back in order. I go to Sadie's bureau. Makeup lies strewn across the gleaming wood surface. It reminds me of when the five of us would gather in someone's dorm room or apartment and get dressed before going out, hair spray hanging thick in the air, makeup and clothes everywhere.

Kimiko's still waiting for one of us to answer. I glance at Em, who's now folding sweaters into tidy rectangles, stacking them one on top of the other. She hasn't replied, so I guess it's up to me.

"We figured, if the cops found our prints everywhere, it might look bad." I don't want to get into our half-baked memories of trashing this place.

Kimiko watches me, her mouth curved into a shrewd little smirk.

"We're not hiding anything. I mean, not really. We just don't want them to get the wrong idea, in case—" I hesitate.

"Sadie turns up dead," Kimiko finishes.

"Or hurt. Or whatever," I agree.

Kimiko sighs, grabbing a pillow and hugging it to her. "How do you think it went with that cop?"

"I don't know." I turn my attention to the makeup,

closing the lids on eye shadows, capping lipsticks. "I couldn't tell what he was thinking."

"I'll tell you what he was thinking: this Asian chick with the broken nose and bad attitude is suspect numero uno."

"We're all afraid of looking sketchy," Em says from the closet. "None of us is in the clear."

"Except only one of us is a minority with signs of having been in a knock-down, drag-out fight."

I keep my back to her, organizing the makeup into piles—lipsticks in one corner, eye shadows in another, eyeliners and brow pencils lined up in a tidy row. She's got a point, of course. Still, I can't help feeling a little annoyed that it's all about her.

I change the subject. "Do you have any memory of how you broke your nose?"

"Not really. There's something I do remember, though. I can't stop thinking about it." Kimiko stares at the floor, her eyes glazed as she tries to dig up the memory. "I was outside. It was dark. There were trees. I'm pretty sure I saw a car heading down the drive."

Em comes out of the closet. "What sort of car?"

"I couldn't see the color or the make, but I have a vague impression of a sports car, something compact and low to the ground. It must have been a dark paint job, because anything light would have shown up, and it was just a shadow. But the weirdest part?" She squints in concentration. "I could swear it was driving with its lights off, like whoever it was didn't want to be seen."

We all mull this over, trying to fit it into the patchy equation of what we know. A faint glimmer of hope shines like a distant star. Maybe Amy was right. This could have been an outside job. It's a grim sort of hope, clinging to the notion that a stranger abducted Sadie. Still, it's a thousand times better than thinking one of us did.

"The gate was closed though, right?" Em picks up a strand of pearls from the floor, wiping them absently with her washcloth. "That means someone here must have let the driver in."

Another silence blooms as we chew on this.

I wipe the makeup down, then transfer each tube, pencil, and brush to the top drawer of Sadie's bureau, using the washcloth like a clumsy mitten. "I wish you could tell the cops about that. It might sound weird, though, since we've already said we slept through it. Maybe we should have just told them the truth."

Kimiko makes a sound in her throat. "Full disclosure doesn't pay when it comes to cops. Believe me."

A gust of wind rattles the glass doors to the balcony, making us all jump.

"What were you doing outside last night?" Em asks Kimiko. Her tone is mild, but I can hear the note of suspicion woven through it.

Kimiko's fingers tighten around the pillow. "No idea. Why?"

"Just wondering…"

"I'm not going to tell you guys stuff if this is the reaction I get." Kimi's voice sounds too loud, bouncing off the massive windows.

Em turns her back and busies herself arranging Sadie's jewelry. "Don't be so defensive."

"You're the one who's making it sound like going outside is a capital offense." Kimiko's eyes narrow.

"Why were *you* digging through Sadie's writing studio?"

Em spins around, her mouth forming a surprised *O*.

"Ethan told me he caught you. What was that about?" Kimiko clutches the pillow like she's prepared to use it as a weapon.

"Look, let's not turn on each other." I employ a conciliatory tone, trying to diffuse the mounting tension.

"Whatever. This shit's making me crazy." Kimiko stands, tossing the pillow onto the bed and heading for the door. "I don't know about you guys, but I'm going outside to smoke a bowl."

"You think that's a good idea? What if Fisher comes back with more questions?" I ask.

Kimiko ignores me. She's already halfway down the hallway, heading for her stash.

As Em and I finish cleaning the bedroom, her phone rings. It's her boyfriend Reggie's signature ring tone, "Super Freak."

"You mind if I take this?" Em says, pulling it from her pocket.

"Of course not."

She darts out of the room. I hear her murmur, "Hey, babe." Then she hurries into her room and closes the door.

I wonder what she'll tell him. For a second, I think about calling Pete. Then I remember with a sick jolt that Pete's in Amsterdam with Allegra, his twentysomething golden-haired paramour. I grab my sweater and head down the stairs, craving fresh air.

The rain's let up to a slow, misty drizzle. Patches

of blue appear between the clouds. The cold feels delicious. The pines and cypress glitter with raindrops. I pull on my coat and head toward the water.

I catch a whiff of weed as I pass the garden. Only the top of Kimiko's head is visible above a tangle of jasmine. I consider going to join her. Right away I reject the idea. I require a clear head. The last thing I need is a paranoid stoner lens clouding everything.

My feet carry me down the drive, a long black twisting ribbon. When the pavement stops, I step onto the sand that stretches like a strip of suede in either direction. Driftwood litters the shoreline. The voluptuous bay glows a deep, melancholy blue.

I'm not surprised when I see Leo pull up at his yurt. He must be just getting back from Port Townsend. His old blue pickup truck swings into the dirt driveway. The smile on his face when he spots me sends a warmth through me I don't expect.

"June Moody." He says my name like an incantation.

"You heard about Sadie, right?" I'm beyond social graces. I know I'm being abrupt and artless, but I don't care. Sadie left Leo's yurt last night pissed off. Now she's missing, leaving only bloodstains in her wake. I can't fall for this guy just because his smile liquefies me. For all I know, he's a murderer.

He backs up a step, caught off guard by my greeting. "I did. Ethan said she's missing."

"Did he tell you about the bloodstains?" I sound shrill, high-strung. I make a conscious effort to lower my voice. "Did he mention that?"

Leo shakes his head, brows pulling together in concern. "What bloodstains?"

I explain about the splatter at the top of the stairs and the stain on the landing. His expression darkens. He's got a couple days of stubble. I remember, with breath-taking clarity, the feel of that stubble against my skin. I stop explaining. My mouth goes dry.

"Was I with you last night?" Again, not subtle, but I'm too frazzled for finesse.

Leo cocks his head, eyes sparkling as he watches me blush. "You messing with me right now?"

"It sounds bizarre, I know, but I might have been drugged." I stare at the ground, sheepish. "I have a few memories, but none of them fit together."

He runs his open palm down his face like he's hav-ing trouble taking this in.

"There's a lot of missing time," I say.

Leo's eyes are baffled. "What do you remember?"

"Just fragments: the woods, the beach, clothes, a scream…" I hesitate. "A kiss."

He grimaces and looks around at the bay like he ex-pects to find an answer there. "This is awkward."

"Believe me, I'd remember if I could."

Out of nowhere, I imagine gripping Sadie's Kwan Yin statue like a bat. My muscles tense as I swing, putting my weight into it, making contact with Sadie's skull. A rooster tail of blood on the wall. Did I hate her that much? If that's the big reveal my brain's hiding from me, I'd rather keep it hidden.

Leo puts a hand on my arm. Even through my coat, I can feel the warmth of his fingers. "Do you want to come in?"

I think of his yurt, so circular and cozy. Yearning breaks open inside me. Something about being in an enclosed space with him right now seems too risky, though. It's not just the unanswered questions. It's not even the pall of danger hanging over the property like a shroud. It's the realization that I don't trust myself with him. The current of heat running between our bodies is palpable. You could power a city off us. I can't be distracted by lust right now. Sadie's missing. This is real.

"Maybe we can just walk?" I gesture toward the beach.

He nods, but I catch the look of wounded confusion in his eyes. "Sure."

We stroll in silence a moment, navigating the driftwood strewn about the beach like dismembered body parts.

"Why was Sadie here last night?" I can hear the thread of fear in my voice. I try to steady it with a mask of calm. "She left pissed off. Why?"

"That's a big question."

I sit on a muscular trunk of driftwood, its branches snarling off toward the water. "Tell me. I've got time."

Leo sits beside me, the fog curling in his hair, forming dewdrops. "How do I know I can trust you?"

"Trust me?" I blink at him, stung.

His smile is sad. "Come on, June. You came here twice yesterday, knocked me on my ass, and now you tell me you don't remember?"

"I remember the first time." I try to make my face look trustworthy. "Around sunset, we had whiskey. We talked."

"But the second time?" He winces at my blank look. "Holy shit, nothing?"

"A kiss. But I wasn't sure who—"

"A kiss," he repeats, his expression pained.

I nod.

He gets up, kicks at a strand of seaweed. "This is unbelievable."

"What?" I'm alarmed by Leo's distress, but I'm at a disadvantage here. I'm walking in during the last five minutes of the movie, trying to get someone to explain the previous two hours. "Tell me."

His breathing is ragged. He stands on a burl lodged in the sand like a crashed spaceship. "I have no idea what to do with this. Drugged? Who would—?"

"I don't know. None of us remember much. We're trying to figure it out."

He stares out at the water, looking like someone who has just realized he's the butt of an enormous cosmic joke.

"We have bigger things to worry about." It comes out sharper than it sounded in my head.

He whips around to face me. For a second, I think he's angry, but then his expression softens. "You're right. I'm sorry."

"What did you and Sadie argue about?" I know I sound like a broken record, but I don't care.

He sits beside me again, his face angled toward the sand, elbows on his knees. "If I tell you, I need to know you'll keep it to yourself."

"Of course." Our secrets have become commodities, traded on the black market like illegal weapons.

Leo turns to take me in. There's a new watchfulness there, a wariness at odds with the wide-open smile he gave me climbing out of his truck. I wonder what passed between us last night to make that smile possible. It feels wrong to squander such tenderness. At the same time, I have no way to claim it. Whoever he kissed last night, whatever happened between them, that wasn't me.

He runs a hand through his hair, smearing the drops of mist. "What's going on with the cops? Have they been here?"

"Yeah. Officer Fisher left a couple hours ago."

"What does he think?" He squints at me, his earlier playfulness vanished.

I shake my head. "I don't know."

"You don't know?"

"We didn't tell him about the missing time."

He puffs out a breath. "Why not?"

"How would that sound to you? 'Oh, hey, our friend's missing, there's a big spray of blood on the wall, another on the floor, and by the way, we have a collective case of amnesia, which may or may not be the result of drugs we may or may not have unknowingly ingested.'" My voice rises with each word, hysteria and defensiveness blurring together.

His hand lands on my knee. "Okay. Sorry. I'm just trying to catch up here."

"Join the club."

I stare at his hand on my leg. It's strong and brown. Veins form faint bulging lines from his wrist to his knuckles. It's a beautiful hand, capable and masculine and so reassuring I want to cry. I want to press it to my racing hummingbird heart, certain that, if I do, the frantic beating in my chest will go still.

He must interpret my gaze as a reproach, because he removes his hand, shoving it into the pocket of his jacket. Instantly, I miss the weighty warmth of it.

"They're looking for her, I assume?"

I'm not sure what he's asking, having lost the thread of the conversation. I refocus my attention. "The cops? Yeah. Ethan, Dakota, and Amy are out there, too. They're driving around to her usual haunts."

"How are Ethan and Dakota?"

"Freaked out. Like all of us, only more so."

"And Amy?"

"Same."

"I bet." He shakes his head, his gaze turning back to the water with a searching intensity.

I clear my throat. "I can't help but notice I'm the only one answering questions here."

He smiles, but there's no joy in it, only apprehension. "Right. Sadie. Last night. Look, I'll tell you, but I need you to swear—"

"I already said I won't tell anyone." I can't keep the note of impatience from my voice.

"Everything I've got here depends on keeping my distance." He levels his gaze at me, willing me to understand. "I live here, I work here, but I'm not part of their world. That's the secret to my survival. You get what I'm saying?"

I nod, though I sense I'm missing something. There's weight to his words, a gravity that goes beyond that of an employee talking about his employers. I remember Sadie leaving his yurt last night, dark hair flying behind her as she sprang out the door like an angry genie released from her bottle. Nothing about this implies Leo managed to keep the distance he claims to value, but I say nothing, waiting for him to continue.

"I came here three years ago because I needed this."

He gestures at the water, the beach, the trees sparkling with rain. "I was in a bad place. Sadie offered me a second chance. I knew, if I didn't take her up on it, I'd be dead in a matter of months."

I can't help raising my eyebrows at this. There's no hint of hyperbole in his tone; he's just telling it like it is.

"As soon as I got here, it became clear this family has problems. Serious problems." Leo glances at me, assessing my reaction before resuming his study of the water. "Sadie tried to enlist me as her confidant. I told her straight up that wasn't going to happen. I've got my own stuff to deal with. The last thing I need is to get tangled in their web."

"So you rejected her," I say.

He looks at me, something flickering behind his eyes. "I guess."

"And last night? Was she trying to enlist you again?"

"In a way." He winces, remembering. "Except this time it was different. She didn't want a confidant. She wanted someone to tell her she's still got it."

"She tried to seduce you?"

A quick bark of laughter, dry and humorless. "That's not how I'd phrase it, but okay. Yeah. She tried to kiss me, and I shut her down. Whatever's happening in her marriage, there's no way I'm going to put myself in the middle of it."

"Seems like weird timing," I say, puzzled. "Why would she make the moves on you when we're all here?"

He looks embarrassed. "That might be my fault."

"What do you mean?"

"I kind of messed up." His cheeks go pink.

"Messed up how?"

He hesitates. "I asked about you."

"Oh." It comes out startled.

"She came down here to tell me about—I don't know—some plants she'd ordered, some kind of bullshit. Anyway, I guess I seemed a little too interested in the mysterious June Moody." He shoots me a sideways glance, studies the water. "She's threatened by you."

I remember the feeling I got, stepping onto Leo's porch. Was it paranoia, that sense that Sadie watched us from the dark enclosure of the forest? Did I feel that telltale prickle on the back of my neck? If she was watching, what passed through her mind?

I can picture it all too clearly. She makes a pass at Leo; he pushes her away. She leaves in a huff, feeling worse than ever, bruised and humiliated. Then she sees me slipping through his door, a welcome guest. She remembers all the times I got the thing she'd been denied: the better grade on an essay, the scholarship we both applied for, the first proposal from Ethan. She broods out there in the cold, damp forest. She vows to get her revenge.

We meet at the top of the stairs later that night. She confronts me, calling me names, hurling invectives with the venomous intensity only Sadie can manage. In her blind fury, she's missed something important. She's not prepared for the anger I've stored up, equal in its toxicity. I grab the statue to defend myself, and when she comes at me I lash out, unleashing years of pent-up jealousy. Blood explodes from her head, spraying the wall. Her knees buckle and she tumbles down the stairs, landing with a hollow, sickening thud on the landing.

Is this memory or paranoid hallucination?

"June?"

I snap out of my reverie and find Leo staring at me, a question in his eyes.

"Sorry. I'm just really—" I break off, unsure how to finish. What am I? Confused? Scared? Guilty?

"This whole thing is scary." His voice is gentle.

There's a throbbing sound in my ears. I think it might be my heart. "Yeah."

He stands, rubbing his hands together. "It's cold out here. I'm going inside. You're welcome to join me."

I get to my feet. The memory of that kiss assails me. It occurs to me that I still don't know what passed between us last night. In my current state of miserable self-doubt, pursuing this line of questioning seems doomed. I decide instead to focus on the essentials.

"Look, I know something happened between us and now's probably not the time to get into it." I push my hair out of my face, avoiding his eyes. "I just need to know. Is there anything you can tell me that might have some bearing on Sadie's disappearance?"

He considers me for a long moment. An entire universe of memories plays out behind his eyes—a universe I can't access.

"Nothing I can think of, no."

My phone chimes. I pull it from my jacket pocket. It's a text from Em. Where are you? Cops asked Ethan to station for questions.

"I've got to go," I say.

"What is it?" Leo looks a little queasy.

"The police asked Ethan down to the station." I tuck my phone back into my pocket. "They'll probably want to talk to you, too."

Something closes in his face, a heavy steel gate pulled down over a shopfront at night. I can almost hear the decisive click as it locks into place. "They know where to find me."

TEN

As I WALK in the door, the smell of burnt toast floats toward me. Angry voices in the kitchen grate against my ears. A part of me wants to make a beeline for Dakota's old room, hide away upstairs and bypass the drama. God knows I'm in no mood to look each one of them in the eyes, wondering which one of us is responsible for whatever happened to Sadie. My stomach writhes like a fish inside me.

I check my reflection in the hall mirror. I'm wild-eyed, my cheeks flushed with cold, my blond hair unkempt. I try to smooth the flyaway strands. Nothing I can do about the eyes, though. There's something feral in my face I don't recognize.

When I get to the kitchen, the argument's reached a fever pitch. Amy's wearing the same incredulous, pissed-off expression she's worn since Sadie went missing. Her hands grip the counter so hard her knuckles have gone white. Dakota's jammed her fingers into her hair, her face conflicted. Kimiko's between them, her body angled toward Amy, her hands splayed out to the side like she's ready to throttle someone. Em's in the corner, her eyebrows arched and her arms folded.

"She's an adult." Kimiko's voice is low and dangerous as I walk in. "She can make her own choices."

Amy barks out a laugh, a hard, mirthless syllable that slaps the air. "Shows what you know! She's seventeen."

"Close enough," Dakota puts in.

"You're seventeen, and your mom is missing, and drugs are not the answer here, I promise you."

Kimiko shakes her head. "You smoked so much weed when you were her age, Amy."

"And look how that turned out."

Kimiko holds a finger up. "Whatever's going on with you, don't blame it on weed."

Amy's head jerks back like Kimiko has slapped her, but she lets it pass. "Sadie wouldn't stand for this. In her absence, I'm the closest thing Dakota has to a mom."

Dakota lopes over to Amy, wraps an arm around her waist. "Come on, Amy. You were always cooler than Mom. Don't get all uptight. I'm fine. It's just weed."

Amy's mouth pulls into a martyred frown. "If I have to be the bad guy here, fine. I'll do it."

"Nobody has to be the bad guy." Dakota fusses with Amy's hair, smoothing a place where Amy's anxious fingers have worked it into a tangle.

"Believe me," Amy insists, "when you're our age, you'll be glad you had somebody setting limits for you."

"That's such bullshit!" Kimi explodes. "Kids have to make their own choices."

"Really worked out well with Jacob, huh? He's a model citizen."

Kimiko lowers her chin, her stare going dangerous. "Don't you dare bring my son into this."

Amy's too worked up to stop, though. She's found a vulnerable spot, and she can't help plunging the knife in with everything she's got. "What's he in for? Oh, that's right. Selling drugs. Twelve years old, and he's pushing crack on the corner. Nice work there, Kimi."

It happens so fast, none of us have time to react. Kimiko grabs a coffee cup and hurls it across the room. It's not quite aimed at Amy's head, but it's close enough. Amy ducks. The mug smashes against the wall behind her, shattering into a thousand pieces.

Silence.

Amy grabs Dakota's hand and pulls her toward one of the doors to the veranda, giving Kimiko a wide berth. She glances over her shoulder at Kimiko. "You're out of control, Kimi. Get your shit together, or get out."

They clamber out the door, practically running toward Amy's house. As they hurry through the garden, Dakota peeks back over her shoulder at us, her expression bewildered.

I glare at Kimiko. This is the second time today she's hurled an object in anger. This time she threw it at Amy—not close enough to show serious intent, but too close for comfort. How much of a stretch is it to imagine her picking up a statue in anger and bringing it down on Sadie's head? God knows they fought. They always did, even back in the day.

One night, when we were stumbling from bar to bar, Kimiko slapped Sadie across the face. Kimiko claimed Sadie had passed out and she needed to wake her up, but it wasn't the gentle pat you might apply to someone's cheek in an effort to rouse her. It was a full-on Scarlett O'Hara–style slap. Even though we were all wasted at the time, laughing like hyenas, I remember being frightened by her capacity for violence.

"What the hell was that about?" I go to the coffee-pot and find it's empty.

When I meet Em's eye, she shakes her head. "Don't look at me. I walked in a few seconds before you did."

Em shovels beans into the grinder, preparing to make a fresh pot. She glances at Kimiko, obviously waiting for an explanation.

"If there's one thing that sets me off, it's hypocrisy." Kimiko hops up onto the counter, her body still bristling with anger. She rummages in her bag and pulls out a glass pipe. Then she produces a silver tin, opens it, and starts filling the pipe with weed.

"Is that supposed to explain something?" I sound impatient, but I don't care.

Kimiko sighs. "I suggested we smoke some weed, take the edge off while we wait."

"Let me guess," I say. "Dakota wanted to join you, and Amy freaked out."

"Exactly! Like we didn't get high as fuck when we were her age. What's the big deal? The girl's mom is missing. The least we can do is offer her premium medicinals."

Em pushes the top down on the coffee grinder, filling the room with its high-pitched whine. When she's finished, Em scoops the grounds into the coffeemaker. Something changes in her expression.

She looks up, startled. "I just remembered something."

"What?" I swallow. My mouth has gone dry. Every memory that surfaces is potentially incriminating. What if Em points the finger at me?

Em leans against the counter, the coffee temporarily

forgotten. She looks at Kimiko, who is carefully packing her pipe. "We were outside smoking weed. Last night sometime. I don't know when. We were in the backyard."

"And Sadie caught us," Kimiko finishes.

Another loaded silence falls over us. Kimiko studies her pipe like it's a delicate experiment requiring her full attention.

"If you'd already remembered that, why didn't you mention it?" Em asks.

Kimiko shrugs, petulant. "Didn't seem relevant."

"Sadie yelled at you. Oh my God." Em studies the air, grasping at the gossamer threads of memory. "Dakota was out there, too. Sadie was furious. She called you a lowlife druggie. She pulled Dakota into the house and slammed the door."

"And then I killed her because she was an uptight bitch." Kimiko's voice is hard.

"I'm not saying that."

"Then what are you saying, Em?"

Em turns her attention back to making coffee. "If you remember that and you didn't say anything, what else are you not saying?"

"I think I took a crap around midnight. Is that important? Is that the detail that's going to break the case wide open?" Kimiko's mouth twists in distaste. "The fact that Sadie's got blinders on when it comes to her daughter and acted all injured because we got high did not lead to her getting killed."

"You don't know that." Em pours water into the coffeemaker, her shoulders tense. "Any scrap of memory could lead to another, and another."

"And then what?" Kimiko pushes off the counter and stalks toward the back door. "Then we know who did this, whatever *this* is. So what? What good is the truth going to do us?"

"At least we'd know," Em says, her voice quiet.

"Yeah, so we can torture ourselves with it for the rest of our lives."

"Hey," I snap, my voice a warning. "That's enough."

Kimiko makes a sound of disgust and slams the door leading out into the yard, one hand digging in her pocket for a lighter.

A FEW MINUTES LATER, I tap at Em's door. I can hear her bustling around inside, banging drawers shut. It takes her a moment to respond. When she does, her voice is tired.

"Come in."

I push my way inside. Em has her silver suitcase on the bed, already half packed.

"Hey," I say.

She goes on packing, her slim frame tense as a guitar string tuned several octaves too high.

I decide not to address the packing issue just yet. "So Ethan's down at the station answering questions?"

She nods. I wait for her to elaborate, but she doesn't. I watch as she yanks a shirt off a hanger and folds it into her suitcase.

"Look, I know what you're going to say," Em tells me.

I sit on the edge of the bed. Everything in here is a smoky lavender, a bruised color somewhere between purple and gray. The silk pillows sit propped up against the leather headboard in an immaculate line. A chande-

lier dangles from the center of the room, crystal drop-
lets quivering from the silver candelabra. The overall
effect is that of a classy boutique hotel, one that leaves
chocolates on your pillow.

"What am I going to say?" I flop onto the bed, kick
off my shoes, and stretch out, my body going limp after
the chaos of the morning.

"That I have to stay." Em knocks over one of the
vintage perfume bottles on the nightstand in her haste.
She's always been the steady one in our group, cool
and methodical. Now her fingers tremble as she sets
the bottle upright.

"I'm not going to say that." Of course I need Em to
stay, but she doesn't react well to direct confrontation.
It's essential that I play my cards right here, easing her
toward the decision so she doesn't feel cornered.

She looks at me, a wary frown on her pixielike face.
"You're not?"

"I get it. This situation is completely messed up."

"It's not just that."

I twist onto my side and prop my head on one hand,
though it takes effort just to move. My bones ache with
exhaustion. I could happily curl up right here and sleep
for days. "What is it, then?"

"I thought we were in this together," Em says. She
goes to the window and looks out, one hand against
the glass.

"And now?"

"Typical Kimi, you know? She has to do her own
thing. God, that used to drive me crazy back in the
day. Remember how she'd always flip-flop at the last

second? We'd come up with an idea, be all ready to go, then—bam!—last possible moment, she'd flake."

I nod. One incident in particular comes to mind. It was winter break our junior year. Kimiko, Em, and I were supposed to spend a week exploring the Oregon coast. Em planned for months, making reservations, mapping out our route. Then Kimiko fell for this Spanish exchange student who invited her to go snowboarding. She bailed on us two days before we were scheduled to leave. I was perfectly happy doing the trip with just Em, but she stewed and pouted about it for months. Em doesn't do well with last-minute changes.

I watch her face in profile as she gazes out the window. The furrow between her brows is more than irritated. Kimiko may have been the one to flounce out in a huff, but Em knows how to nurse a grudge. She doesn't act out, doesn't yell or cry or throw things. She just quietly removes you from the circle of people she trusts. Once you cross that line with Em, there's no going back.

If Em leaves, I'll be stranded up here without a ride back to California—not an insurmountable obstacle, but an irritating detail to be dealt with on top of everything else. The more serious issue is what her disappearance might do to this whole equation. Em's the closest thing we have to a cool head. I can't face this mess without her.

"I see what you're saying." I have to start with empathy and work the problem logically, step by step. "You feel betrayed by her."

"Exactly. She's the one who was all into talking it through, making a plan. Now suddenly she's all, 'What does it matter what really happened?' But it does matter." She looks at me. "It matters, right?"

I sit up, choosing my words carefully. "Of course it matters. We all want to know the truth."

"Knowledge is power." She turns to the window again, her gaze far away.

"On the other hand, I also see Kimi's point. Since all of our memories are sketchy and we can't share them with the cops, maybe we should focus on the logistics."

Her jaw tightens. She shoots me a sideways glance. "The logistics?"

"Look at it this way: we're not in an episode of *Law and Order*. We're real people in a dangerous situation."

"I never said this was *Law and Order*."

I hold up a hand. "Hear me out. What's the most important thing we've got to deal with right now?"

After a beat, she says softly, "Finding out what happened to Sadie."

"Exactly. And, if something bad's happened, we have to make sure none of us gets blamed."

She raises an eyebrow. "If one of us hurt her, that person deserves to—"

"Okay, yes." I nod in agreement. "If one of us really did hurt her, and the cops figure that out, sure. But none of us should be blamed for something we didn't do. Avoiding that is going to require calm, deliberate actions. We have to make it impossible for anyone to pin this on us. Regardless of who resented Sadie or even hated her, that's the bottom line. The rest of this"—I wave my hand vaguely, a gesture meant to indicate the house and everything that's gone down under its roof—"is just drama."

She doesn't respond.

In the silence, I worry it might sound like I don't care who did this to Sadie. There's a sliver of truth in that. My loyalty to Sadie pales in comparison to my concern for Amy, Kimiko, and Em. If one of us attacked Sadie in a drugged frenzy, then yes, I'd rather cover it up than see one of us spend the rest of her life in jail. It's not something I'm especially proud of, but sometimes knowledge *isn't* power. Sometimes the truth is too devastating to bear.

I roll my shoulders, conscious of the tension creeping into my neck. "Just because you're pissed at Kimiko, that's no reason to leave."

"It's not just Kimiko, it's everyone. Ethan's been all weird since he found me in Sadie's studio. Dakota's treating us all like suspects. Amy keeps asking why I was wearing Sadie's jewelry. Even you asked me if I—" She breaks off, leaning against the wall, her cheeks puffing out in frustration. "We're all turning on each other, you know? I don't see any reason to torture myself by staying."

"Taking off right now won't look good, Em." I hold her gaze. "I don't think it's smart."

"But the cop said we could go home if—"

"I know, but things could change." I try not to plead with her, but I can hear the strain of desperation creeping into my words. "If you go, I'll be all alone up here without any allies."

"You could come with me." Even as she says it, I know Em's conviction is slipping, the doubt creeping in like hairline fractures.

She's right. I could leave with her. I see us driving down I-5, music blaring, the wind in our hair. Just the thought makes me feel like my lungs have more room, like I can take a proper breath for the first time in days.

It's a fantasy, though, a mirage. We can't go back, not without repercussions. Leaving this mess in our rearview mirror will solve nothing; it will just draw out the torture. Better to leave only when we know exactly what we're dealing with.

"If you and I go home right now, we lose any say in what happens. We basically hand the reins over to the others. What if they tell the cops their insane mish-mash of drugged recollections? And if it turns out Sadie's hurt—or worse—we're the ones who took off, too scared to face the music. If I were the cops, I'd look long and hard at you and me."

She doesn't respond. The furrow between her brows deepens. It's not anger there now, but concentration. I can see her analytical brain kicking in, turning the puzzle over, examining it from every angle.

I push my advantage. "What's to stop the others from banding together and coming up with a plausible story that pins her disappearance on us?"

Her expression darkens. "You think they'd do that?"

"There's no telling what people will do when their backs are against a wall." I let this hang in the air.

She comes over and sits beside me on the bed. I can smell her moisturizer, lavender and mint. It's comforting—the smell of my friend. The best friend I've ever had.

"You're smarter than me," I say. "So…you tell me: it makes sense, right? When you look at it logically? Leaving right now is the stupidest, most dangerous thing we could do."

She gives one quick, reluctant nod.

I grin. "Remember Ziegler's logic class? How he used to go on and on about the ancient Greeks and their tenses?"

"The past tense is forensic. It's all about blame. The present tense is demonstrative. It's all about values."

I put on his thick German accent to make her laugh. "'But the future tense—that's where the real magic happens. The future tense is deliberative. Only when you turn your attention to the future are you entering the realm of choice.'"

Em does laugh, but weakly. I can see in her face the strain of the last few hours. The stress. The fear. The weight of our choices.

I grab her hand. "That's what we have to focus on now: the future. I need you here, Em. I'll go crazy without you. We have to see this through. Promise me you won't bail."

She nods. It's all I need. Em never goes back on a promise. I just hope my theory is right—that staying here will give us some control over the madness creeping like a dark tide over the house.

If I'm wrong, then I just talked us out of our last chance to escape.

"WHAT EXACTLY DID the cops say to Ethan?" Em and I are back in the kitchen. It's half past three, and I haven't eaten anything all day. Though I have no appetite, I doubt mainlining coffee on an empty stomach is helping my nerves. We busy ourselves warming up leftovers from last night as the coffeepot gurgles.

Em pulls a plate of mushroom ragout from the microwave and hands it to me. Her face is lined with exhaustion. "Not much. They just asked him down to the station, said they've got more questions."

I push the steaming food around on my plate. "Did he seem freaked out?"

She shrugs. "No more than the rest of us."

My cell rings. I look at the number. It's a local area code, but there's no name. "This might be the cops."

"Answer it," Em whispers, as if they might hear.

"June Moody," I say in my crispest voice.

"Ms. Moody. Glad I caught you. Officer Fisher here. We got a hit on your friend's car. We've informed Mr. MacTavish, but I thought you and the other guests would want to know."

"Oh." It comes out a dry croak.

"We've got Mr. MacTavish down at the station. There's a detective there asking him some questions. I'm afraid we're going to need you to meet us down there next. Can you do that?"

I press my palm against the cool, smooth counter top. The word *afraid* registers in big block letters inside my brain. Why did he phrase it like that? My whole body feels cold, then hot, then cold again.

"Sure. Anything in particular you need to ask me about?"

I remember Ethan saying he planned to tell them about our... The words light up inside my head like a neon sign: *midnight rendezvous*. It flickers and pops, buzzing like a vacancy sign at a sleazy motel.

But Fisher's not taking the bait. "Let's leave it for later. Can you meet us there in, say, thirty minutes, around four?"

"Okay." There's a salamander making slow, steady progress through my intestines.

"Just standard procedure." He tries to sound reassuring, but for some reason this only scares me more.

"Of course."

Em's staring at me with an urgency that only adds to my growing panic.

"Where did you find her car?"

"Deception Pass. Rangers found it. State Park. It wasn't too far from the bridge."

"Was she…in it?"

"No, it was empty."

I nod, though of course he can't see this.

"My partner and I are headed over there now. Just wanted to keep you in the loop."

"Okay. Thank you."

He hesitates.

"Was there something else?" I ask, my eyes widening, all innocence, though he can't see this either.

He clears his throat. "I thought you might have more questions. People usually do."

"I figured, if you're on your way, I should let you get there."

"No problem with that. My partner's driving." He sounds amused.

"Oh, right." I try to swallow, but there's a lump of fear in my throat the size of a walnut. "So, was her purse in the car? Was there any sign of a struggle?"

"Yes and no. Purse in the front seat. No sign of forced entry."

"Well, that's good." I wait for him to respond. When he doesn't, I add, "Right?"

"Could be, yes. We'll know more when we get there."

"What about footprints? Any sign she left the car and went into the woods?"

"Hard to tell with the rain." Terse now. Abbreviated. Jesus, what does this guy want from me? First he's chiding me for not asking enough questions; now he's acting like I've used up my allotment.

Another half beat. His tone goes casual—too casual. "So you're familiar with the area?"

"Not very."

"It's just—you said *woods*, so I thought maybe you knew the place."

The little hairs on my arms stand up. I watch the gooseflesh spread from wrist to elbow like a wind shadow sweeping across the bay. "I went there once or twice. In college. And we kayaked under the bridge yesterday."

There's a brief, staticky silence. Should I even be talking to this guy without a lawyer? Then I realize how ridiculous I'm being; nobody gets a lawyer because their friend disappeared. It would look suspicious—absurdly so.

"Ms. Moody?" When he says my name, there's an edge of impatience. I realize he may have said it more than once.

"I'm here. Sorry."

The smell of the ragout is making me want to throw up.

"This morning, your friend mentioned that you both need to head back to California. We'd prefer you stick around another day or two. Will that be possible?"

I try to decode his inflections. He's polite, respectful, but I detect a steely edge that wasn't there before.

Earlier today, his tone was bland as milk. Now there's a hardness there, like a disappointed teacher preparing to meet with a student who cheated on an exam.

"Em has to work Monday, and it's a fifteen-hour drive." There's a long, awkward pause. "But I'll talk to her. She's my ride."

"You do that." He exhales into the phone, or maybe it's a gust of wind. I feel at a disadvantage, not being able to see his face, read his expressions. At the same time, I'm grateful he can't read mine. "The station's in Anacortes. You think you can find it? About ten, fifteen minutes from the MacTavish place. We can send someone to pick you up if you need a ride."

"No, I'm okay," I say. "I can get there."

"See you in half an hour?"

"Sure. Thanks, Officer." I end the call. My hands are sweating so badly my phone almost slips from my grasp. "They found her car."

"Really?" Em says. "Where?"

I relay the basics of the conversation. She chews on a fingernail, that old nervous habit resurfacing again. It makes her look twelve.

"God, what was her car doing in Deception Pass?" she asks. "Why would Sadie go there? You don't think...?"

I try to imagine Sadie jumping off that bridge. Before I came here, I couldn't stop fixating on how perfect her life seemed. Now that I'm here, though, I see how wrong I was. Sadie sits at the center of a web, one woven from resentment and manipulation. Under every shiny surface of Sadie's world lies a tangled knot of angst. Would she take her own life, though? Surely, she must know she has options. Her daughter's got one foot out the door. Her marriage is falling apart. She has the money and freedom to reinvent herself if this isn't what she wants.

I flash on that old saying: *Wherever you go, there you are.* Sadie's the puppet master pulling the strings of this imperfect life. Even if she did start over somewhere, she'd take her need to control people with her.

It takes me a moment to realize Em's asking me a question.

"Sorry, what?"

"Was her car close to the bridge?"

I nod. "Yeah. But the bloodstains on the wall and the floor. What's that about if she jumped off a bridge?"

Em sucks in a breath. "I've been thinking about the blood. It could have come from Kimiko, right? Her nose looks really bad."

I consider this, trying to run the scene in my head like a movie. Kimiko's injured nose spraying blood on the wall. It still raises the question of who or what inflicted the injury, but I decide to skip that for now. Do noses bleed like that? Maybe. But then what about the puddle on the landing? Maybe she grabbed something—a tissue, say, or her shirt—and used it to stop the blood? Then she paused at the landing—maybe checking to see if she was still bleeding—and this time it formed a pool instead of a splatter. I feel a little sick even thinking about it. Something about the scenario doesn't track right, though I'm hardly a blood-splatter expert.

"Em, what if...?" I know what I'm about to say will sound ridiculous.

"Just say it," she prompts, leaning closer.

I glance around, unsure of who might be listening. The house is so open and expansive, each room spilling into the next. It fosters paranoia. My voice drops to a whisper. "What if Sadie staged all of this? What if she's faking her death so she can start fresh?"

"Pulling a *Gone Girl*, you mean?"

I nod. "I know it sounds crazy, but wouldn't it be her style?"

"How so?"

"Think about it. Her marriage is basically a sham, Dakota doesn't need her anymore—at least not emotionally. Amy needs her but doesn't want her raising her kid. Maybe she just looked around and thought, 'Screw it, I'm not happy here, I'm going to stash a load of cash in a Swiss bank account and reinvent myself in Barbados or Mallorca.'"

Em stabs a mushroom but doesn't raise the fork to her mouth. "Come on. Really?"

"She's losing control here. The peasants are in revolt." The more I think about it, the more I like my theory. "This way, she's controlling them from afar, but she also doesn't have to deal with their shit. She can find a fresh batch of people to manipulate."

Em puts the mushroom in her mouth, chews, and swallows. "You're saying she did it all—drugged us, cut herself, ditched her phone, left her car at Deception Pass—?"

"It's possible, right?"

"But she's famous. People will recognize her."

"Reconstructive surgery?" Even as I say it, I know I'm spinning a story that barely makes sense even on badly written television, but I can't help myself. It's the only answer we've hit on so far that means none of us killed or hurt Sadie.

Em gives me a hard look. She pushes the plate of ragout at me. "You need to eat something."

"But—"

"You can't go to the police talking like this. You sound nuts. Why do they want to talk to you, anyway?"

With a deep sigh, I push the plate away and slump over, pressing my hot face against the cool marble counter top. "I met up with Ethan Wednesday night."

"What?" she snaps.

"He texted me, asked me to come to the beach house." I don't lift my head. My body feels like a deflated balloon. "I was curious."

"You're not still hung up on him, are you?" The disgust in her voice fills me with shame.

"No."

"Nothing happened, right?"

I jerk upright, my spine going straight. "Of course not. What kind of person do you think I—?"

"Okay, okay." She moves closer, watching me carefully. "Calm down."

"We decided to tell the cops about it. If we don't, and they find out somehow…" I wish I could press rewind and undo everything about this trip. Why did I even come here? What was I thinking?

"Right." Em makes an effort to sound calm and reasonable, but she keeps chewing at her fingernail. "So that's fine then. You'll just tell them the truth."

We look at each other, both of us thinking the same bleak thought. The truth is, we don't know the truth.

THERE'S SOMETHING ABOUT being trapped in a small, windowless room with two barrel-chested men that sends my lizard brain skittering.

Officer Fisher watches me with thinly disguised repulsion. His attitude has changed since the last time I saw him. He's gone from polite to suspicious. Behind him stands a man in a charcoal-gray suit. He must be the detective. This new guy has a quiet, menacing air, like a snake biding its time, coiling tighter. He's very good-looking, in his thirties, lean and athletic. His shaggy haircut, piercing blue eyes, and olive complexion lend him a chilling beauty, as delicate as a Greek god.

"This is Detective Marcus Bledek." Fisher nods over his shoulder at the man. I hear the note of respect as he adds, "He's joining the investigation."

Bledek glances up at me, his eyes meeting mine for only a second. Even so, I note the precision of his blue gaze; it's a laser, homing in on telling details. Sweat breaks out on my forehead. Adding a detective to the mix can't be a good sign.

Fisher's use of the term *investigation* also worries me. This morning he was full of bland platitudes. *Sometimes people just need space.* All that reassurance is gone. Now that he suspects something more sinister has happened, he knows the eyes of the whole world will be on him.

They just want to ask some questions, I remind myself. *No need to panic.*

But why are they questioning only Ethan and me, not the others? Why does Fisher's thin upper lip lift in a sneer when he looks at me?

The walls are inching closer every second, a trash

compactor squeezing the airless space. The top of my head tingles, and I can't feel my hands or feet. I sit like a statue, motionless, my face impassive. At least, I hope it's impassive. I can't feel my cheeks or chin or my lips either, come to think of it. I've got no idea what my expression communicates.

Detective Bledek pivots and takes a seat so quickly I flinch.

Fisher continues, his notepad in one hand. "This conversation will be recorded. Do you understand?"

I nod in mute agreement. My hands start to tremble, so I rest them in my lap, under the table.

Fisher gets up and turns on a video camera mounted near the ceiling. He says all three of our names and the date for the camera. Then he strides back to his chair and sits, his eyes locked on mine.

"Do I need a lawyer?" I ask.

Bledek leans forward, resting his elbows on the table. He doesn't speak.

"Lawyers tend to complicate things." Fisher darts a quick glance at Bledek, like he expects him to jump in. When he doesn't, Fisher continues, his tone swelling with confidence. "I'd like to think we can keep this simple."

I'm not sure I'm breathing. My heart has wrenched its way into my throat.

When I say nothing, Fisher goes on. "Here's the thing, June. May I call you June?"

I nod again.

"We understand you and Mr. MacTavish met up the night before last. In secret."

I say nothing. My eyes move to Bledek. He sits perfectly still. His gaze never leaves my face.

"Is it true you had a relationship back in college?"

"Sort of." I shrug. "It didn't last long."

"But you met him Wednesday night anyway."

I bristle at the officer's condescending tone. "He asked me to come. I was curious."

"Curious?" Fisher cocks his head, as if listening for some far-off signal.

"Nothing happened," I snap. Instantly, I regret my defensive tone. I dial it back. "I had a crush on him, back in the day. Everyone did. It wasn't serious."

"But you were 'curious.'" Fisher shoots a sardonic look at Bledek.

"I went to see an old friend." I fold my arms, then instantly unfold them, knowing I'll only look like I'm hiding something. Cops must study body language. They know what to look for.

Fisher glances at his notes. "After midnight."

"Yes." I resist the urge to add that this doesn't mean I had sex with him. The maddening string of knowing glances between the two of them has me on edge, but I know better than to call them on it directly.

Bledek cocks an eyebrow, tilts his face toward the table, taking this in. I wonder if he will ever speak. I've heard of good cop/bad cop, but angry cop/silent cop? I feel like a bug under a microscope; I will myself not to squirm.

I decide to turn the tables and ask a question of my own. "You said you found Sadie's car at Deception Pass. What do you think happened to her?"

Fisher stands and steeples his fingers on the table,

leaning toward me. Sweat glistens on his forehead. "We saw scuff marks on the cliffside. We're searching for her body."

I put my hand to my mouth. I can feel the blood draining from my cheeks.

"I'd prepare yourself for the distinct possibility Mrs. MacTavish is dead."

At Fisher's suddenly gentle tone, a frightened sound escapes my throat. "Do you think she might have killed herself?"

"We're looking at all possibilities." Fisher darts another glance at Bledek, who only shifts his gaze back to me again.

"Why would she do that?" I ask, my voice hoarse.

Fisher cocks his head, shoulders rising. "Any theories?"

I bite my lip, thinking. Ethan was open with me about the problems in their marriage. Would he be as honest with the cops? Maybe he played up his marital problems to me. Who knows. This is a grenade. I need to lob it with care.

"I think there were some issues in her marriage." Even as the words form themselves inside my mouth, I wonder if I'm being a total idiot for speaking without a lawyer, but clamming up now will make it seem like I've got something to hide. I just want to get through this and get out.

"Was one of them having an affair?" Fisher asks, his tone neutral.

Bledek stares at me, his eyes burning. His silence is now a third voice in the conversation—the loudest.

"Not that I know of." I hesitate. "I think they were just…estranged?"

Fisher searches the ceiling. "And how do you fit into this, June?"

"I don't know." I can feel sweat trickling under my bra. "I'm not that close to either of them. I just came up for a few days. I haven't been to Washington in years."

"Have you and Mrs. MacTavish known each other long?" Fisher wears a puzzled frown.

"Since college," I say. "We all know each other from college."

"Did Mrs. MacTavish know about your meeting with Mr. MacTavish?"

I hear Amy's words in my head: *You're not as stealthy as you think. If I saw you go down there, God knows who else did.* "I don't think so, but it's possible."

"Did she confront you?"

I shake my head.

"Mrs. MacTavish never accused you of sleeping with her husband?"

This throws me. I try to keep my voice steady. "She knows I had feelings for him a long time ago. Everyone knew. I never tried to hide it."

Fisher's mouth twists into an ironic smirk. "Would you say she was *salty* about it?"

I stare at him, confused by his odd use of millennial slang. Is he deliberately trying to throw me? "Upset, you mean? No, I don't think so."

He nods. The room fills with a dense silence. I stare at my hands on the table, reminding myself not to fidget. Seconds tick by; each one feels like an eternity. I know this trick. They're daring me to break the silence with something stupid—push over the pile of silent moments like a toddler swiping at a tower of blocks. Blurt out some desperate confession. I refuse to give in.

I force myself to think of the ocean—the glassy curves of a breaking wave. I imagine the sun sinking into the water at Natural Bridges, my favorite beach in Santa Cruz. I watch the gold melting into the horizon like butter melting on a skillet, spreading out in amber rivulets. It calms me.

Bledek gets up and leaves the room without a word. His chair scrapes once against the floor, but otherwise he moves with the silent agility of a cat. As soon as he's gone, my lungs manage to pull in twice as much air. The dizzy fear clouding my mind begins to dissipate. By comparison, Fisher is easy. It's Bledek I have to worry about.

"I think that's all for now." Fisher stands.

It takes all my willpower not to race out of the room.

I'M HEADING BACK to Dakota's old room when I see Amy darting out the door. She shoots a furtive glance my way.

"What's up?" I can hear the hardness in my voice. What the hell was she doing in my room?

The cagey gleam in her eye does nothing to assuage my suspicions.

"I just wanted to see if you were back yet."

"A knock usually does the trick."

She looks shamefaced. Her fingers work at her sweat pants; there's a rabbity twitchiness to her mouth.

"Amy, come on, tell me." I sigh, impatient. "What were you looking for?"

"I just wanted to see if you were here. Really." Her eyes tell me how much she's hiding, but without resorting to physical threats, I've no idea how to force the truth from her.

We regard each other a moment, both of us suspicious.

"It's exhausting, isn't it?" I'm suddenly so drained, I want to lie down and sleep forever.

"What is?"

"Always suspecting everyone." I feel tired in my bones. My back slumps against the wall. My knees struggle to hold me up.

She nods. "Totally."

"The cops just grilled me. I'm running on adrenaline."

She frowns. "They're asking about your thing with Ethan, huh?"

"Which is not a thing."

"It looks pretty damning." She hesitates, as if deciding whether to say the rest.

"Go on," I prompt.

"It doesn't look good. It's motive." She shrugs. "That's where they're going to look; who does Sadie's disappearance benefit most? You guys win the prize."

My mouth goes dry. She's right, of course. I think of Detective Bledek—his silence, his intensity. His ice-blue eyes slicing through my defenses, his silence more ominous than any words.

"That's a pretty shitty prize." I can hear my voice, but it sounds far away. I slump to my ass, looking up at Amy. Her swollen belly floats between us like a balloon.

"You're in a terrible position." She has enough humanity to look compassionate, but it can't pierce the thick bubble of terror I'm encased in.

I manage a weak "Yes."

"If I were you, I'd lawyer up."

This phrase, redolent of TV procedurals, makes me itch.

Amy looks down at me on the floor. "Maybe I can find you someone."

"I'll think about it." I manage to slither to a standing position, relying on the wall as my support.

Sweat beads on her upper lip. I wonder what she's so nervous about, considering she's not likely to be the cops' favorite suspect. I feel a sudden, violent need to lie down.

"Want me to ask around?" Amy's still talking as I lurch past her toward the bed.

"Sure." My voice is a whisper.

"I really think you should get someone good."

I lie on my back, my head pounding. "I need a minute."

"Okay." She sounds uncertain.

"I've got a headache." I feel like I'm watching the scene from deep inside a swimming pool. The light wavers before me, and I have to close my eyes. My temples throb.

Amy lingers in the doorway, her voice growing even fainter. "I'll look into it. Ask around."

"Okay." I mouth the syllables more than voice them. I kick off my shoes and try to block everything out.

ELEVEN

FISHER AND BLEDEK show up just before sunset with a search warrant. They flash it at us, just like on TV. I've still got a headache, though it's dulled to a gentle throbbing inside my skull. I've fought it off with a healthy dose of Advil, but I can feel the pain hovering at the edges, still looking for a way in.

They move with purpose through the rooms, a team of uniformed assistants in tow. There is a terrifying efficiency to their search, dispassionate and methodical. I can't bring myself to watch them.

Looking for an escape, I slip into the backyard. I yearn for something to do, somewhere to go. I glance in the direction of Leo's yurt, but I can't go there. It's too confusing seeing him. The missing time and the odd sense of intimacy between us will only deepen my unease. I still haven't eaten much of anything all day. My head swims as the cool air hits my face.

I spot Em and Ethan at the far edge of the pool. They're hunched together, deep in conversation.

I shield my eyes, trying to get a better look at them. No doubt about it, they're conspiring. There's no other word for the skulking postures, the cagey glances. What do Em and Ethan have to say to each other that requires such a secretive powwow?

A messy sunset has erupted across the bay. It's all

purples, reds, and pinks, the palette of an open wound. I try to breathe normally, but it feels like I'm running a marathon, like I have been for days.

I study them a moment longer, then cross the patio. It takes them forever to notice me. For furtive people, they're clueless.

"Hey," Em says, overly bright.

"June." Ethan's just as awkward.

I surprised them, I tell myself. That's all. They could have been talking about anything.

But what was it? My headache looms, pain pounding at the Advil barrier.

"What were you guys talking about?" I don't see any point in beating around the bush. If they know something, they need to share it with me.

"Nothing," Em says, just as Ethan says, "Books."

Really, they'd make hopeless criminals.

"You guys obviously weren't talking about literature." I know I'm being nosy, but my freedom's at stake here. "You're both terrible liars. Just tell me."

Em sighs and looks away. Ethan holds my gaze. There's something in it I can't quite read.

"We were talking about the manuscript." Ethan sounds exhausted. "I'm sure Em's told you all about it."

Not *all* about it. The bare minimum. Her reluctance to confide in me still stings, but I just nod.

"She wants to destroy it." Ethan looks at me, imploring. "You're a writer, June. You should know, a book isn't something you can just throw away. It's like killing someone's child."

"What about my relationship with my mom, Ethan?" Em's seething. She spits the words out with cold precision. "My relationship with every single person I grew up with? Is that worth nothing? She never should have written it in the first place."

Ethan keeps his eyes on me, ignoring Em. "Sadie's been slaving over this book for two years."

"And there's a big fat royalty check with your name on it." Em takes a step toward him. "But we're not going to talk about that, are we? No, it's all about the art, isn't it?"

"Don't do that," Ethan says. "You know it's not about the money."

Em's face is so distorted by anger, I hardly recognize her. "A posthumous novel by Sadie MacTavish? Imagine the sales. You'll be set for life. As if you weren't already."

I recoil. "How do you know it's posthumous?"

Em looks at me, her expression blank. This is not the Em I know. I glance at Ethan. The muscles in his jaw are clenched, like he's holding back—what? Anger? Tears? I suddenly feel like I don't know either of them at all.

My headache is back with a vengeance. It's not a slow, steady entry, but a rush of pain like a torrent of water breaking through a levy.

Just then I see Fisher marching toward me, Bledek in his wake; I see the aggressive swagger in their movements and the grim lines of their mouths. My stomach fizzes with acid.

They think I'm a murderer. The words tear through me. I'm not sure I can keep it together. This is bad. I can see by Fisher's determined stride he's got something.

"Ms. Moody, we'd like a word back at the station." He's not smiling.

The world spins a little, and I wonder if I'm going to faint. "It's after nine. Isn't it sort of late for—?"

"It would really be best if you complied." His tone suggests things will go badly for me if I resist.

"Did you find something?" Em gets straight to the heart of the matter.

Fisher looks at her, then at Ethan, his expression unreadable. "I'm afraid we can't discuss an ongoing investigation."

She persists. "But if you found some—"

"Do you want us to drive, Ms. Moody, or can you make it there on your own?" He eyes me warily.

"Um, yeah, I can borrow a car or get a ride." I sound like a little girl. With effort, I force my register lower. "See you there in ten minutes?"

He nods, his expression grim.

When he's gone, Em, Ethan, and I don't say anything for a long moment.

My lungs tighten. Even outside, I feel cornered, like the house, the trees, and the sky itself are closing in around me. I sit on the lawn chair, woozy, and glare at Ethan. "What did you tell the cops earlier?"

He's shamefaced. "At the last second I decided to call in my lawyer."

"Wait, what?" His answer lands like a sucker punch to my stomach.

"I didn't like their tone. It felt unsafe to tell them anything without legal counsel."

"But you told them about Wednesday night." My tone is accusatory; I can't help it. I feel like the sacrificial lamb.

He shakes his head. "My lawyer wouldn't let me say much of anything."

Sickness washes through me, a tingly vertigo.

"Did *you* tell them?" Now Ethan looks sick.

I shake my head. "They already knew. I assumed it came from you. You did say you planned to come clean about that. We agreed."

Em covers her mouth with one hand. "Who would tell them that?"

"Amy." I look at Ethan. "She saw me that night. And earlier today, when I got back from the interview, I caught her coming out of my room. She was super weird about it. God, I think she's trying to set me up."

Ethan leans in close. The blue of his eyes startles me. "You didn't do anything wrong. You have to remember that."

"I don't know that for sure." It comes out faint.

"You don't remember doing anything wrong." Ethan changes tack. "That's enough. Stick to that."

"You can do this." Em keeps her eyes on mine.

"I can, right?" I don't sound convinced.

She offers a brave smile. "Of course you can."

"You can plead the fifth to anything," Ethan reminds me. "I'm calling my lawyer right now."

"Wouldn't that also be Sadie's lawyer?"

His eyes are on his phone, but he looks up at my question. "The family lawyer, yes."

"Is that a good idea?" Em sees where I'm going with this and steps in. "Wouldn't he feel too much loyalty to Sadie to defend someone accused of harming her?"

Ethan scoffs. "*Loyalty* and *lawyer* should never be uttered in the same sentence. He's a gun for hire. I'm sure he can recommend a colleague, though, if you're more comfortable with that. Don't worry about the expense. I'll cover it."

I haul myself to my feet. The lawn wavers, but after a couple of deep breaths I feel steadier.

"You can do this," Em repeats.

I try to stand tall, to fill my lungs with the pure, rain-washed air. "Looks like I have no choice."

THEY TAKE ME to an even smaller room this time. After the svelte receptionist ushers me in, I sit in the silence and wait. The walls gleam white. The fluorescents flicker overhead, casting a ghoulish green pallor over everything. I can feel sweat breaking out all over my body. My scalp prickles with fear. The camera eyes me from its perch in the corner, watchful.

Fisher and Bledek burst through the doors, charging into the cramped space with the energized gusto of football players invading a locker room at halftime. I watch them, fear turning my saliva gummy, and wonder what's got them all worked up. Was my DNA found someplace damning? But wouldn't they need a DNA sample to determine that? I'm not in their system, since I've never committed a crime—right? I did get fingerprinted when I first started teaching at Cabrillo. Is that it? They found my fingerprints someplace incriminating?

There is no cat-and-mouse foreplay this time. Bledek has relinquished his role as mute observer. He tosses two sealed bags onto the table between us. His icy glare pins me to my seat. "Do these look familiar?"

I study them. Through the clear plastic, I see a prescription pill bottle with no label. The other contains a white T-shirt. Something about it catches my eye. I pick it up. It's a nondescript shirt, but not cheap. I notice the Dolce & Gabbana label. It's folded neatly, like a mail-order package that hasn't been opened. Then I see what pulled my attention. A spider web of dark red snakes from the fold. As I turn it over, the web becomes an ugly smear, rust colored, repulsive.

"No." I keep my answer simple. The T-shirt could be anyone's, in theory, but I know it's not mine.

"Really?" Bledek takes a seat, his expression interested. "Can you explain, then, why we found both of these in your luggage?"

I raise my eyebrows, trying to think. My body goes cold, as if a tap's been turned on inside my bloodstream, ice water gushing through my veins. I remember Amy leaving my room, her eyes furtive. Was she in there planting the evidence in my bag?

Then Fisher lurches forward, grabs the white T-shirt in its plastic bag. He jabs it at me. "You're saying this isn't yours?"

"That's right." It takes everything in me, but I keep my voice calm.

I try, with great effort, to steer my mind back to the ocean. The surf pounds in my ears. I can taste the salty mist on my tongue. The sand beneath my feet feels firm and warm. I dig my toes in, feeling the cooler, damper sand beneath the surface. This is my calming place, my safety zone. For some reason, I flash on Leo's yurt—the golden curves and the sapphire-blue rug, the green velvet chair. I can feel the highball of whiskey between my cupped palms, sweating. The layers of brown in Leo's eyes. I cling to this image as if my life depends on it.

"Have you ever seen it?" Bledek taps his fingers on the table, head tilted to one side.

I shake my head. "Not that I can remember."

"You're sure about that?"

I cast my mind back to last night, to my last clear memory of the evening: talking to Em in her room before we decided to do shots. Was anybody wearing a white T-shirt? All I can picture clearly is the top Kimiko wore, the sequins flashing like the scales of a mermaid.

"Ms. Moody," Bledek says, his quiet voice edged with menace, "please answer the question."

"I'm not positive. But I don't think I've seen it." I take the shirt from him again, studying it. There's a small fleck of something straw colored clinging to the sleeve. My fingers probe at the plastic. I wish I could smell it. That would help. I'm pretty olfactory. I notice how people smell, but it seems like a weird request, so I keep quiet.

"If you had to take a guess, who would you say it belongs to?" Bledek's jaw flexes. "Hypothetically."

I stare at him. "I really couldn't say."

"Couldn't?" He murmurs the word, his teeth touching. "Or won't?"

"I mean, it's an expensive brand." I point to the label. "Very high end, Dolce and Gabbana. Like, three hundred bucks for a plain white T-shirt."

"This T-shirt costs three hundred bucks?" Fisher looks skeptical.

"I would never spend that much on something so simple," I say, trying to sound reasonable, but I have the vague sense I'm speaking a foreign language. "It's not my style."

Fisher grimaces and looks at the wall, shaking his head. I can't tell if he's reacting to the uselessness of this information or to the privilege of people who spend hundreds on a T-shirt. Bledek stares me down, his eyes unreadable.

"Designer inflation," I continue. "It's stupid. I shop secondhand, mostly. So does Kimiko. Em likes high-end stuff, but quirky, you know? Obscure brands that cater to sporty people with money." Fuck, I'm babbling.

Bledek blinks like I've put him into a trance. We should stay on this topic. They're so out of their comfort zone, I want to keep them here forever. It's much more bearable than the question I know we're cruising toward like a missile trained on its target: what was this stuff doing in my suitcase?

But then Bledek pushes the pill bottle toward me. "What about this?"

"Never seen it."

"You're sure?"

I meet his gaze. "Positive."

"You don't take any medications?"

"No. Advil now and then, but that's it."

Fisher paces, agitated.

Bledek casts a quick, annoyed glance at his colleague before training his gaze on me again. "So you have no idea what it is or how it got into your bag?"

"I have a guess." I force myself to keep my tone civil, but a hot, acrid anger's starting to build inside me like a plume of lava bubbling up through my core. It's turning my diction staccato, each syllable landing harder. I'm not sure if I'm more pissed at these two for questioning me about planted evidence, or at someone—Amy, most likely—for planting it. Either way, it feels good to have righteous indignation on my side for once, something to drive my words other than the queasy urge to lie.

Bledek raises his eyebrows at me, inviting me to go on.

"If I were guilty of something sordid, why would I stash the evidence in my own suitcase? Clearly somebody's trying to set me up."

"What makes you think this is evidence of something sordid?" This comes from Fisher; his mouth twists into a grin, like he's caught me incriminating myself.

I stop myself from rolling my eyes. "Well, for starters, it's a bloodstained T-shirt in a missing-person case."

"How do you know it's blood?" Fisher persists.

"I don't, but I doubt you two would get this excited about spaghetti sauce."

"And the bottle?" Bledek leans back, his expression thoughtful.

"I don't know what was in there, but you obviously think it's damning, or you wouldn't have rushed me down here and started pelting me with questions."

"Interesting." Bledek's tone is cryptic.

I sigh. "All I know is…neither of those are mine, so I can't help you."

"One more thing." Bledek produces a third bag, concealed until now under the table. "Have you ever seen this?"

My heart stops cold. It's the Kwan Yin statue. Part of her head is missing. It's stained with blood. A few dark strands of hair cling to the gore.

I cover my mouth. I think I'm going to be sick.

They wait, watching me with predatory stillness.

When I'm sure I can speak, I say, "That's the missing statue."

They say nothing. Their eyes bore into me.

"It used to be in Sadie's house. At the top of the stairs."

They continue staring at me, motionless.

"Where did you find it?" I whisper.

Bledek's reply is terse. "In your bag, with everything else."

"I don't—why would I put that in my suitcase?" Tears drip from my lashes to the table. "It's got blood on it. Hair—" My voice breaks. I cover my mouth again, too choked up to continue.

"We're sending these to the lab for analysis." Bledek takes the evidence back and casts one last look at me. "Once we get the results, we'll have more questions, I'm sure."

WHEN I GET back to the house, it's almost ten. Kimiko and Em are in the living room. As soon as I enter, they look up with anxious expressions.

"How did it go?" Em stands, wiping her palms on her jeans.

I shake my head. "Where's Amy?" I know it doesn't answer Em's question, but at this point I have no idea who I should trust.

All I can think about is confronting Amy. She was in my room a few hours before the cops searched the house. I kick myself again for not insisting she tell me the truth about what she was doing in there. Did she know the cops would appear hours later with a search warrant? I should have gone through the whole room,

searched for planted evidence, but I wasn't thinking
straight. I felt overwhelmed by my first interview with
the cops, sick from all the subterfuge. I hadn't yet
learned to assume the people I considered my friends
might frame me for murder.

It occurs to me with a lurching queasiness that Amy
might have planted the evidence, but that doesn't mean
others weren't in on it. Any of them could have conspired with Amy. Everyone has a motive—namely, pinning their crime on someone other than themselves.
Pinning it on me.

"She's resting, I think." Em's face is tight with worry.
She seems to have aged in the last few days. I notice
the lines around her eyes, tiny commas bracketing her
mouth. "Why?"

I shake my head again, my legs already propelling
me toward the sliding-glass doors. I step outside and
hurry across the veranda. There's a cool breeze swirling through the trees, rustling through the shrubs. I
take a deep, gulping breath of it, relishing the momen-
tary cold. I feel a moment of fleeting relief, like a diver
pulling air into her lungs before plunging again into the
murky depths.

Amy doesn't answer when I pound on her door. I
find it unlocked and make my way inside. "Amy?" No
answer. "It's June. I need to talk to you."

I listen to the silence in the small house. Only the
insistent whisper of the trees swaying in the wind
penetrates the dense quiet. Something in me twinges
at the stillness. Fired up by my need for answers, I
didn't consider the delicate state Amy's probably in.
My imagination conjures a terrible image of Amy's

pregnant body sprawled in a tub filled with blood. The thought makes my mouth go dry.

"Amy?" My voice sounds hoarse. I clear my throat and try again. "You in here?"

A branch ricochets off the window, rattling the glass behind me. A tiny yelp escapes my lips before I can clench my jaw and swallow it. My heart's speeding down the autobahn, gears shifting.

I stride to the stairs and mount them, my shoes pounding on the hardwood steps.

"I'm coming up," I call. It's hardly necessary. I must sound like an army ascending the stairs.

I pause at her closed bedroom door. If she's asleep, I don't want to be the one to wake her. I don't want to see the look on her face as she emerges from unconsciousness and remembers, at the sight of my face, what's happened. My heart's still pounding. I rap on the wood with gentle knocks.

A voice behind me makes me jump. "Over here."

I spin around. She's lying in her candlelit bathroom, splayed out in a deep, beautiful clawfoot tub. Mounds of iridescent bubbles surround her. Amy's belly breaks from the froth like a pale island.

"There you are." I put my hand to my chest, willing my pulse to stop racing.

I find a yellow velvet chair beside the bath and pull it closer. *God, Sadie thought of everything when she decked this place out. She's even anticipated the possibility of a cozy bathroom chat.* I can't decide if this level of attention to detail is touching or creepy. Maybe a little of both.

Amy eyes me warily. "What's going on?"

"Why were you in my room?" I cut to the chase.

Her blue eyes go wide. I don't know what she expected me to say, but this wasn't it. "I told you, I was checking to see if you were back yet."

"I call BS." Amy's been weird with me all weekend. My gut tells me she's the one behind the planted evidence. That whole thing about helping me get a lawyer was just subterfuge to distract me from the truth. "You and I both know there's more to it."

"I can't—" She falters.

"You can't what? Admit you snuck in there to frame me for murder?" I know it sounds outlandish, but I'm way past worrying about melodrama.

She recoils. "What? No, I didn't—"

"The cops found a bunch of incriminating stuff in my bag. You were in there a few hours before they searched the house." I have to pause to catch my breath. Anger and desperation burn inside my throat like smoke. "Tell me the truth, Amy. I need to know."

She sighs. A ridge of bubbles floats along on the tide of her breath.

"This is serious," I whisper.

Up close, she looks more tired than anyone I've ever seen. Even in the candlelight, I can see dark circles rimming her sad eyes. A surge of empathy wells up, but I manage to tamp it down. Survival trumps compassion when you're a murder suspect.

"I swear, I didn't put anything in your bag. I was looking for something."

"What?"

She runs a hand through the bubbles. "It's humiliating."

I sit there, biding my time, fighting the impatience that makes me want to shake her.

After a long silence, she finally speaks. "I need to know what's going on with you and Ethan."

"Ethan?" I echo, confused.

"Please don't tell me nothing happened between you two, because I don't believe it." Her mouth thins as she meets my gaze, a stubborn tilt to her chin.

I take a deep breath, searching for patience. "I don't get it."

"What don't you 'get'?" A layer of sarcasm coats her words.

"I'm asking you about planted evidence—a missing-person investigation." I try very hard to keep my voice calm, but even I can hear the ragged frustration turning my words sharp. "Ethan is beside the point."

She blinks at me. I can see her deciding how much to tell me. "I don't know why I bother. You'll just go on lying."

I reel back, thrown off guard. "I'm not lying, Amy. What does Ethan have to do with—?"

"He's got a thing for you. He always has." Her face takes on a flinty, accusatory look. "I went to your room to see if I could find out what's really going on."

I can't hide my confusion. "What did you think you would—?"

"I don't know." She runs wet hands through her hair, exasperated. "Emails, love notes, photos on your lap-top, condom wrappers—whatever. I know it sounds desperate, okay?"

"But why? So you could use *that* to frame me?"

She gives me a pitying look, like I'm the one missing the point.

"Did you tell the cops I met with him?" I ask, changing tack.

She shakes her head. "No. Why would I?"

"Somebody did. You're the only one who knew I went down there."

Her look of patronizing disbelief only deepens. "Everyone knows you're still in love with him, June."

My head falls back as I let out a groan of frustration. "Look, the only thing I care about right now is figuring out who planted that evidence. I swear to you, I'm not in love with Ethan; I'm not sleeping with him; I don't want to sleep with him, okay? I don't get why we're even talking about this—"

"Because I am." She flares her eyes at me, defiant.

"You are what?" I look up. "Sleeping with Ethan?"

She gestures at her belly, an impatient wave of her hand, like she can't believe she has to spell it out for me. "Yes, June, I slept with him."

All at once, I feel stupid for not seeing this sooner. I recall the awkward tension between them this morning when he first came into the house, the resentful way she looked at him when he neglected to tell the cops she lives on the property, her bogus-sounding story about a one-night stand in Walla Walla. Why didn't I add those things up and come to the natural conclusion?

The only answer I can offer is that back in the day, Amy was the one woman on campus who seemed one hundred percent immune to Ethan's legendary charisma. She never even *liked* him. Her barbs were always sharpest when aimed at Ethan. Her sarcasm about him was never ending. Was all that just a smoke screen to hide her attraction?

"But you were always so disdainful of Ethan," I say.

She shrugs. "You know what he's like. When he gets you alone, it's like you're the only woman in the world."

"How does he feel about you?" I ask.

She shrugs. "Hell if I know. He's not exactly a stellar communicator."

"He knows you're pregnant with his kid?" This is so surreal. I can't believe the words coming out of my mouth.

"If he doesn't, then he's incredibly stupid." Amy looks like she's thinking the same thing about me.

I'm almost afraid to ask, but I have to. "What about Sadie? Does she know?"

Amy grabs a washcloth from the side of the tub and runs it over her face. "Honestly, June, I'm not sure. Sometimes it felt like…" She trails off, staring into space.

"Sometimes it felt like what?"

"Like she was pushing us together." She shoots me a quick look, as if gauging my reaction.

"Really?" I find this hard to imagine. Sadie's always been so possessive of Ethan, at least around me. Then again, given our history, it makes sense she would be. "How so?"

"The week we got together, she was in New York. Normally he'd go with her, but she insisted he stay here." She bites her lip, lost in thought. "Before she left, she kept saying I should check in on him every day, make sure he was okay, that sort of thing. She even texted me with suggestions about what he liked for dinner."

I find myself with my hand over my mouth, as if to hold back the idea forming in my mind. It's too outlandish. Not even Sadie would go that far, would she?

Amy looks at me. A knowing, wry smile forms on her face. "She'd been trying for three years to get pregnant again. No luck. A month before her New York trip, a doctor confirmed that it was definitely a problem on her end, not Ethan's. Even in vitro wasn't going to work. She was shit out of luck."

"You're not suggesting…?"

"I never had the balls to ask, in case I was wrong, but yeah." She lifts a shoulder, lets it drop. "After I got knocked up, she barely asked about the dad. And Ethan will hardly give me the time of day."

I shake my head, at a loss for words. My stomach flips over at the bizarre implications of what Amy's telling me. I recall the phrase Amy used the day we went kayaking. *Sadie's planted a flag in my womb.* At the time, I assumed she meant Sadie would be overly involved in raising Amy's child. I pictured Sadie going on about the importance of breastfeeding, pureeing organic carrots, paying for private school. I never imagined a *Handmaid's Tale*–style plot twist.

"Are you saying…?" I clear my throat, start again. "You're saying Sadie wanted Ethan to get you pregnant so she could raise the child herself?"

Amy blinks at me. There are tears in her eyes, but they don't fall. She's trying to be brave. "Ding ding ding. Finally, June gets the right answer."

God. How many dark surprises about my oldest

friends can I handle in one weekend? Sadie's writing a book about Em having sex with her mom's boyfriend, and now this? I want to curl up in a fetal position, cup my hands over my ears, and block it all out. What kind of insane power trip was Sadie on, anyway? Using her cousin as a surrogate without her consent, forcing Em to relive her secret history by writing about it—she pushed everything and everyone to the breaking point. I'm starting to think the question isn't *why would someone want to harm Sadie?* but *why did it take so long?*

The second I think it, I feel guilty. No matter how controlling and manipulative Sadie is, she doesn't deserve to die.

With a jolt, I realize what this new information does to Amy's motive. It's one thing to resent your cousin's proprietary attitude about your child. It's something else entirely to become ensnared in a plot to have a baby *for* her.

I can picture it all too easily. Ethan can be so charming when he wants to be. When Amy got pregnant, she must have imagined their life together—she and Ethan, raising the child together. Sure, there would be some messy fallout, a complicated reshuffling of their lives, but these things do happen. Amy's just delusional enough to imagine it could all work out in the end. Then Ethan turned his back on her, and Sadie carried on like nothing had changed.

Amy must have lost her mind when she realized how thoroughly she'd been used. There would have been only one way to get what she wanted, one path to winning the man she loved: getting rid of Sadie. Our little reunion provided the perfect subterfuge, too. She drugged us, disposed of Sadie, and played dumb with the rest of us. Then she planted that evidence in my bag, making me the perfect fall guy. Since she perceives me as her one remaining rival for Ethan's affection, I'm the ideal patsy. It's ingenious.

Amy yanks me back to the present. "What are you thinking?"

I turn to her. In the candlelight, her face is unreadable, a mask of dancing shadows. A chill runs down my spine.

I stand so quickly, I almost knock the chair over in my haste. My hands are shaking as I right it. "I've got to go."

"Really?" Her eyebrows arch in surprise. "No more questions, Nancy Drew?"

She's mocking me. I think of all she's put me through—those terrifying interviews with the cops, her eagerness to offer me up as the clueless sacrifice. I lean forward, gripping the edge of the tub, glaring down at her smug face. She's every bit as manipulative as Sadie. There's a reason they've been locked in such a toxic relationship all these years. They're two sides of the same coin—the power-hungry monster and her helpless victim. Only this time, the fly has swallowed the spider.

"You're not going to get away with this," I hiss.

"Come on, I was only—"

"Do not mess with me, Amy. I'm not going to prison for something you did."

She opens her mouth to respond, but I turn on my heel and stride to the door before she can get the words out.

TWELVE

When I get close to the house, a mighty crashing sound greets me. It sounds like shattering glass, something weighty smashing into a thousand pieces. Even as I trot toward the house, I'm tempted to bypass whatever new fiasco's under way and head straight for my room. I don't think I can handle more drama tonight. My skin feels fragile, my heart swollen like a balloon ready to pop.

The minute I pull open the kitchen door, I see what's happened. One of Sadie's blown glass sculptures—a huge, abstract jellyfish that dominated the mantel—has shattered. It's now a sea of sparkling shards flung across the pale wood floor. Ethan, Kimiko, and Em form a circle around the wreckage. They're all staring at it, but with very different expressions. Ethan looks angry. A twinge ripples inside his jaw, a muscle clenching. Em looks a little thrilled—maybe even vindicated. Kimiko's amused, like a kid who's just done something wrong and expects to be punished but can't help feeling pleased with her own daring.

I pause, taking them in. Nobody moves for a long moment, the silence stretching on like the final note of an opera.

Ethan looks up first, sees me coming through the

door. When I catch his eye, he seems to decide something.

"Fuck it," he declares. "Let's get drunk."

"That's what I'm talking about." Kimiko points a
finger at him, and they march to the kitchen.

I look at Em, who goes on staring at the ruined sculpture with avid fascination.

"What the hell was that about?" I ask her.

Though I direct the question at Em, Kimiko tosses
over her shoulder, "We broke it."

"I can see that." I turn to face her. "On purpose?"

"Yep." Kimiko offers no further explanation, so I
turn to Em.

"Are you okay?" I put a hand on her arm. It's hard
to read her expression. She's still gazing at the mess,
her eyes glossy.

Finally, she looks up at me. "We broke something
of hers."

"I don't get it." I look from Em to Kimiko to Ethan,
confused. "Why?"

"Call it *the imp of the perverse*." Ethan pours himself a shot of Patrón and downs it in one quick toss.
"We felt compelled."

"She controlled us." Em's eyes beg me to understand.
"She controlled all of us, in any way she could."

I can't help noticing Em's use of the past tense. Do
they know something I don't? It's hard to imagine them
destroying her sculpture if they thought she might walk
in the door any minute. Their assumption that she's gone
for good makes me queasy.

"We had to break the spell." Kimiko pulls a fresh
bottle of gin from the freezer. She sways slightly as

she throws a couple of ice cubes in her glass and fills it halfway.

The thought of a drink has my mouth watering. I need something to take the edge off, to soften the sting of my day. Getting drunk isn't a luxury I can afford right now, though. I still don't know for sure who planted that evidence. All signs point to Amy, but how can I be sure she's not working with one or more of the others? If that's the case, partying with them would be a serious mistake.

Then again, maybe their tipsiness can work to my advantage. If I *pretend* to get drunk with them, it could yield valuable information. *In vino veritas*.

"You want one of these?" Kimiko waves the bottle of gin at me.

"Sure."

Ethan still grips the tequila bottle. "Shot for you, Em, or a civilized mixed drink?"

"Shot, please." Em breaks from her trance, lunging toward the kitchen unsteadily.

"How many have you guys already had?" I ask.

Ethan pushes a shot across the bar to Em, who downs it in one.

"Not enough," he says. There's something unhinged in his smile. He throws back another shot and winces, wiping his mouth with the back of his hand.

As I take a seat at the breakfast bar, I can't help noticing that all three of them already seem a little drunk. That might explain the perverse logic that led them to break Sadie's sculpture. I feel that uneasy sense I always get walking into a party where everyone's got a serious head start on me. They've already slipped into a different world, one where the rules are looser, the consequences hazy. But there's an air of desperation to their drinking, too. Their grins look more like snarls, their lips peeling back from their teeth. Still they keep pouring. It's unnerving, how vacant they seem—not the friends I know and love, but ghoulish stand-ins.

Kimiko hands me a perfect G&T. A slice of lime hangs suspended in my glass as I hold it up to the light. Bubbles shiver loose from the porous green skin. We clink glasses. Her smile is loose and sloppy. She tilts her head to the side, studying me.

"What?" I sip my drink, suddenly self-conscious.

"You're not going to jail, June."

I bark out a nervous laugh. "I sure as hell hope not."

"For real." She puts on a serious face, but it comes off a little goofy. "We can't let that happen."

I decide to go ahead and tell them about the evidence the cops sprang on me at the station, starting with the T-shirt and the pill bottle. Like Bledek, I hold back on the statue, wanting to focus on their reactions to the less shocking stuff first.

Em and Ethan continue with the shots, knocking them back with grim determination as they listen to my retelling.

"Dolce and Gabbana," Kimiko says, squinting in thought.

Ethan pulls a bottle of olives from the fridge and unscrews the top with an audible pop. "That's Sadie's brand."

I turn to him. "What do you mean?"

"Only T-shirts she ever wears." He flashes a crooked, vacant grin. "She's particular."

Em leans over the breakfast bar. "So somebody was wearing Sadie's T-shirt?"

I stare at her, trying to decide if there's anything more to this statement—a hint of guilt, or signs that she knows more than she's let on. We were both in Sadie's closet, after all, trying on her clothes. I don't remember Em in a white T-shirt, but there's so much I don't remember.

"And there was definitely blood on it?" Kimiko looks a bit sick. "Could it have been something else?"

I shrug. "Hard to say. The way the cops acted, though, blood seems the most likely."

"You think the pill bottle contained traces of whatever you were dosed with?" Ethan's question comes out a little blurry. I can tell he's trying to enunciate, but his speech is starting to slur.

"Again, I'm only guessing, but it hardly seems like evidence otherwise."

I think of Bledek and his icy blue eyes; something in the pit of my stomach turns over, a slow, queasy motion as heavy and slimy as an eel.

Em looks scared. "They know we blacked out?"

I shake my head. "I didn't tell them. It casts too much doubt on everything we say."

"I don't know." Em clutches at her empty shot glass. "Our credibility's already in question. Maybe it's time to tell them that part."

"Change our story?" I stand up, too agitated to perch on the chair another second. "That's not a good idea. They won't believe a word we say if we do that."

"Still, what if we—?"

"No." I cut her off, unwilling to negotiate. "We stick to our story. Otherwise, we're screwed."

Kimiko breathes out an ironic laugh. "I think we're already screwed."

I hear the unspoken addition, though she's too tactful to say it aloud. *Or at least you are.*

"There was something else," I say.

"What?"

"Another piece of evidence." I look from face to face, trying to decide if any of them already suspects what I'm about to say. I can't tell.

"June, just tell us." Kimiko winces like she's bracing for a punch.

"The Kwan Yin statue." My voice sounds thick, unnatural. "With blood on it. And a few long, dark hairs."

There's a stunned silence. Ethan grips the counter like he's trying to keep his footing on a boat that's tipping side to side. Em's eyes are wide and wet with tears. Kimiko looks like she might throw up.

Ethan breaks the silence with a long, gusty sigh. "I can't believe this is happening."

I stare at him, thinking about all the crazy things I've learned about him in the last hour. An image of Amy flashes through my mind, alone in her clawfoot tub, pregnant with his child. Amy has plenty of reasons to want Sadie dead, but Ethan has even more. He already told me their marriage was on the rocks, and Kimiko implied Sadie would leave him penniless if he asked for a divorce. If Amy's telling the truth about their affair, he might want to be with her, to raise their child without the complication of Sadie in the way. He doesn't seem to be pining for Amy, but maybe he's trying to keep their relationship under wraps during the investigation. It's possible luring me down to the beach house the other night was all part of a plan he cooked up with Amy, a way to confuse the cops and cast suspicion on me.

I sip my drink, enjoying the way it warms my chest. Even so, I'm determined not to have another. Ethan seems drunker than Em and Kimiko. His eyes have a glazed, unfocused look, and his speech is getting sloppy. If I can lure him away from the others, there's a good chance I can get him to talk.

It's likely the cops will have enough to arrest me soon. The clock is ticking. I need to get Ethan alone, apply a little pressure, and pray he'll tell me something I can use.

ETHAN IS PRETTY far gone by the time we're splayed out on the lawn chairs two hours later. I pretend I'm a little drunk myself, even though I had only one G&T. After that I poured myself Perrier and let everyone assume I was keeping up with them, drink for drink. Em stumbled upstairs half an hour ago, and Kimiko's passed out on the living room couch.

Ethan's smoking a joint Kimiko offered us before she conked out. When he hands it to me, I put it to my mouth long enough to give the impression of taking a hit, but I don't inhale. He's too wasted to notice.

The cushion of the lawn chair is soft as a down pillow and cool through my shirt. An owl hoots in the distance. I spot the shape of it against the stars, moving with balletic grace from tree to tree. We sit in silence for a long moment, watching the breeze ripple along the surface of the pool, the lights from the house casting amber shapes along its turquoise surface.

This will all be Ethan's if Sadie's dead. He won't have to live with her rules, her schemes. He could revel in this palace, or sell it and start fresh someplace else. He could go back to Scotland, something I suspect he yearns for more than he lets on. He could swan off to an exotic island in the West Indies or the Caribbean. He could drift from one holiday hot spot to the next, charming new women every night amid the sparkle of cold, fruity drinks spiked with rum.

It's easy to imagine a whole new life for him, especially now that Dakota's almost off to college. With Sadie's money, he could be anyone, go anywhere. He could reinvent himself after years of bending to Sadie's iron will.

Ethan burps into his hand and grinds the butt of the joint into the teak coffee table. Watching the dark scar form on the pristine wood makes me feel like a teenager getting away with something. I guess this feeling—the childish urge to rebel against Sadie's tyranny—is why they tipped over Sadie's sculpture. It's why Em and I went straight to Sadie's room last night and messed it all up. The perfection of Sadie's world is like a stretch of fresh, powdery snow. Anyone halfway human wants to destroy that virginal whiteness, to mar its immaculate beauty by plowing right through it.

Sadie really is a force of nature. Amy might be the one with the mental health diagnosis, but I suspect Sadie's got a pathology of some kind, too, though I'm not sure what it would be. Narcissist, probably, or borderline personality disorder. She has a knack for making the people around her crazy. She's so oppressive, the tentacles of her wants and needs reaching out to ensnare everyone in her orbit. Even a couple of days in her presence reminded me of how toxic she is, poisoning the moods of everyone around her. I know that's uncharitable, but all the suffering I've seen in the last couple of days confirms it.

"I thought we'd never be alone." Ethan slants me a sideways look.

I'm in no mood for Ethan's charm, but I'm determined to play nice. Anything else would be counterproductive. He'd just clam up. I know him well enough to realize accusations will get me nowhere. He hates confrontation, which is probably why he and Sadie stayed together so long. She could never tolerate someone who would stand up to her.

"You okay?" I try to make my voice warm, sympathetic.

He exhales loudly. "Not really. You?"

"Same." I flash on Fisher and Bledek. I see myself dangling from a thin thread over a deep pit, with Bledek and Fisher snarling like wolves beneath me.

"Life is so crazy, isn't it?" Ethan swivels his gaze to the stars, which fill the sky tonight like a thousand shards of glass. "You ever feel like there's no way out?"

I nod. The lump in my throat won't let me speak.

"I'm so fucked right now. It's a good thing I'm numb with tequila, or I'd be howling in pain." To my surprise, he fishes a pack of cigarettes from his pocket, taps one out, and lights it. He gestures with the pack, offering me one.

I shake my head. "I didn't know you smoked."

"Bought a pack today." He waves out the match and tosses it down. With his face still tilted toward the stars, he takes a greedy lungful and exhales an extravagant plume. "Haven't had one in fifteen years."

"What made you start?"

He looks at the cigarette like he's just now noticed it between his fingers. "Don't know. Just wanted one, I guess. Sadie would have a fit. I know it's perverse, but her inevitable disapproval made me want one more than ever."

"You've always wanted what you can't have," I observe.

He studies me, his head tilted like he's trying to work something out. "You're the only one who's managed to stay free of her grasp. Do you realize that?"

"What do you mean?" The smell of tequila is so strong on his breath, you could light each word on fire.

"You don't owe her anything. Every other person here is tangled in her snare. Even your friend Leo."

It's possible he's referring to Leo's allegiance to Sadie as an employee. Still, it's not hard to read something more into his tone—something nastier.

"Is there something going on between them?" I try to sound casual, like I couldn't care less either way.

Ethan chuckles, but it's hollow. His smile doesn't reach his eyes. "She thought he'd make a better dad than me. You know Sadie. If at first you don't succeed…"

This blindsides me. "Wait, what? Leo—?"

I stop, images slotting into place. Sadie bolting from Leo's yurt. Her angry words: *Fine! Stay miserable. That seems to be what you want.* When I asked Leo about it, his explanation felt incomplete, like he was holding something back.

I try to find just the right question to guide him toward the truth without seeming like I'm digging. Ethan's not stupid, but he might be drunk enough to say more than he means to.

"You and Sadie have a smart, beautiful daughter." I ease out onto thin ice, feeling for the telltale crack beneath my feet. "Why would she want to 'try again'?"

Ethan scoffs. His voice goes bitter. "Sadie thinks we failed with Dakota."

"How so?"

"Who the hell knows? She's got a thousand secret tests she applies to everything and everyone. Nobody measures up. Least of all me." He takes a long drag from his cigarette and watches the smoke with the fascination of a child. "God, I've missed this."

I see Amy floating in her tub, eyeing me with a calculating gleam in her eye. *Ding ding ding. Finally, June gets the right answer.* It's so convoluted, I wonder if I'm jumping to crazy conclusions. I try to hit just the right note of casual assurance. If he thinks I already know, maybe he won't hesitate to confirm. "So her plan was to raise Amy's baby with Leo. Start fresh."

Ethan leans back in the lawn chair, putting his feet up. "That's pretty much the shape of it."

My pulse races. "Did she tell you that?"

"Not directly." He shrugs. "You know Sadie. It's all about the subtext."

"Didn't it bother you?"

"Why would it?" He closes his eyes, the cigarette dangling from the tips of his fingers.

"She's your wife, Ethan." I decide to push it one step further. "And it's your kid."

His eyes fly open. I can see his shoulders tense. "*My* kid?"

"Isn't it?" I say it like I'm asking about the coat nobody's claimed after a party, not a human being.

"Amy's baby? You think it's mine?"

I don't say anything. My gaze fixes on the water, shimmering in the moonlight.

"Amy's baby has nothing to do with me." He's adamant now, defensive, the insouciance falling away. "Why would you even—?"

"So you two never...?" I let it hang there.

"What kind of monster do you think I am?" He sits up, swinging his legs over the side of the lawn chair and facing me directly.

"You and Amy never got together?"

"God, no." His lip curls into a sneer. "She's my wife's cousin. And anyway, I would never—I'm not—she's not the least bit attractive to me."

Maybe it's stupid to believe anything Amy said, since she's out to get me, but right now her confession is all I've got to work with. I forge ahead. "Amy says you're the father."

"Come on, June." He gives me a look like I'm too naïve for words. His gaze goes beyond me, to Amy's house. "She's delusional. I get that you all love her, but Amy's mentally ill, okay? I know it's not PC to say it like that, but it's true."

"So she's lying?"

He gives a helpless shrug. "For all I know, she believes it. But let's face it, she wants Sadie's life. She always has. It's her raison d'être. She wants every single thing Sadie's got, from her Dolce and Gabbana T-shirts to me. It's not even flattering, really. I'm just part of the package."

I mull this over. Could he be telling the truth? The doctors have been adjusting Amy's meds to accommodate her pregnancy. Maybe her mental illness tipped over the edge into true psychosis? She seemed to believe what she told me earlier. There were no signs she was lying. If she's created an elaborate fantasy and lost touch with reality, though, her conviction would be absolute.

If that's the case, and if Amy's delusion runs deep enough to justify murdering Sadie, there are still two huge questions left unanswered. Her pregnancy is clearly not imaginary, so who's the father? Some random one-night stand she's blocked out and replaced with Ethan? Leo's the only other man on the property. Could the child be his? He claims to keep a distance from the drama he's steeped in, but I've known the man less than forty-eight hours. I can hardly take him at his word. If Ethan's right, Leo's more involved in all of this than he claims. The way Sadie stormed out of his yurt last night implies he's ensnared in the Mac-Tavish web, like it or not.

The other question is at once simpler and more complex. Assuming Amy did kill Sadie—as part of a premeditated plot or in the heat the moment—what did she do with her? Amy's five feet tall and eight months pregnant. How could she dispose of the body?

As soon as I've posed the question, I conjure a scenario. Amy bakes a cake with Sadie's special French chocolate, knowing she'll get a rise out of Sadie. She's already drugged us, so she knows we'll be unreliable witnesses. Amy and Sadie fight. Sadie storms off, up the stairs. Amy follows her. She picks up the statue at the top of the stairs, hits her with it. Sadie tumbles down to the landing, bleeding profusely. She's not dead, though. She's just disoriented. Amy tells her she'll take her to the hospital. They get into Sadie's car, Amy behind the wheel. Amy drives out to Deception Pass. Maybe she has a weapon, or Sadie's so drugged and concussed she's pliable as a child. Amy coerces Sadie out of the car, leads her over to the cliff. One push, and Sadie's gone. Amy leaves the car there, hoping to confuse the issue further and raise the possibility of suicide. She gets a taxi or hitchhikes home.

But then, where does the bloodstained T-shirt fit in? Could Amy have faked that? Maybe she took one of Sadie's shirts and smeared it with blood. Amy used to hurt herself in college. She'd slice herself in places that wouldn't be visible, the tops of her thighs, mostly. Maybe she stained the shirt with her own blood. Wouldn't that be risky, though, if they have it tested? Maybe she managed to get some of Sadie's blood before she pushed her off the cliff...

"You don't believe me, do you?" Ethan's petulant voice pulls me back to the moment. He's reclined in the lawn chair again, his eyelids starting to droop. "Nobody believes me around here. I've got to say, though, that's a new one, casting me as the baby daddy."

"Do you know who the father is?" I know I sound too sober, too lucid, so I add a breathy, "The real baby daddy?"

"One-night stand. That's what Amy says. I've got no

reason to doubt it. It's not my business. Unlike my wife, I've got no plans to be involved in the whole mess." He tries to look at me, but his eyes refuse to focus.

The window of opportunity with Ethan seems to be closing. He's too drunk to keep talking much longer, let alone offer something useful. Time to cut my losses and retreat. "I'm wiped out. I've got to go to bed."

"I know. I could fall asleep right here." He closes his eyes.

"Don't. You'll catch a cold." I stand, surveying him. I can't help thinking he looks mighty relaxed for a man whose wife is missing.

"Sweet dreams, Juney." He hasn't called me that since the summer we dated. Back then, his nickname made my heart race. Now it makes my skin crawl.

I go inside, make my way up the stairs, pull off my clothes, and fall into bed. Even under the thick down duvet, though, there's a chill in my bones that won't leave me. I can't stop thinking about Amy. I picture her lying in her own bed, her belly cupped protectively under one hand, spinning delusional fantasies about her new life free of Sadie.

THIRTEEN

HOURS LATER, I'm still staring at the ceiling. My mind
is buzzing with thoughts of Amy and Ethan, trying to
figure out whose version of events I can trust. One of
them is either lying or delusional. Ethan's version casts
Amy as a Single White Female, a crazed psycho obsessed with taking over Sadie's life. According to Amy,
though, she's just a pawn in a sick MacTavish game.

I try to decide which story rings true. I recall the
simmering tension earlier today when Ethan showed
up. He and Amy never even made eye contact. It's not
that hard to imagine Ethan sleeping with Amy once
and regretting it. I know that's not a flattering view of
a guy I spent years obsessing over, but I see Ethan more
clearly this weekend. My youthful, starry-eyed self is
gone. If he did regret hooking up with her, it's easy to
picture him acting like it never happened.

The window's open a crack, and the gauzy curtains
dance in the cool, damp breeze. I can smell the bay. I
try to clear my mind, taking refuge in the thought of
the glossy curves of a deep blue wave, but before the
image fully crystallizes, a bloody Kwan Yin shoves it
out of the way. I see the strands of black hair clinging
to dried clumps of blood on her stone face. Then I see
the amber pill bottle; it glows like it's radioactive. The

bloodstained T-shirt pulses beneath the plastic evidence bag like a beating heart.

A light tapping sound on my door makes me sit bolt upright. I get up and pad to the door, heart pounding. When I open it, Em's there in the shadows of the hallway, her bloodshot eyes bruised with exhaustion.

"I thought you might be awake," she whispers. "Can I sleep in here?"

"Of course." I pull the door open wider.

We crawl into bed together, though neither of us attempts to sleep.

"I'm surprised you're not passed out after all those shots."

She groans. "That was stupid. This always happens to me when I drink too much. I zonk out for a few hours, then wake up at two in the morning, full of regret."

I want to ask her about her mom's boyfriend, but she's made it clear that's not a conversation she's willing to have. I decide to ask her something more neutral, something that won't put her on the defensive.

"Have you told Reggie that Sadie's missing?" My voice is quiet, but it pierces the thick silence.

Em breathes out. It lands somewhere between a sigh and a scoff. "Are you kidding? If I had, he'd be up here already. We've got enough trouble without Reggie antagonizing the cops and ranting about a rigged justice system."

"I'm going to prison, huh?" I say it to the ceiling.

"No." Em spits out the single syllable with a ferocity I'm not expecting. "That's not happening."

My shoulder muscles, coiled tight, relax a little at her words. Then I think of Bledek's wolfish eyes, and they tighten all over again. Em might be loyal to a fault, savage in her urge to defend me, but her protectiveness won't change the evidence. My stupid, incriminating meeting with Ethan. That bloody shirt, the pill bottle. That grisly statue. To a jury, I won't be the June Moody Em knows and loves. I'll be the opportunistic *other woman*, driven by my twenty-year obsession with a famous writer, eager to claim the spoils of her glamorous life.

I think about the media circus that will erupt. It's a miracle the paparazzi haven't sunk their claws into it already. If they find her body and the media gets wind of it, that's it. We'll be hounded by reporters; a throng of journalists with cameras and microphones will press in on the house, littering the yard with their coffee cups and cigarette butts. We'll be trapped. The headlines flash before my eyes. I see a blurry picture of my pale, frightened face on the cover of a supermarket tabloid: *Crazed Mistress Murders* Dakota's Garden *Author.*

"June?" Em reaches out and brushes my hair back from my forehead. "I'm serious. We're going to clear your name. You didn't do anything wrong."

"We don't know that for sure."

She props her head on a splayed palm. "If anything, this planted evidence is further proof you didn't kill her. Somebody wants you to go down for it. We just have to figure out who."

The sound of footsteps in the hall makes us both sit up. Whoever it is stops outside the door. After a moment, the knob turns and the door swings open. A figure stands in the shadows, hard to make out in the gloom. My heart's pounding so hard I'm sure it must be audible.

"I thought I heard voices." Kimiko steps into the light, her hair wild, eyes blinking like a sleepy child.

Em and I let out a collective breath.

Kimiko sits on the edge of the bed, rolling her shoulders and massaging her neck. "Can't sleep. Got up for a glass of water and now all this is running through my head, you know?"

"Yeah," we say in unison.

She touches her nose, wincing. "Plus my nose is killing me. I had this dream. At least I think it was a dream. It might have been a memory."

"About last night?" Em whispers.

Kimiko ignores Em's question and looks at me. Her eyes sparkle with tears. "Do you remember being in the woods?"

I bite my lip. "Kind of. I have this vague sense I was out there, in the trees, barefoot. I think I screamed."

"Exactly." Kimiko nods. "That was in my dream. I came looking for you, and when you saw me, you screamed."

A memory floats up from the depths. Somebody was following me, and I was running through the forest barefoot. Kimiko's face appeared from out of nowhere, covered in blood. I shudder.

"I think we went to the beach after that." Kimi studies my face as if looking for signs of recognition.

Before the memory is fully formed, I hear myself saying, "We braided each other's hair."

"Yes!" She slaps the bedspread. "So it wasn't just a

dream. We went to the beach and braided each other's hair. You kept saying it would calm us down."

"But then why didn't we wake up with braids?" I ask, confused.

"We must have taken them out again. Or maybe we were too high to get them right." She smirks. "You always did them too loose."

"What else was in your dream?" Em hugs her knees, watching Kimiko with interest.

Kimi suddenly bursts into ragged sobs. Em and I both huddle closer to her, exchanging worried glances over her head.

"I think I know how I hurt my nose," Kimi manages.

I rub her back, tracing circles.

"It was when I had that fight with Sadie about smoking up with Dakota." Kimiko searches the ceiling, as if the memories are up there, playing out like a movie. "She went apeshit on me. I did what I always do with Jacob when he's like that. I grabbed her from behind and held her, tried to keep her from lashing out."

Her words jog my own memory. I can smell the fog mixing with smoke. I'm laughing. We're out on the patio, surrounded by garden lights. I remember how magical they looked, like benevolent fairies hovering all around us. Em's choking on too big a toke, making us laugh harder.

Kimiko can barely get the words out, she's so upset. "While I had my arms around Sadie, trying to contain her, she head-butted me. It hurt like a motherfucker. I remember blood pouring down my face. After that, it all goes black."

Nobody says anything.

"I wanted to hurt her." Kimiko looks at me, tears streaming down her face, naked fear in her eyes. "I remember that."

We sit there in silence for a long moment, sifting through our own private memories.

"Maybe I should tell the cops." Kimiko looks at me.

I stare at her, amazed. "It's not relevant, Kimi. They don't need to know about a random argument."

Her hand finds mine, squeezing. "It could get them off your back."

I'm so moved by her courage I can't speak.

Em says, "What about the car you saw? Did you remember anything more about that?"

Kimiko swipes at her tears. "I don't know. It was hard to see, but I think it was a sports car. Definitely dark—black or dark gray."

"Was it headed towards the house, or away from it?" I ask.

Kimiko thinks about it. "Towards the house, for sure. With its lights off."

I think about the theory I worked out earlier. I picture Amy driving an injured, disoriented Sadie to Deception Pass, shoving her off a cliff, and leaving Sadie's car there. Could this be the vehicle that brought Amy home? Maybe she called a friend or an Uber. Would they drive with their lights off, though? If she was trying to normalize the situation, would she dare ask the driver to do that? If she really wanted to keep a low profile, she would have them drop her at the gate and walk the rest of the way. Maybe in her condition the walk was too far, though.

Or maybe she was driven by an accomplice. Ethan,

maybe? He drives a Land Rover, though. It would be hard to mistake that for a sports car.

A part of me wants to tell Em and Kimiko my suspicions—about Amy, Ethan—just pour out the whole crazy mess. But until I know more, my instincts tell me to keep it to myself.

Besides, my Amy theory is starting to seem a little ridiculous. If she drugged us, that implies premeditation, but then why did she carry out her plan in such a sloppy way? Were the bloodstains part of her plan to cast suspicion on the rest of us, or did she attack Sadie only when her original plans fell through? Either way, pulling all of this off would take a cool head and a certain amount of physical stamina. At eight months pregnant, it would have been a serious strain on her.

After a while, Kimiko sighs and stands up. She wipes her eyes and stretches, shaking off her sadness. I remember that about her, how her moods pass like storms. "I doubt we're going to figure it out tonight."

"Not after all those drinks," I say.

"I'm going to get a snack, try to soak up the booze," she says. "You guys want anything?"

We both shake our heads.

"Okay. 'Night." She heads back out the door, closing it behind her.

Em looks pensive. "That car is important. It has to be. Who would be driving here with their lights off in the middle of the night?"

"It doesn't sound like any of the cars on the property," I say, thinking aloud. "Nobody here has a dark sports car."

"So it had to be an outsider." Em crawls back under

the covers, fluffing the pillows behind her and leaning against the headboard.

I join her. Maybe she's right. This car could be the key to everything.

I turn to face Em, an idea forming. "What about Dakota's boyfriend? Doesn't he drive a black Porsche?"

"That's right," she agrees. "He drove up in it when we first got here."

We both stare at the ceiling, thinking. Shadows cast from tree branches dance around the ceiling. Somewhere in the night, a fox barks out a hoarse, haunting scream. I shiver, pulling the comforter up to my chin.

Freedom. Dakota wanted her freedom. She saw herself as a prisoner. I recall our conversation in Ethan's study. *Have you met my mom? She's a total control freak. Babies are her favorite because they have no will of their own.*

How far will an inmate go to escape?

"What if the drugs had nothing to do with the murder?" The words are out of my mouth before the thought's fully formed.

Em hesitates. "What do you mean?"

"Maybe Dakota drugged us so she could sneak out."

"That sounds pretty farfetched."

"Go with me a second. Dakota's stuck in her room. It's the beginning of summer break. There's a party; all her friends are already there. Her phone's blowing up—they're having an awesome time, and she's missing it. Her mom's made it clear if she leaves the house she's grounded, meaning more prison time. More missing out."

I sit up again, hugging my knees as I picture it. Dakota

slipping something into our drinks, waiting in her room, gleefully listening for the sound of our party winding down—or for the opposite, the party ratcheting up, but with us too out of it to notice her tiptoeing toward the door. It's an extreme way to win a night of freedom, but Dakota doesn't strike me as a kid who does things halfway.

Em inserts a question as I pause. "So she drugs us? She just happens to have a bottle full of date-rape specials sitting on her nightstand?"

"Her boyfriend's in med school."

"You think they give that to med students? I doubt it." She stops, circling back. "Wait, Dakota's boyfriend is in med school? Doesn't that make him way older?"

"Five years." I think back to the conversation we had at the spa. It seems impossible that was only yesterday; it feels like decades have passed. "It was something she and Sadie fought about, apparently. The point is, maybe she had access to drugs. Or I don't know, maybe she got them wherever rapists do—on the street, right? It's not impossible."

"True," Em concedes. "Let's assume that's what happened for now. Where does that leave us? She drugged us, and then what happened?"

"Her boyfriend's home for the summer, and she's determined to go to this party with him. Or it could be the other way around. Her boyfriend's putting pressure on her to sneak out with him, so he suggests she drug everyone. Either way, he drives in here with his lights off, creeps into the house to get her."

"Wouldn't they just text?" Em asks. "Why would he come in?"

"The signal can be spotty out here—haven't you noticed? Or maybe the battery died on his phone, or he's trying to be romantic. Maybe he's drunk or high, not thinking clearly—I don't know."

She nods. "Okay, so he sneaks in, and then…?"

"Sadie, who's not as out of it as everyone else because she hardly drank, catches him at the top of the stairs before he can make it to Dakota's room." I pause, picturing it. Sadie flying at the intruder, ready to attack. The boyfriend picking up the statue, defending himself with it instinctively in the dark. Sadie's long fall down the staircase, the pool of blood on the landing from her head wound.

"And then what?" Em sounds skeptical. "They fight?"

"Maybe Sadie came out of nowhere, thinking he's some random intruder. He might have been acting on instinct, trying to fend her off."

Em picks up the thread where I left off. "So the boyfriend kills Sadie—accidentally, reflexively—"

"And Dakota helps him cover it up," I say, finishing her sentence.

"Dakota drives the body out to Deception Pass in Sadie's car, they dump it off a cliff, leave Sadie's car there, and he drops Dakota off here."

I nod. This story is easier to swallow than the one featuring Amy lumbering around in the middle of the night, pregnant and winded, ordering Sadie around. It also explains the weird mixture of premeditated and impulsive behavior—the drugs and the bloodstains.

"Maybe he told her to pin it on one of us to save his ass," I say, thinking of the evidence stashed in my suitcase. Just because Amy was in my room, that doesn't mean she was the one to plant it. Dakota could have snuck in there the second the cops arrived with their warrant. That's the only way she could be sure I wouldn't find it in my suitcase before they did.

I think of that T-shirt again, wrapped in plastic. Something about it keeps nagging at me. I scan my memory of it and stop at the sleeve. There was a fleck of something golden there—a plant of some kind. Hay. It was a tiny piece of hay.

"Dakota's the only one who spent time with the horses since we've been here," I muse, more to myself than Em.

"Yeah. So?"

"I saw a piece of hay on that T-shirt. The one with blood on it," I say.

In the faint moonlight, Em's expression is hard to read. "You think Dakota planted the evidence?"

I feel my heart picking up speed. "If her mom wears Dolce and Gabbana, maybe she does, too. It could have been her shirt, stained with her mother's blood."

"It's possible."

Now that I've started down this road, the pieces begin to slot into place. "There's something else. When Fisher questioned me about my relationship with Ethan and whether or not Sadie suspected anything, he used a word that seemed really out of character: *salty.*"

"Salty?" she repeats, perplexed.

"He asked if Sadie was 'salty.'" I can't believe I didn't think of this earlier. "We know Ethan didn't tell the police about us meeting Wednesday night—his lawyer wouldn't let him—so maybe it was Dakota. I heard her use that exact word at the spa yesterday. Maybe she told them Sadie suspected we were having an affair to throw more suspicion onto me."

We listen to the pines murmuring as the breeze becomes a steady wind. Em stays frozen in place, still staring at the ceiling, deep in thought.

She sits up and faces me. "We have to find out more about this boyfriend. Right now it's just a theory, but we need more than that. We need proof."

IT's FOUR IN the morning when Em and I sneak down the hall to Dakota's room. We spent half an hour trying to research her boyfriend online, but her accounts are set to private. Without a name or much information about him, we didn't get very far. Borrowing her laptop and phone is the only way to dig deeper.

My hand feels clammy as I grip the doorknob. There's a thickness to the silence, a heaviness. I can hear an owl hooting in the distance, faint but determined. Otherwise, the house is filled with pure stillness. Usually the pipes murmur inside the walls, the wind rattles the windows. I can't help but take the quiet personally. It's as if the sprawling mansion is protecting its youngest resident, conspiring to expose us by giving us zero margin of error.

I release my grip on the doorknob and whisper into Em's ear. "You sure about this? Maybe we should sneak in tomorrow when she's out."

"She won't leave without her phone." Em's response is instant, decisive. "If she wakes up, we'll say she called out in her sleep and we came to check on her."

I take a deep breath, reminding myself this is necessary. It feels like the worst kind of betrayal, feigning maternal concern. We're not out to protect her. We're trying to prove her boyfriend killed her mom.

Then I think of that Dolce & Gabbana T-shirt, the blood smeared across it. I think of Kwan Yin, her head partly caved in and bloody. I picture Dakota stuffing it all into my suitcase, the prescription bottle and the statue wrapped inside the T-shirt, careful not to leave fingerprints. I see her pretty blue eyes darting to the door, listening for footsteps. She's prepared to watch me spend my life in prison for something her boyfriend did. If this is true, I have every right to arm myself with knowledge.

With a fresh surge of determination, I turn the knob. The door lets out a creak as I push it open. This damn house again, working against us. We hold our breath, poised in the doorway, eyes glued to the lump under the duvet. Dakota doesn't stir. Em nudges me forward. We're in.

There's a pink night-light near the window that casts a soft rose glow. I wait for my eyes to adjust to the dimness. I scan the room's surfaces quickly: a storage chest at the foot of the bed, a small nightstand, and a dresser against one wall. I spot her laptop on the dresser.

Clothes lie scattered across the floor. I move toward the laptop, careful to avoid the clothes in case heavier items are concealed beneath the mounds. I grab the laptop and unplug it from its charger. With the computer tucked beneath one arm, I wade into the room a little deeper, looking for Dakota's phone. It's right where I would expect it to be, but the last place I want it—perched on her nightstand, inches from her face.

Damn.

I hand Em the laptop. As she takes it from me, I nod toward the phone. In the shadows, I can just make out her pained expression. I gesture at the door, trying to communicate that she should go. If Dakota wakes while I'm attempting to nab her phone, it will look less suspicious if it's just me. Em, who has years of experience communicating with me telepathically, gets my point and slips out the door, stealthy as a shadow. I breathe a sigh of relief, a little surprised we've gotten this far.

Dakota stirs in her sleep, flipping over beneath the duvet. One arm reaches out from the covers, a hand hanging limp over the edge of the mattress right by her phone. I consider giving up and making do with her laptop. Maybe we can glean something from her computer, but the real treasure trove is her phone. Anyone under the age of thirty stores all their secrets there. It's the holy grail of evidence, as every jealous lover knows.

I take a deep breath and let it out slowly, sliding my socks along the floor in an effort to move silently. I pray she's out cold. I creep closer, my gaze darting between the bed and the phone. When I'm close enough to touch it, I extend my arm slowly, avoiding her limp hand. I grip the silver-studded phone case and pick it up, not even daring to breathe. I turn toward the door, ready to make a quick getaway, but as soon as my back is turned, I hear a rustling sound. I stuff the phone into the pocket of my sweats and spin around to see Dakota sitting up, her hair mussed and her eyes bewildered.

"What the—?"

"Hey." I sit on the edge of her bed, forcing my voice into a warm, soothing register. "You okay?"

She ignores my question, blinking at me owlishly. "What the hell are you doing in here?"

"You were having a nightmare." I'm hyperaware of her phone pressed just below my right hipbone; I angle my body and hope she can't see it bulging in my pocket. I silently thank Em for thinking up a cover story, making improv a little easier. "You called out, so I thought I'd come check, make sure you were okay."

Dakota regards me. It's hard to read her expression with only the pink night-light and a thin wash of moonlight to see by. I tell myself her frown is inquisitive, not suspicious. Anyone would demand answers, waking to find a near-stranger prowling around her bedroom.

"What time is it?" She looks to the nightstand. For a heart-stopping moment I'm afraid she'll reach for her phone. Luckily, there's a brass clock there with a glow-in-the-dark face, circumventing her need to search further. Still, how long will it be before she checks for texts? Isn't that what any seventeen-year-old would do the second consciousness takes hold?

I've got to lull her back to sleep. If she barrels through this hypnopompic state to full awareness, she's sure to notice her phone's missing. We need time, or this whole venture will be fruitless. Worse than fruitless—it will warn Dakota we're onto her.

"It's late," I say, willing my voice into what I hope is a reassuring tone. "Go back to sleep."

To my enormous relief, she flops back against the pillows, letting her breath out in a gusty sigh. I can see her blinking, though, still struggling to regain clarity amid the haze of lingering dreams.

I recall what my own mother did when I couldn't

sleep; she used to stroke my hair. Feeling like a world-class ass, I reach out and gently push several strands away from her forehead. At first she tenses, and I worry I've made a miscalculation. Then she rolls onto her side and snuggles more deeply into the pillows, surrendering to my touch. I stroke her soft, honey-colored hair until her breathing deepens.

"Shhhh," I murmur, the only lullaby I dare. "Shh."

At last, she starts to snore, a gentle wheezing sound that floods my body with relief. I get to my feet and scurry out the door.

EM WORKS WITH intense concentration, going back and forth between Dakota's phone and her laptop, fingers flying across the keys. She's set up shop on the bed, the laptop before her, phone beside it. Since she's the one who works for Google, there's no way I'm going to get in her way with my inferior tech instincts, but I hate feeling so useless. I'm too restless to sit. I pace the room, pausing to hover near her now and then, trying to read the screens over her shoulder.

"What are you doing?" My gaze moves to the door, my body still charged with adrenaline. I'm sure Dakota will wake any second now, notice her pilfered stuff, and barge in, demanding answers.

Em sits back against the pillows with a sigh. "I'm trying to hack her passwords. Her computer's not protected, but her phone is."

"Damn."

"Any ideas?" She studies the phone. "Most people use birthdays."

"Let's see…do you know Dakota's birthday?"

"Already tried that. Poached it from Facebook." Em's fingers fly across the keyboard. "I also tried Sadie's, but that didn't work. Do you know Ethan's?"

"April thirteenth," I say automatically.

She looks at me, her mouth curved into a little smile. "Year?"

I do the math in my head. "He's six years older than us, so…seventy-three?"

She picks up the phone and tries again, but no luck.

I rub my forehead. "You're not thinking we use her thumb, are you?"

She shakes her head. "Too risky. We need to be careful with random guesses, though. If we try too many times with no success it could lock, depending on her security settings."

"I have an idea." I sit down next to her, pulling the laptop closer. Her relationship status shows Ben Cole as her boyfriend. His profile picture reveals a handsome young guy in his early twenties—strong jaw, bright-blue eyes, sandy brown hair cut short. I look for his birthday. "Try May seventh, 1996."

"What's that?"

"Boyfriend's birthday."

Em types the numbers in. I know when I see her smile we've struck gold.

"Nice work, Poirot." She scrolls, her face tense with concentration.

I huddle closer, trying again to read over her shoulder. She's opened Dakota's texts and is scrolling through the contacts.

"There," I say, when I see Ben Cole. "See what they texted about."

She obeys, scrolling through their messages too quickly for me to glean more than a word here or there.

"Hmm...not much here. Looks like Dakota and Ben haven't texted for days."

"That seems unlikely," I say.

"She could have deleted them." Em looks away from the phone, staring out the window. "If there was anything incriminating, that's what a smart girl would do."

We ponder this in silence, and cold dread creeps around my belly.

"If she did delete them, does that mean we're screwed?" I ask.

Em snaps out of her reverie and springs back into problem-solving mode. "Not at all. I've got a few tricks up my sleeve." She takes the laptop from me. "They might be backed up in the cloud. Not too likely, if she was trying to erase all traces, but worth a look."

"And if there's no backup?" I can hear the anxiety in my voice.

"Like I said. I've got tricks." She tries a reassuring smile, but it doesn't quite reach her eyes. "Why don't you get some sleep? This will be boring."

"I'm not sure I can. I'm too freaked out."

"I bet if you close your eyes, you'll be out in a few seconds. You look like you haven't slept in years."

"Thanks a lot."

"Seriously." Em pulls the covers back, a mother coaxing a reluctant child after a nightmare. "I'll wake you when I find something."

I climb under the covers and plump the pillow, relishing the soft, cool pillowcase. She's right, as usual. My body feels leaden; my eyes ache with exhaustion.

I burrow in deeper, comforted by the tapping of her fingers on the keyboard. Before long, I've fallen into a deep, dreamless sleep.

FOURTEEN

I WAKE TO find Ethan leaning over me. His face fills my field of vision. I jerk my head away, disoriented and bleary-eyed. My skull knocks against Em's, deepening my confusion and eliciting from her a low, throaty moan of protest. She flips away from me, pulling the covers over her head.

I sit up, lean against the headboard, and blink. "What time is it?"

"I don't know. Early."

A glance out the window confirms the sun's just coming up; the sky is a cold, arctic blue. I shiver and hug myself. Ethan's wearing a black T-shirt and plaid pajama pants. I can tell from his bloodshot eyes and bedhead he hasn't been up long. His complexion is pale, and there are creases of worry lining his forehead.

With alarm bells screeching at the back of my brain, I force myself toward lucidity. I'd much rather hear whatever he's going to tell me after coffee, or—better yet—another few hours of unconsciousness, but I have a bad feeling this is too urgent to wait.

"What's going on?"

Ethan glances at Em, who is now just a mound beneath the covers. The sight rouses a memory. With a jolt of adrenaline, I scan the room for Dakota's phone and laptop. Neither one is visible, at least not in this light.

I have a vague memory of Em saying she'd wake me if she found anything. Did she decide to put them back, or are they hidden someplace out of sight?

"Can you come to my room?" he asks.

Sadie's room, I think automatically. The thought of being surrounded again by her most intimate belongings makes my skin crawl, but I'm too groggy to suggest an alternative. I have a feeling this is a private conversation, and no other room in the house will do. I nod and follow him out into the hallway.

In the early-morning light, the hallway is dim, the floor cold beneath my bare feet. As we pass the top of the stairs, I can't help glancing at the wall where the blood splatter is still visible. I see Dakota's boyfriend picking up the stone statue and swinging it at Sadie's head. I hear the sickening sound as it makes contact, blood bursting from the wound and flying through the air, freckling the wall.

Ethan pushes his bedroom door open and waits as I slip inside. A small bedside lamp fills the room with golden light. As I hover beside him, hesitant to venture any farther, he shuts the door with a barely audible click. He looks at me a moment, his expression unreadable. Then he runs one hand over his face and wanders to the bed, his knees buckling as he collapses onto it.

I can smell Sadie in here. She's everywhere, the delicate scent of violets. It's suffocating. There's a silk kimono hanging from the door to the en suite bathroom, a bright floral confection rich with lavender and periwinkle. A ghostly presence lingers; I wrap my arms around myself, fighting the chill. It's probably just the vulnerability of half consciousness, my defenses not yet kicking in, coffee not yet arming my system with artificial optimism. I feel naked and unprotected, laid bare.

"The cops called a few minutes ago." Ethan sounds hoarse.

I wait for him to go on. Taking a step closer, I try to make out his expression.

Finally, he looks into my eyes. "They found her."

The words hang in the space between us, fragile and dangerous.

"Oh my God. Where?"

"She washed up on a beach near Deception Pass." He swallows hard. "I've got to go down to the morgue and identify the body, but it's almost definitely her."

I cover my mouth, unable to speak.

"Her skull was fractured. It could have happened in the fall."

"The fall?" I repeat.

"They think she fell—from the cliffs, maybe, or the bridge." His voice is flat, drained.

"Do they think it was suicide?" I'm surprised at the steadiness of my tone.

He shakes his head. "They seem to think she was already dead when she hit the water. They're treating it as a suspicious death." His voice breaks on the last word.

I stare at Ethan, reading his eyes. There's fear there, though I can't tell if it's for himself or for me.

"I take it I'm still their favorite suspect."

His frown is an apology. "They didn't say as much, of course."

I hug myself tighter, cold seeping into my feet through the floor. Sadie's dead. It's a kick to the gut.

I wish it were simple grief racing through me, but it's more than that. The feel of handcuffs clamping around my wrists is so real, I rub my wrists to assure myself it's not happening. Not yet. It's just a matter of time, though. Once I'm arrested, I won't be able to fight back.

"The last person I want to suffer for this is you," he says.

Not quite, I think. *The last person you'd want to suffer is your daughter.* I wonder what he'd do if I told him our suspicions. How do you explain to someone that his daughter might have conspired to cover up the murder of his wife?

"Hey." When I don't look at him, he stands, gripping my biceps like he's trying to hold me up. "We're going to figure this out. I promise."

"You can't promise that," I croak.

"You have to trust me."

I look down, unable to hold his gaze. A strand of Sadie's hair catches my eye. It clings to the cream bedspread, long and dark. A sob tries to escape from my pursed lips. I can't go to prison—I just can't. Any sadness I feel about Sadie's death is eclipsed by the claustrophobic panic of a cornered animal. My mind spins with images: mug shots, orange jumpsuits, steel bars closing in.

"June." Ethan ducks lower so I can't escape his eyes. "We're going to get through this."

"They're so sure it's me, and I—"

He cuts me off with a kiss. His mouth is insistent, his lips parting mine.

I jerk away from him. "What are you doing?"

His eyes search my face, questions quirking his eyebrows. I see how thrown he is by my resistance. Did he really think it would work like this? They've just found his wife's body, Amy may or may not be pregnant with his kid, and he's kissing me.

With a blinding flash of insight, I realize how right I was to say no to Ethan's proposal. It's like a lightning bolt to my brain, incinerating any doubts I've nursed over the years. Ethan's weak. He's an opportunist. He's not someone I admire or even like.

I back away from him, inching toward the door, keeping my eyes glued to his face. I try to see the man I worshiped all those years, but he's vanished. What I see is a frightened, hollow-eyed ghost.

He must see something in my face, because he reaches out a hand to stop me. "Please don't look at me like that, June. I'm in so much pain."

"Did you ever love her?" The question pops out before I can stop it.

His shrug is the saddest thing I've ever seen. All those years of marriage, and the only thing he can offer is a minuscule movement of his shoulders.

"I'm not your answer," I whisper, reaching for the door.

Ethan closes the distance between us, his hands gripping my biceps again, tighter than ever. His touch is repugnant, his fingers clammy and desperate. The smell of violets hits me with fresh intensity. With effort, I yank free of his grip and grope again for the door. I feel dizzy, my head swimming.

"Please don't go." His voice is raw.

I risk a quick glance back at him. He looks helpless

there, a man standing alone in a room filled with his dead wife's beautiful things. I jerk the door open and hurry back down the hall.

I CRAWL BACK into bed, trembling. The realization that Sadie's dead sits like a stone in the pit of my stomach. We've been bracing ourselves for this moment ever since we found the bloodstains, but before they found her body, it was still possible she'd turn up, that this whole thing would go from tragedy to misunderstanding. Now that hope is gone, and in its place is a dark, sickening dread.

The danger of my situation crashes over me, all traces of brave optimism evaporating like steam. Sadie's body floats to the surface of my mind, blue and bloated, chunks of flesh torn loose by underwater predators.

The chill in my bones is impervious to the thick down duvet. I look at it as I wrap it tighter around me. The pale-gray comforter is as subtle and luxurious as everything else in this house, a thousand-thread-count artifact of understated elegance.

Sadie wanted beauty like this all around her, everything expertly crafted. She had the determination to forge her own exquisite reality. Her books, her movie deals, her public persona—she willed it all into being. Now Sadie's lying in a morgue, splayed out on an autopsy table, all that spirit and tenacity leached from her. I picture her sightless eyes staring up at the ceiling and shudder.

Do I fight tooth and nail to get out of this mess? Am I willing to do whatever I can to ensure the cops arrest someone other than me? I feel sick. Scared. Dirty.

My values, my moral compass, have existed on some rarefied plane until now. They've never been tested. At thirty-eight, I'm facing a bona fide moral dilemma for the first time. But the alternative, spending the rest of my life in prison, makes my body tremble harder than ever. I grind my teeth together to keep them from chattering.

Em's still fast asleep. She probably stayed up for hours hacking Dakota's accounts. I don't have the heart to wake her, and I know I won't be able to go back to sleep. After that encounter with Ethan, I don't feel safe in this house. Between him and Amy and Dakota, even this sprawling mansion feels too small.

I recall the memories Kimiko and I unearthed last night. It's like digging in sand; we found the edges of something, and now I have the sense that, if I just pull hard enough, the whole thing will emerge. I can feel the sand falling back into place, though, trying to keep the night buried. I need help to see the rest.

There's only one person I know who can help me.

I slip out from under the covers, careful not to disturb Em. After pulling on my jeans, a wool sweater, and boots, I step out into the frigid dawn and hurry down to Leo's yurt.

As I walk, I flash back to Ethan's attempt to use me as a distraction. He's got to be in shock. I suppose I should have some compassion, but the memory of him groping me like a drowning man lunging at a life preserver makes me sick. I can't believe I wasted all those years wondering if I should have married him. He never brought Sadie real happiness. I spent so much time longing for him in college, I never stopped to look at him with the clear-eyed objectivity of an adult. Now that I'm finally capable of doing this, what I see floors me.

Sadie didn't have it all. Far from it. She had a disloyal husband and an inner circle of people who resented the hell out of her.

A curl of smoke rises from Leo's chimney as I draw closer. He must be awake. As I make my way up the steps, he opens the door wearing army fatigue cargo shorts that aren't quite buttoned and an inside-out, gray, threadbare sweat shirt.

"Sorry to show up so early," I say.

His hair stands up at hectic angles. He tries to smooth it, but it springs up again under his palm. For some reason, a painful stab of tenderness shoots through me.

"You want to come in?" His voice is gentle, tentative.

I nod, passing by him as he holds the door open for me. He smells of sleep—warm sheets and wood smoke.

"You want some coffee?" Leo nods at a French press on the counter.

I take a seat in the green velvet chair. "Love some."

I watch as he fills two rough-hewn mugs. "How do you take it?"

"Black is fine." Usually I take milk and sugar, but I'm imposing enough as it is. In spite of the weirdness of me showing up like this at dawn, though, there's a comfortable silence between us as Leo delivers my mug and takes a seat in the beat-up leather armchair across from me.

He blows a whisper of steam from his cup and watches me, waiting for me to speak.

"They found Sadie's body," I say into the silence.

He doesn't look surprised. I try to read his expression, but it's blank.

"Where?"

I fill him in. His face remains impassive.

"How are you doing?" His eyebrows pull together with concern.

I consider the question. "I don't know. I'm too freaked out about being a suspect to feel much sadness about Sadie, to be honest. I guess that sounds awful, but it's the truth—at least for now."

"Why would you be a suspect?"

I tell him about yesterday's police inquiries. As I do, I can feel my pulse quickening. I stick to the truncated, bullet-point version. Laying it out like that, point by point, a fresh wave of fear sloshes through me. I don't mention the suspicions Em and I harbor about Ben and Dakota. He doesn't need to know everything.

"How are Ethan and Dakota?" He sips his coffee, those dark eyes studying me over the rim of his cup.

I sigh. "I don't think Dakota knows yet. She's probably still asleep. As for Ethan, I guess he's in shock."

Leo nods; his eyes never leave my face.

I take a sip of my coffee. It's strong and bold, full of flavor. "Listen, the reason I came down here is because I need answers. Last night, talking to Kimiko, I remembered a little more about what happened Thursday, but you're the only person who can help me fill in the blanks."

It's his turn to sigh. He puts down his coffee and leans back in his chair, arms folded behind his head. "You really don't remember, do you?"

I shake my head. "I know this is awkward, but the

stakes are high. The more you can tell me, the more prepared I'll be to face the cops."

His brown eyes glint in the morning sun. There's a whiskey-colored streak in one of them. "I was asleep. You showed up after midnight, maybe closer to one. When I woke up, you'd already crawled into bed with me."

I almost choke on my coffee. "Seriously? How did I get inside?"

He shrugs. "I never lock my door. Nobody does around here. Guess you let yourself in."

"But why would I—? God. I can't believe I did that." I press my palms to my cheeks, trying to cool the sudden rush of shame making my face burn. I'm not sure I want to hear the rest.

The hint of a smile plays at the corners of his mouth. The dimples I noticed earlier appear again, bracketing his barely contained grin. "Don't look so horrified, June. We didn't have sex, if that's what you're worried about."

A memory comes back to me. The heat of his skin against mine. Lips, fingers, glimmers of moonlight through the skylight, casting ghostly beams along the fine planes of his face.

"What happened?" I whisper.

"I'm a pretty heavy sleeper. I don't wake up that easily. For a few minutes, I just went with it."

"You went with it," I repeat, my voice cracking slightly.

"I wasn't fully conscious. To be honest, I thought it was a dream." He stares up at the skylight as if remembering.

A part of me longs to know what he's seeing. The other part of me is pretty sure I'd implode with shame. I can't believe I'd be that forward. More than forward— aggressive. I think of what Em said about whatever we took lowering our inhibitions. I guess it's no secret what I wanted to do with Leo from the first moment I met him.

"It was the best dream I've had in a very long time." He takes his time saying this, his voice low and gentle. His face is a complicated mixture of desire and something else. Wistfulness? Regret?

I lick my lips, unsure if I can make any words come out. "How long did I stay?"

"Not long. Once I woke up, I realized something was off." He runs a hand over his face and drinks more coffee. "There was something strange about you."

"Oh, you mean aside from the fact I broke into your house and tried to rape you?" It sounded funny inside my head, but once the words hit the air, I want to suck them back into my mouth.

"I haven't known you very long, but yes, it seemed out of character." He pins me with his gaze. "I wanted to keep going, believe me. I wanted it so much I surprised myself."

I can feel heat flooding my cheeks again.

"I asked you a couple questions. Your answers didn't make a lot of sense. When I turned on the light, you got scared, disoriented. The more I tried to calm you down, the more agitated you got."

"Could you tell I was high?"

He thinks about this. "Like I said, I'm not the sharpest tool in the shed when I first wake up. I was still pretty groggy, but I was starting to suspect you were on something, yeah." He shifts in his chair, pushes the sleeves of his sweat shirt up, and looks out the window. "A couple minutes after I turned on the light, you bolted. I tried to stop you, but you went tearing through the woods barefoot. I followed you, but you were fast. You kept looking over your shoulder at me, terrified. I could tell I was scaring you, so I hung back. But then I heard you scream, so I picked up my pace again. By the time I caught up with you, your friend was with you. The two of you headed towards the beach. I figured she'd take care of you and I was only freaking you out, so I went back."

I drink the rest of my coffee and stand up, too embarrassed to sit there another second. I can't look him in the eye. Instead I busy myself depositing the empty coffee cup in the sink. There's a colander filled with freshly washed strawberries. They look impossibly red and juicy.

I run my hands through my hair, groaning. "God, Leo, you must think I'm certifiable."

"I guess that's one way of putting it." There's that voice again—gentle, amused.

"There's something else I need to ask you about." Though I'm eager to shift the focus away from my craziness, I'm not sure how to broach the tangle of contradictory stories Amy and Ethan handed me. "Last night, I was talking to Ethan. He was pretty drunk, but some of the stuff he said…"

"Like what?" Leo looks relaxed, hands cupped around his coffee cup, but I hear a note of tension in his voice.

"He implied Sadie wanted more from you than just—how did you put it? 'Someone to tell her she's still got it'?" I stare at the strawberries in the sink, unable to look at him. "He said she wanted to raise Amy's child with you."

Silence. After a long moment, I tear my gaze away from the strawberries to check his reaction. His expression is unreadable.

"I wouldn't put it that way," he says at last.

I look down. "How would you put it?"

"Sadie had a lot of ideas—fantasies, I guess—about who I am and what we could offer one another." He sighs. "She knew about my past. As soon as Amy got pregnant, she kept trying to involve me, but I made it pretty clear it's got nothing to do with me. In some twisted way, I think she saw this baby as a chance for all of us to start over again."

I turn his words over in my head. There's so much he's not telling me; that much is clear. What he's saying confirms Ethan's bombshell, though. The exact outline of Sadie's plan is still hazy, but between their two versions, it's easy to glean that she talked to Leo about it.

He gets up and walks toward me, puts his coffee cup down near the sink. The top button of his fatigues is still distractingly undone. He stands near me, close enough for me to catch his scent again. A wave of longing washes through me. I lean a hand on the counter, steadying myself. I study the collar of his sweat shirt, afraid to look up into his face. More memories assail me. I can taste the salt of his collarbone under my tongue, feel the heat of his hands tightening around my waist. My thighs straddle him, hips rocking, one hand on his chest, my head thrown back. I remember the sea of tangled dark sheets, the warmth of his bed, the view out the windows of the water in the moonlight.

"I know this is probably the worst timing ever," he says. "But I'm just going to come out with it, okay? I like you, June Moody. I haven't liked anyone in a very long time, but there's something about you."

When I finally meet his gaze, he's staring down at me, his expression so intense it takes my breath away. Without thinking, I reach for him. Our mouths collide, both of us leaning into it, tasting each other. I lose myself in the kiss for a long, precious moment.

I pull away. "I can't, I—Sadie's dead. I'm sorry. I can't deal with this right now."

Leo gives me a solemn nod and steps back.

I hurry toward the door. I'm already out on the porch when I hear Leo's footsteps behind me. To my surprise, he hands me my beat-up Converse. I never even noticed they were missing.

"You left these the other night," he says, handing them over. "I meant to give them to you yesterday, but then our conversation kind of messed with my head."

"Thanks," I murmur.

He clears his throat. "Let me know if there's anything I can do to help."

I mumble something incoherent and stumble down the steps.

FIFTEEN

"HEY." EM'S SITTING up in bed when I return. She takes one look at me, and her expression goes from groggy to alert. "You okay?"

"They found her body." I shudder. "They're treating it as a suspicious death."

Em sucks in a deep breath, lets it out slowly. When she speaks, it's in the steady, calm voice of someone digging deep for courage. "I kind of figured it was just a matter of time."

"Yeah. It's just…more real now."

"Yes." She rakes her fingers through her hair. "It is."

I set down my Converse, kick off my boots, and lie on the bed beside her, staring at the ceiling. "I'm really scared."

"I know." She squeezes my arm. "We all are. We just have to block everything else out and concentrate on clearing your name."

"How?" The tears I managed to keep at bay all morning break free now. I can feel them tracing hot trails along my temples.

Em looks down at me. "I'm more sure than ever we're right about Dakota's boyfriend. I was able to access their deleted texts. It's not definitive, but everything implies our theory has legs."

I look at her. She's got dark circles under her eyes,

but there's something new in her face, something that wasn't there last night. Not just her face—her whole body radiates fierce determination. In spite of the collapsed, hollow feeling in my chest, the ice in my veins, I feel a tiny brush fire of hope sputtering to life in my belly.

Em is brilliant. I know that much. If she believes we can get out of this mess, maybe she's right.

I sit up and wipe my tears. "Do we have enough to take to the cops?"

"I don't think so. My gut says we need a little more evidence if we want them to take us seriously." She's careful to keep her tone positive. "But I have an idea about how we can get it."

"How?" I glance toward the door, keeping my voice down.

Em holds my gaze. "We need to talk to Ben."

"He's not going to confess if he thinks he can get away with it," I say, spirits plummeting.

"If our theory's right, he didn't mean to kill her," she points out. "Manslaughter or self-defense is a lot less serious than first-degree murder. Maybe we can pressure him into telling the cops what happened."

I shake my head. "Pressure him with what? We don't have any solid evidence."

"I've got screenshots of all their texts." Em reaches for her phone with that determined, steely look of hers. "We've got some pretty damning intel we can turn over to the police; we just need a little more. They were planning to run away together Thursday night."

"Wait, really?" I cup my hand over my mouth.

Em nods. "Dakota was going with him to LA. She

figured it was her only chance to decide her own fate, not get bullied into going to Yale."

"Whoa." I feel a rush of hope. "So that's why she drugged us?"

"I think so. The drugging thing isn't spelled out, but it's implied." She starts scrolling through her phone, brow furrowed.

"How would we even get him here?" I ask.

"We can text him, pretend to be Dakota," she suggests.

This sounds a little crazy. Sadie's body is lying in the morgue, waiting to be identified. Everyone is in shock. The idea of luring Ben here and confronting him is so ridiculous I almost laugh. "How would that work? And don't you think it's too soon? I mean, they just found Sadie and—"

A keening sound tears through the house, cutting me off midsentence. It's coming from downstairs. We scramble off the bed and race down the hall.

WE FOLLOW THE sound to the kitchen, where we find Ethan holding Dakota in a tight hug. She's sobbing with the abandon of a child, gasping for breath before letting out another high, piercing wail. Ethan's face is unnaturally pale as he strokes her hair and whispers in her ear. The moment is too intimate. We back out of the room, trying to give them space.

Kimiko stumbles down the stairs and comes over to us, looking hungover. "What's going on?"

"They found Sadie's body," I whisper. "At least they think it's her."

Her eyes fill with tears. "Oh."

After another few seconds, Ethan comes out of the kitchen, one arm wrapped tightly around Dakota as if to hold her up. They almost collide with our little huddle in the hallway. Dakota's still crying.

"I have to go down to the morgue," Ethan says, his tone terse.

Dakota sputters, "I—I'm coming with you."

"That's not a—" he begins, but she cuts him off.

"I won't go in with you. I can wait in the car." She shoots me a poisonous look. "I'm not staying here with *her*. Fucking psycho."

I'm tempted to respond but bite my tongue. It's out of the question to fire back a retort that might reveal our suspicions. If she knows we're onto her, that will only work against us.

My lack of response, rather than diffusing the tension, seems to goad Dakota into an even more accusatory tone. "Look at her. She's not even bothering to deny it."

Em tenses beside me. "You're way out of line, Dakota."

"*I'm* out of line? This bitch killed my mom, so don't tell me I'm—"

"Ducky." Ethan finally steps in. "You're upset. Let's not say things we don't mean."

Her gaze pierces me, cold fury coming off her in waves. "She shouldn't be here. It's insane that you're letting her stay. She killed Mom. Doesn't anybody care about that?"

I can't stay silent another second. The words erupt from me, unbidden. "I didn't kill her, and you know it."

Dakota breaks away from her father and lunges at me, pushing me hard in the chest. I feel my back hit the wall behind me as I stumble away from her, too shocked by her violence to do much more than hold my hands out to shield myself.

"That's enough!" Ethan yanks Dakota back, pulling her toward the door.

I guess I should feel some sympathy for her; she's seventeen and she just found out her mom's dead. At least, that's what we're supposed to believe. If Em's right and the texts reveal she's involved, though, this is a performance, the ingenue playing shock and rage. For the first time since I met her, a visceral hatred of this girl washes over me. It's easy to see echoes of Sadie in the stubborn angle of her jaw and the feverish intensity in her eyes.

Ethan glances at me in apology as he strides toward the garage door, one hand wrapped around his daughter's arm in a firm grip.

"Hold on," she says, when they're halfway out the door. "I need my phone."

"The coroner is waiting," Ethan snaps. "We're going right now."

Dakota's response is muffled as they disappear into the garage. A moment later, we hear the roar of Ethan's Land Rover starting up, the sound trailing off as they head down the drive.

Kimiko's barely awake, sleep still crusting her eyes as she rubs them, groggy and dazed. "Man, she's losing it."

I bark out a nervous laugh.

Kimiko looks at me. "Where did they find her?"

I fill her in on the details. As I tell Kimiko everything I know, tears slide down her cheeks. I hug her for a long moment, feeling a dull ache behind my eyes. This isn't the time for me to break down, though. It's time to fight.

When Kimiko pulls away from me, she clutches her head. "God, this is crazy. Does Amy know?"

I shake my head. "I think she's still at her place. Unless Ethan told her—and I don't think he did—she's clueless."

"You want me to go break it to her?" Kimiko's voice shakes a little.

I grab her hands. "Would you?"

She nods, though I can see dread in the tired lines of her face. Without another word, she goes to the sliding-glass doors and lets herself out, trudging in the direction of Amy's.

Once Em and I are alone, I pull her up the stairs and into Dakota's room. "I think you're right. We need to get this over with."

Em looks uncertain. "What do you mean?"

"Dakota's openly accusing me. That little performance downstairs tells me she's no longer content sneaking around, leaving clues for the cops. Things could escalate. The cops could show up any second to arrest me. The press could get wind of it, making everything harder. We need to stay one step ahead of Dakota or we're screwed." I can feel panic creeping over me, trying to steal my breath, but I refuse to give in. I can't afford to freak out right now.

"What do you want to do?" Em asks.

"Ethan and Dakota should be gone for at least an hour, right? This might be our only chance to confront Ben, see if we can get him to confess." I pick up Dakota's phone. "We can text him from her phone, invite him over."

Em nods. "His parents' house is only a few minutes away. I looked it up on Google Maps."

"If we're lucky, he'll come over right now." I hand Em Dakota's phone. "Here, unlock it, will you?"

Em's fingers fly through the code and she hands it back. "What are you going to say?"

I bite my lip, thinking. It has to sound like Dakota, and it's got to be urgent enough to get him over here fast. I type, I'm going to tell the cops everything if you don't come over now. I show it to Em. "What do you think?"

She purses her lips, head tilted to the side as she reads. With one hand she takes the phone from me, types something, and hands it back. The word *now* has been changed to all caps, and she's added an angry-cat-face emoji.

"You think it'll work?" I whisper, heart pounding.

She looks at me, her forehead glazed with sweat. "Only one way to find out."

I hit send.

BEN COLE IS the kind of guy whose beauty reveals itself only up close and in person. We saw him from a distance the evening we got here, but I didn't get a good look at him. His pictures on Facebook don't do him justice. He's standing on the doorstep, wearing silky gray track pants and a black T-shirt. My eyes fall on a tattoo around his bicep, some kind of tribal armband—a mark of hipness that can be displayed at Coachella but hidden for job interviews. His eyes have the piercing blue intensity of a romance-novel hero. It's easy to see why Dakota might go full Juliet, willing to sacrifice everything for love.

"Morning," Ben says. He folds his hands under his armpits. There's something quintessentially jockish about the way he moves, even the way he stands. It's easy to picture him as a high school quarterback, throwing the winning pass. "Is Dakota around?"

"She'll be down in just a minute," I lie, my voice bright. "It's Ben, right?"

He scratches his chest and nods. "Yeah. I thought she—"

"I'm June," I say, cutting him off. "This is Em. We're friends of Dakota's mom. Come on in."

His brow creases in confusion, but he doesn't resist as we usher him into the living room. "I just got her text. She said it was urgent."

"She told us to let you in," Em says. "She's upstairs, getting glamorous."

"Oh. Okay." He's visibly uncomfortable, but he takes a seat in one of the plush blue chairs.

"While we wait, we have some questions for you," I say.

A silence falls over the room, the air going dense. We let him squirm in the confusion. He perches on the edge of his chair as if he regrets coming in, like he hopes to push rewind so he can erase his entrance.

"Okay." One hand grips the armrest. "What about?"

Em and I take a seat on the couch opposite him.

Her expression goes from friendly to serious. "We need to talk to you about Thursday night."

The hand on the armrest flies up like a startled bird.

It lands in his hair, raking through it roughly. His face takes on a panicky expression. "Who are you, again?"

"I'm June. This is Em." I repeat it slowly, like he's not too bright. "We're friends of Dakota's mom."

"Except Dakota's mom is dead," Em says.

Ben looks surprised, but a beat passes first, like an actor realizing half a second too late what his emotional response should be.

"You already know that, though, don't you?" I pin him with my gaze.

He stands. "I—no—what are you talking about? How did she die?"

"It's no use lying." Em pulls her phone from her pocket. "We've read all the texts, even the ones Dakota deleted. We know she was planning to run away with you Thursday night."

His face drains of color. He takes a few steps toward us, wandering like a man in a dream. I've never seen someone's face go from a healthy tan to a sickly white so quickly. It's alarming, but also a little gratifying. I've been the one in the hot seat lately, answering the detectives' questions, feeling the bottom of my stomach drop when I see the doubt and suspicion in their faces, when I remember that anything I say *can and will* be used against me. I know what he's going through. At least now the person in the hot seat actually belongs there.

"We know you killed Sadie, Ben. But it was self-defense, right? An accident?" I try to infuse my words with just the right blend of cut-the-crap and compassion.

"No! That didn't—no way." He rolls his fists in the hem of his T-shirt. "Why would you think that?"

Em reads from her phone in a prosecutor's voice—

relentless, accusatory. "At twelve forty a.m., you texted, 'On my way to your place now. Is everything ready?' Why would you just happen to be coming over here after midnight? What did Dakota need to 'get ready'?"

"I didn't—I mean—that doesn't prove—" he stammers.

Em continues. "The very night Sadie died, you came here, driving with your lights off. We have a witness who spotted you. Don't you think that will look suspicious to a jury?"

He darts a panicky look toward the door. "I don't have to listen to this."

"Except you want to know what we've got on you," I say. "Anybody would."

With a roll of his shoulders, he starts toward the door. "Screw this."

"You could go," I say to his back, my tone reasonable, "but we're taking this to the cops. They'll be a lot tougher than us. Maybe if you just tell us the truth, we can figure out a game plan, give you advice on how to minimize the damage."

He stops in his tracks, pulls out his phone. One finger stabs at the screen. Dakota's phone blares a pop song in my pocket.

As he whips around, Ben's face registers something other than panic for the first time. He stares at us with pure loathing. "Dakota never texted me. It was you."

"That's right," Em confirms. "We wanted to hear your side of the story."

"What did Dakota tell you?"

"Nothing," I say. "She's been too busy trying to frame me. Was that your idea, too?"

His blank look tells me nothing.

I push the point further. "Dakota wants to protect you. For now. But if the cops start looking at her too closely, I'm sure she'll give you up. If that happens, you'll wish you'd come forward with your own version of the facts."

He tosses me an incredulous look. "So you're on my side, huh?"

"Not really," I reply. "We just want to know the truth."

"The *truth*? You stole Dakota's phone and pretended to be her. Sounds to me like you're a couple of goddamn liars. Where is she, anyway?" He's belligerent, his voice getting louder with every word.

I scowl. "Down at the morgue with her dad, identifying her mother's body."

"Bullshit."

"I promise you, that's where they are," I say, my tone solemn. "Which means this whole investigation is about to get way more intense."

He crosses the space between us so quickly, I have to resist the urge to flinch. Em and I remain seated on the couch, holding his gaze with what I hope is cool indifference. He towers over us, muscles twitching. If he can't flee, he wants to lash out. In my peripheral vision, I scan the room for possible weapons: the heavy lamp by the couch, the ceramic bowl on the coffee table.

"You don't have anything on me," he insists.

Em reads again from her phone. "At twelve fifty-five a.m., you texted, 'Outside now. Where are you?' That didn't go through until later, though, did it? Sketchy reception out here. You must have known that. Is that when you went inside to get Dakota? Except you didn't find Dakota, did you? Instead you found her mother, pissed off and waiting to confront you at the top of the stairs. Was she armed, Ben? Did you—?"

"No!" he cuts her off, his voice too loud, his whole body bristling with anger. "I never went inside the house. I swear to God."

"That's going to be a hard sell in court, Ben." I shake my head sadly.

"Stop saying that!" He takes another step toward me, his hands flexing like he wants to wrap them around my neck.

Again, the instinct to flinch away from him flares, but I force myself to stay rooted to the couch, my voice calm and rational. "You can't hurt us, Ben. It's no use threatening. The cops are very aware of us right now. They probably have this place under surveillance. Anything you do will only drag you deeper into this mess, okay? All we want to do is talk."

"I don't talk to people who accuse me of murder," he growls.

With a flash of inspiration, I decide to try a new angle. My instincts tell me Dakota wasn't honest with him about her age. Would he really run away with a minor? Sadie could have had him arrested for statutory rape. "You know Dakota's underage, right?"

I didn't think it possible for him to lose more color, but he stares at me, his complexion going gray. "She turned eighteen last summer."

I shake my head. "Nope. She lied. She's seventeen."

"You're full of shit."

I keep my tone sympathetic. "Think of how it will

look, Ben. Boyfriend in his twenties, manipulating an innocent child. Conspiring to kill her wealthy mother for a substantial inheritance."

"I'd never—no way. Are you serious? I'd never do that."

I nod, leaning back into the cushions of the couch. "We believe you, but it's not us you need to convince."

The fight seems to go out of him as quickly as it kicked in. He collapses into the armchair opposite us again, slumping like a petulant child. The blue of the chair matches his eyes, which are feverish and bright. His tone is truculent when he mumbles, "What do you want to know?"

"What happened Thursday night?" I try to make my voice gentle. "We know Dakota drugged us so she could get out of the house. We know you came here to pick her up, take her down to LA. We know someone hit Sadie hard enough to kill her. Was it you?"

He rubs his forehead. "I was out in the car. She told me to keep the motor running and the lights off. She ran out of the house with her suitcase."

Em leans forward, her elbows resting on her knees. "Did she tell you what happened?"

"I saw blood on her shirt, and I was like, 'What the hell, Dakota?'" He looks at us, an apology in his eyes. "I wasn't sure about her whole plan, to be honest. I mean, I'm into her, but sometimes…"

"Sometimes?" I whisper, trying not to push him too hard.

"Sometimes I think she's not quite right, you know? Like she's not a hundred percent human." He searches my face, a cornered look quirking his brows. "I kind of freaked out."

A couple beats pass as we wait for further explanation.

When he still doesn't say anything, Em asks, "Freaked out how?"

He shakes his head. His mouth moves as if to speak, but no words come out. Some color floods back into his face—two high, bright spots on his cheeks. He's embarrassed about something.

I decide to leave the nature of his freak-out for a moment and see if he'll confirm the drugs. "Did you give her the drugs?"

He looks confused. "What drugs?"

"The ones she used on us," I say.

"No way. Are you crazy? I could get kicked out of med school. That was all her idea, and she didn't tell me about any of that until after."

"But she admitted she drugged us?" I ask. Until now, this was just a working theory.

"Yeah." He darts another self-conscious look in our direction. "She wanted to make sure nobody stopped her from leaving. Her mom can be a little…controlling."

We don't correct his use of the present tense.

"So what happened after she came out with her suitcase? You drove off and left her there?" Em keeps her tone carefully neutral.

Ben goes on the defensive anyway. "What else was I going to do? She had blood all over her."

"Did she tell you her mom was dead?" I ask.

He shakes his head. "Not exactly."

"What did she say?" I ask.

"She said they got in a fight. To tell you the truth, I didn't want to know. Plausible deniability." He looks at his hands. "I know it sounds bad, but I just—couldn't risk it. I've got a good scholarship. My mom's sick and my dad's riding me twenty-four/seven to pay my own way, and I just—the whole situation was more than I bargained for."

I don't know this kid, but something about the story he's telling us feels true. We were so quick to assume Ben was the killer. It was such a relief to find an outsider to blame, somebody beyond the scope of Sadie's family and friends. We clung to the least horrifying possibility—an impulsive boyfriend who killed her without any motivation except feeling surprised and cornered in a dark hallway, an intruder lashing out. Fight-or-flight.

But if what he's saying is true, then Dakota's the real murderer here. The realization lands in my stomach like a punch. Fresh dread creeps over me. Now I see our mistake. Dakota didn't frame me to cover for her boyfriend. She's not that kind of girl. She did it to protect herself.

"Look, we're on your side, okay?" I've dealt with kids like Ben my whole career—cocky, privileged, with a Machiavellian streak a mile wide. They've been raised to look out for number one. It's not attractive, but it's what they know. If you want something from them, you have to appeal to their survival instincts rather than their humanitarian principles.

I try to sound calm in spite of my racing pulse. "Right now, I'm the cops' favorite suspect. If you don't come forward with what you know, we'll have to do it for you. I know that sounds cold, but I'm not going to prison for a crime I didn't commit."

Ben gives me an anguished look, his hands running through his hair again, making it stand up. "I can't go to the cops."

The truth is, Ben and I are in the same boat now; we'll both have to do what we can to survive, even if it means throwing Dakota overboard.

"If you don't, you could do time yourself," Em warns. "You'll be an accessory to murder, maybe worse. Dakota might claim you're the killer. She's already tried to pin it on June. She's proven she'll lie to save herself. You've admitted you were there. It wouldn't be much of a stretch."

"I never went inside. I—"

"We believe you," I soothe, "but the cops are more likely to buy it if you come forward now. Don't force them to track you down."

"I wanted to be with her. That's all." He huffs out a frustrated sigh. "I didn't know any of the other stuff—the drugs, her real age, how serious this thing was with her mom. She lied to me."

"If you're telling the truth, the cops will believe you." I hope to God this isn't wishful thinking. "You need to come forward, tell them what you know, set them on the right path. They'll find evidence to prove she's guilty. You'll be in the clear."

"I didn't kill anyone," he murmurs, his voice small and scared.

"I get that. And I know what it's like to feel trapped by circumstantial evidence," I tell him. "But it's not me you have to convince—"

"Actually, it's me."

We all jump at the sound of her voice. Dakota's standing in the doorway. There's a gun in her hand.

"Go ahead, Ben." Her voice is tight with anger. "Tell them you'd never turn on me like that."

I can't take my eyes off the gun. I don't know anything about firearms, but it's definitely some kind of handgun. Then I remember the gun safe on Ethan's side of the walk-in closet. Sadie's dismissive words: *A Smith and Wesson, maybe?* Its gleaming black metal catches the light. It looks enormous in Dakota's small, pale hands. She keeps it pointed at Ben.

In spite of seeing this scene play out in countless movies and TV shows, I feel a deep, stomach-wrenching shock at finding myself at the center of this one. Nothing can prepare you for the pure, dry-mouthed fear of staring down a weapon that can blow your body apart at any second.

"I thought you were with your dad," I say stupidly.

"He's being a dick." Her bravado doesn't quite mask the quiver in her voice. "He dropped me at the beach house, told me to calm down. Imagine my surprise when I saw my douchebag ex-boyfriend racing up to the house to conspire with you bitches."

I force my gaze away from the barrel of the gun so I can concentrate on her face. "More violence won't solve anything."

"For a professor, you're not very smart, are you?" Her mouth twists into a condescending smirk. "Oh, that's right, you're just a *community college* professor. I guess that explains it."

She's trying for action-hero swagger, but the tension in her limbs, the tightness in her face—it all makes the

performance unconvincing. I watch her with wary concentration, my mind scrabbling for ways to disarm her.
It should make her less frightening, the fragility beneath
her bravado, but the hair-trigger skittishness makes her
even more dangerous.

Ben stands and takes a step toward her. "Babe,
you've got to calm down."

"I'm calm, *babe*." She spits out the word with an ugly
sneer. "You're the one who's about to crap your pants."

"I'm on your side. You know that."

She gives him an incredulous look. "You *left* me
standing in the driveway with my suitcase, Ben. I had
to call my dad."

"I freaked out, okay? I'm sorry."

"We had to load her body—" Her voice breaks. Tears
glimmer in her eyes.

The final piece of the puzzle slots into place. I could
picture Dakota lashing out and killing her mother on
accident. What I couldn't picture was her disposing of
the body all alone. She's probably only a hundred and
twenty pounds, tops, with the slender frame and thin,
bony limbs of a girl flirting with an eating disorder.
The thought of her heaving Sadie's corpse off a cliff is
almost as ridiculous as Amy managing the task eight
months pregnant. No, it took some muscle and stamina
to accomplish that. Ethan took care of the cover-up, the
attempt to make it look like a suicide.

"So Ethan knows it was you?" I blurt.

I wonder if it was Ethan who framed me, too, or if
Dakota took that part of the plot on herself. Maybe they
cooked up the plan together and divvied up the work
as needed.

Dakota eyes me with disdain. "Of course he knows. God, you people are slow."

Ben tries to soothe her. "Look, I'm sorry I left you there, okay? I just—you need help. We can get you—"

"Don't talk to me like I'm crazy, Ben."

"You're not crazy. That's not what I—"

"I'm not an idiot, either," Dakota says. "I know what 'help' means." She barks out a dry, humorless laugh. "My mom sent me to so many shrinks, it's a wonder I can even think straight."

Ben takes another half step toward her. "You're in too deep this time. We can help, that's all I'm trying to—"

"Oh, you'll help. Just not the way you think." She cuts him off, raising the gun so it's pointed directly at his face. Her hands are shaking violently, and I wonder if she'll drop it. I can hear the effort it takes to keep her voice from shaking, too. "This is what's going to happen. Ben's going to write a suicide note confessing to my mom's murder."

"Suicide—?" Ben starts, but stops when she jabs the gun closer to his face.

"It's the least you can do, after leaving me here all alone. We had a plan, and you completely bailed. You owe me."

Ben looks at the floor, saying nothing. She's obviously beyond reason.

"You're going to confess to my mom's murder and then shoot yourself. But first, we're going to shoot these two." She waves the gun at Em and me. "You'll put them in the note, too. They figured out it was you, blah, blah, blah. Case closed."

I stand, leveling my gaze at Dakota. "That's not

going to work. There are cops watching this place. Kimiko and Amy are right next door."

"Do not talk to me right now," she says, her voice low and dangerous.

I ignore the hypnotic pull of the gun, the need to track the crosshairs. If we can keep her distracted, maybe we can live long enough for someone to come in and get the gun away from her. Maybe I can even manage to grab it myself.

In spite of her warning, I try again. "Why did you do it, Dakota? What happened?"

She points the gun at me. "You're the wannabe detective. You tell me."

I swallow the lump in my throat. "I think you resented the control your mom exerted. You were tired of being an extension of her. You wanted to be your own person."

"You think?" She raises an eyebrow, her tone thick with sarcasm. Underneath the glibness, though, I can see how much she longs to explain herself, to drop the burden she's been carrying.

"But did you plan it? Or did it just happen?"

"I didn't *want* to do it. I didn't even mean to. All I wanted was to get out of here and never come back."

"Why the drugs, though?" I ask. "Couldn't you have just snuck out while we slept?"

She lowers the gun slowly, her voice trembling. "You really don't know my mom at all, do you? I've tried to run away before. She's a fucking stalker. She always catches me before I can even leave the property. I was a prisoner. Just like Dad and Amy."

I'm silent, waiting for her to say more.

Her expression is far away, remembering. "I thought if I knocked everyone out and got to LA that night, at least I'd have a chance. It was supposed to just put you all to sleep. I didn't know you'd turn into freaks."

I notice Ben in my peripheral vision, taking a step away from Dakota, toward the stone fireplace. Em is still on the couch, frozen in place.

I take a step toward Dakota, angling my body in front of Em. "But your mom tried to stop you anyway, didn't she?"

Dakota looks at me, her expression lost. "I was starting down the stairs with my suitcase, super quiet. I saw her coming down the hallway. Her eyes were crazy."

I inch toward her, wondering if the safety on the gun is off. Does Dakota know anything about guns? She clearly knew the combination to her dad's safe. Maybe he taught her how to shoot. I don't want to underestimate her. It could be my last mistake.

Dakota sighs, looking exhausted. There are lavender half-moons under her eyes. "She wasn't normal. You guys are supposed to be her oldest friends, but you have no idea what she's really like. One time, we had this photo shoot for a magazine, something her publicist set up—the happy-family portrait. I was thirteen. I had a pimple on my forehead. It happens, you know? God, she couldn't let it go. The photographer kept assuring her he could photoshop it out, but she got all pissed at Dad and me, accusing us of sneaking out to get dough-nuts. I mean, she controlled everything we put in our mouths, wouldn't let us eat anything normal. It was all kale and whole grains and tempeh and shots of wheat-grass. We were extensions of her, so we had to be perfect. I always knew I had to *earn* her love—I couldn't just have it. Nothing I ever did was enough."

I nod, all sympathy. Am I close enough to lunge for the gun? How fast would I have to be to knock it out of her hand? I need to get closer before I can chance it. "No wonder you needed to get away."

"Now she's planning to highjack Amy's baby. I'm a total disappointment, so she's trying to start again. Dakota two-point-oh. I did that kid a favor," she snarls. "At least now Mom won't be around to screw up the baby's life like she screwed up mine."

"Still, you didn't mean to kill her, right?" I hold her gaze, trying to convey that I'm on her side. I take another step in her direction, but in a conversational way, hoping to God she won't feel cornered. I still won't let myself look at the gun.

"She was flying down the hallway with this look in her eye. I grabbed the statue to defend myself. To show her I was serious this time." She shakes her head, her bottom lip quivering. "And then it just…happened."

Ben is now standing by the fireplace, a good ten feet away from her. "It's okay, babe."

She whips around so fast I flinch. She points the gun at his chest. "You left me here all alone with my mother's dead body, you spineless douche."

"I didn't even know she was dead," he protests.

"Yeah, because you took off as soon as you saw blood on my shirt." She glares at him with pure loathing. "Jesus, who does that? You didn't even ask me what happened."

"Dakota, come on," Ben whispers.

"Shut up," she hisses, fury turning her face ugly. "You always underestimated me. Just like everyone else."

"Your dad wouldn't want you to do this." I pray this will have some sway with her. She obviously loves her dad more than anyone. Maybe if she thinks of him, it will bring her back to earth. "He may have helped you cover this up, but he doesn't want more people to die. I'm sure of that."

"He'll get over it." She studies my face, an avid gleam in her eye. "It's me he cares about. Not you."

My voice comes out hoarse. "But think of how hurt he'll be. How disappointed."

For a moment, true sadness washes over her face. It's like watching a dark cloud pass over a sunlit field. Her smooth brow wrinkles. She's just a confused little girl.

"This isn't going to work." I push her harder. "It's insane. The cops will barge in here as soon as they hear the first shot."

Dakota's moment of doubt passes. She pastes on a confident, deranged smile. "The cops might be watching, but they're idiots, and they're keeping their distance. By the time they get here, you'll all be dead, and it'll be my story they hear. I'll be a media sensation. All because my mentally unstable boyfriend cracked under the pressure of a sick mom and med school." She flashes a pretty pout at Ben. "Poor little rich boy."

"You can't do this." My feet carry me closer to her, even as Dakota jerks the gun up and aims it at my chest. Instinctively, I cast a quick glance behind me to make sure Em's still on the couch, adjusting to make sure my body shields hers. "I won't let you, Dakota."

Dakota's eyes narrow; her hand is still shaking as she

keeps the gun trained on me. "This is not your story. You're just the slut who's sleeping with my dad."

I take another step toward her. The gun's no more than four feet from my breastbone now. "I can take you down before you get to the others. They'll wrestle the gun from you. We've got at least four hundred pounds on you. Three against one."

"Stop right there. I'm serious."

"She's right," Ben says, though he stays where he is by the fireplace. "We've got you outnumbered."

Dakota shoots at the floor. The sound is impossibly loud, an explosion ricocheting inside my skull. The smell of metallic sulfur fills the room.

By the time the roar in my head starts to recede, Ben's dropped to one knee. For a second, I think he's begging, but then I see his bare foot, curled against the floor like a mangled animal. A nimbus of blood gathers around it, a red so deep it looks almost black.

It takes him a moment to realize what happened. He falls back on his butt and stares at his foot. He's wearing flip-flops, and there's exposed bone where his big toe should be. We all gape at it.

Ben lets out a long, agonized scream. Then he looks up at Dakota, incredulous. His voice is thick with pain. "What the hell, Dakota?"

"Nobody gets to tell me what to do anymore." She gives him a look so cold, it makes my skin crawl. "You forfeited that right when you drove off."

Em tosses Ben the scarf she's wearing. "Bind it with that. Put lots of pressure on it."

"This isn't a first-aid course!" Dakota steps around me and aims the gun at Em.

"You're still outnumbered." I adjust my position so I'm blocking Em again and take another step toward Dakota. "You can't win."

She's breathing so hard I can see her chest rising and falling. I'm only a few feet away. She aims the gun at my face, her hands trembling. "Get the hell away from me."

"Please, Dakota." I keep moving toward her, determined to keep my body between her and Em. "Just put the gun down."

Dakota whimpers, her face rigid. Slowly, she lowers the gun. Tears stream over her cheeks. She closes her eyes, defeated.

Just then, the front door flies open with a bang. Two plainclothes cops storm inside, brandishing handguns. "Police!" they shout. "Drop the weapon!"

What happens next is a blur. Dakota raises the gun again, turning this way and that, panicking. Her eyes are wide, that startling navy-blue flashing as our gazes lock. She raises the gun high. Her small, pale finger squeezes the trigger. A shot rings out.

There's a searing pain in my head. I close my eyes, and there are orange flares behind my lids. It's a beautiful orange, as fiery and vibrant as a sunset. I feel myself crashing to the floor.

And then there's nothing.

SIXTEEN

I WAKE TO a blur of white—blinding, antiseptic blankness. I blink, trying to force the world into focus. The walls swim like reflections in water. My mouth is dry, my tongue thick. I try an experimental groan. A pathetic croak is all that escapes.

Somebody crosses the room—a flash of green moving quickly—then I feel someone squeezing my hand. With supreme effort, my brain struggles to arrange the dancing pixels into a shape. The pointillist painting finally resolves into a recognizable face.

Leo.

A tide of emotion surges through the pain and drugs. Gratitude. Relief. Hope.

Dakota had a gun. I grope for the memory, but it's shrouded in layers of opaque mist.

I draw a breath, cool air moving over my dry tongue. Leo holds out a plastic cup of water, pokes a straw into my mouth. Too thirsty to attempt a thanks, I suck at it greedily. In seconds, the cup is empty. He grabs a plastic pitcher and refills it, inserting the straw into my mouth again. I drain the cup.

"More?" His voice is gentle.

I shake my head. My mouth no longer feels like the Sahara. In place of thirst, a driving need to understand why I'm here eclipses everything else. I try to sit up.

Leo pushes me back against the pillows with one hand. "Hold up, Moody. Allow me." He fiddles with a button. There's a whirring sound; then I feel the bed tilting beneath me, raising me to a sitting position.

From this angle, it becomes apparent I'm attached to a dizzying array of tubes. There must be something pumping through my veins, because I feel sluggish and serene in a way that makes no sense. Whatever I'm on lends an extra layer of surreal distance to a scene that's already dreamlike. I'm grateful for the cushion between me and reality.

I open my mouth, unsure if I can find my voice. "What happened?"

His smile is amused. "You survived."

"Thanks. I figured that out on my own."

Leo pushes my hair away from my face, tucks a strand with tender care behind my ear. "You were shot. The bullet grazed your scalp. There was a lot of blood, but no trauma to the brain."

Even in my drugged stupor, I notice his use of the agentless passive. *You were shot.* With a shiver, I see Dakota pointing a gun high, tears streaming down her face. Then I remember who was with me.

"Em. How's—?"

"She's fine. Everyone's fine. Well, Dakota's boyfriend lost a toe."

"I don't think he's her boyfriend anymore," I croak.

His wry smile warms me. "See? No damage to the brain. You're still a smartass."

I can't help grinning back at him, though through the haze of drugs I'm dimly aware this is not a funny situation.

He squeezes my hand. His fingers offer a delicious, pulsing heat against the cold inside me. "You were very brave, from what I hear. Aside from the wonky haircut, you're going to be fine."

I grope at my head, confused. Then my fingers find the shaved patch just to the right of my part. "Shit. I bet I look amazing."

Leo laughs. Then his eyes go serious. "You're stunning. Believe me."

My brain struggles to assemble the memories scattered like puzzle pieces. I see the sparkling, sunlit bay through a collection of massive windows. Ben sitting on the floor, his foot swathed in a scarf that's quickly turning scarlet.

I struggle to pull the right question from the wreckage. "Did they arrest Dakota?"

Leo nods. "Apparently they had a hunch about her, even before all this. The evidence in your suitcase, the claims she made about you having an affair with Ethan—it all seemed a little too convenient. She's got a history of mental health issues. They had their eye on her."

Another question emerges from my brain fog. "I don't understand. She aimed high."

His expression goes from confused to grim. "They said the bullet ricocheted off the stone fireplace and hit you on its way down."

"Oh." I try to work out the physics of this, but I'm too tired to picture it. "Guess that was lucky. Or unlucky, depending on how you look at it."

He takes my hand, studying my fingers, avoiding my eyes. "She confessed. It's all over."

"And Ethan?" I lick my lips. They feel chapped. "Will he be charged, too?"

"As an accessory, at least. He helped her cover it up. It all came out in her confession. How she drugged you guys, tried to run away with Ben, got in a fight with Sadie and hit her with the statue."

"And then what? She called Ethan and he dumped the body?"

"Exactly. Ethan loaded Sadie into her car and drove out to Deception Pass. He threw her off a cliff to make it look like suicide."

"But then…" I try to formulate the question, swimming upstream against the drugs' current. "How did he get home?"

"Dakota followed him out there in his Land Rover, drove him home after." Leo looks sad. "I think he's trying to convince the cops he's the murderer, that Dakota's innocent, but they're not buying it. Not after she told them everything."

I try to imagine what they must be going through. Fisher and Bledek can be intimidating; I know this firsthand. Some of Dakota's words come floating back to me, worming their way through the drugs. *I always knew I had to earn her love—I couldn't just have it.* Sadie's drive for perfection, her need to control the people around her, finally took their toll. Her most cherished creation, her own daughter, pushed back in a moment of raw violence. I think of Dakota, just seventeen, standing on the edge of life, ready to dive in. Now her mother's dead, and she's defined by it. She'll be paying for a split-second decision to lash out, to do whatever she could to escape her mother's suffocating devotion, for the rest of her life.

It's more terrifying, in a way, than the thought of Dakota plotting to kill her mother in cold blood. It will probably earn her a lighter sentence, but to me Dakota's impulsive violence is the most chilling part of the whole story. I picture her raising the statue, brandishing it, wanting only to get away. I think of how trapped I felt in that house even for a few days, suffocated by its opulence and perfection. It feels like it could have been me wielding that statue.

"You okay?" Leo's eyes lock with mine. He's a lighthouse in the fog, a beacon trying to guide me home.

"It's just so awful to imagine."

"Yeah." He looks down. His hand still grips mine. "I knew they were messed up—the whole family—but I had no idea it was this dark."

"For years, I was sure Sadie had it all." I study his brown fingers covering mine. "I really believed that."

"Everybody's got their own stuff to deal with," he says.

"That's what Em kept telling me."

"That reminds me, I should text your friends." Leo pulls his hand from mine and digs his phone from his pocket. "We've been taking shifts, watching over you."

I smile, thinking of Em. She stood by me through this whole ordeal, working her ass off to prove my innocence. I feel a wave of gratitude. All along, I had more than Sadie ever did. I have real friends, people who have my back. Sadie had only indentured servants. Maybe Ethan, Amy, and Dakota loved her in a way, but they also hated the control she exerted over their lives.

"Thank you for staying with me. You didn't have to do that." I flash him a shy smile.

He glances up, eyes twinkling. "I'm the lucky bastard who got to be here when you woke up."

"I thought you had a strict no-drama policy," I tease. "I'm surprised you volunteered."

One eyebrow arches at this, a grin tugging at the corner of his mouth. His dimple appears. "I have a strict policy against MacTavish drama. You're a Moody—that's a whole other animal."

I recall, through the painkillers, that kiss.

"What will you do now?" I ask, the reality of Leo's altered situation hitting me.

His forehead creases in confusion. "What do you mean?"

"Looks like you may have lost your job."

"Oh." Understanding dawns in his face. "Yeah, that. Ethan wants me to stay while the whole legal battle drags on, be a caretaker of sorts, but it's time to move on. Three years is more than enough time to wallow in my misery."

I squint at him. "Are you ever going to tell me about that?" It comes out a raspy whisper.

He gets up, refreshes my plastic cup with water, and puts the straw to my lips. It's obvious he's stalling, but I appreciate the solicitous care just the same.

Once he's settled in his chair again, he looks at the ceiling. I sense a sadness in him so enormous it threatens to rob the room of air. "I lost my son four years ago."

I stare at him in silence, no idea what to say.

"Miles. He was three and a half." He glances at me, then resumes his inspection of the ceiling. "My ex-wife and I couldn't…we didn't make it. We divorced less than a year later."

"I'm so sorry." Even in my drugged state, I know it's insufficient, but I've got nothing else to offer.

He studies his hands. "That's why I came here. I was in a downward spiral in New York. Drugs, alcohol, meaningless hookups. I knew if I didn't make a clean break I'd find a way to self-destruct."

"Good choice," I murmur.

His expression shifts, the worst of the storm passing as he fixes me with a searching look. "I don't want to put too much pressure on you, June. It's just, meeting you, getting to know you—this is the first time I've felt halfway human in years."

I don't look away. "I can handle the pressure."

"Good." The seriousness lifts again, the moment passing. "Let's hope that's not just the drugs talking."

"What will you do next?" I circle back to my original question, trying not to get my hopes up.

He shrugs. "I was thinking I might check out Santa Cruz. It's not a bad town, right?"

"It's a great town." I sit up straighter, jostling the tubes attached to my arms. "You'll love it—"

"Easy, Moody." He puts a hand against my chest, gently pushing me back and checking to be sure I haven't done any damage. "Don't want to summon the nurses. They're a surly lot, I have to warn you."

"Sorry, I just—that's exciting." I know it's uncool, but I can't stop beaming at him. "It'll be fun to show you around."

He smooths my sheets. "I actually have an old friend

there. Texted him last night. He thinks he can get me an interview with a landscape design firm."

"Really?" This is a surprise. I wonder if *design firm* is a fancy name for a gardening business.

He must read the confusion on my face. "That's what I do—what I did, in New York. I design public spaces—parks, campuses, resorts, that sort of thing."

"Oh. Right. Got it."

He leans back in his chair, watching me. "I figured I'd give it a try again. Gardening is great when you're licking your wounds, but I think I'm ready to get back to the real world."

"Welcome back," I say.

His smile is so warm I feel it spread over me like a blanket. "Welcome back yourself."

TWO MONTHS LATER, Em and I sit in her garden, drinking wine. It's an excellent Syrah Reggie picked out for the occasion, velvety and smooth. Em's garden is tucked into the rooftop of their SoMa loft, so we're seven stories above the rumble of rush-hour traffic. It's early August, unseasonably warm for San Francisco. The air smells of Chinese food and jasmine. An expansive peace fills me; I can feel my shoulders melting a little more with each sip.

"I guess you heard about Dakota?" Em puts her glass down.

My shoulders tense a little at this, half undoing the magic of the wine. I take a deep breath, reminding myself how much worse the situation could be. It could be me on trial. It almost was. "About her being tried as an adult?"

"Washington state law is pretty firm on that point," Em says. "If you're sixteen or older, you get treated like anyone else. Of course, it'll probably be at least six or seven months before it actually goes to trial."

Dakota's being charged with second-degree murder. They could have nailed her with attempted murder as well—of me, and possibly of Ben and Em—but none of us wanted to pursue that, so those charges never materialized. I suppose we should be bitter, but it's still hard to get past the idea that she's young and troubled. Maybe that's naïve. She'll have plenty of time behind bars—or in a psych ward—to figure out what made her do the things she did. That's the most important thing for now.

Ethan tried to take the rap, but the cops had too much information to believe him. He's looking at doing plenty of time as an accessory to the crime, though.

Dakota was right about one thing: she's an international sensation. The media went crazy when they got their hands on the story. Imagine a real-life Harry Potter murdering JK Rowling. Dakota's insanely photogenic, which only adds to the media's fervor. She pouts for the cameras with just the right cocktail of petulance and brooding intensity.

The injury to my scalp has nearly healed, though I still feel an ache there, often at four AM, when the nightmare of that weekend swirls around inside my brain like a bad acid trip. I cut my hair short to offset the wonky shaved patch. It's still hard to believe we went through all that. Here in California, far from the sprawling mansion that felt like a prison for a few long, terrible days, it seems more like a movie. I can still see the images, but they play out in a Technicolor haze, made glossy and unreal by time and distance.

Amy had her baby July seventh, an eight-pound girl with dark curls and a cherubic face. She named her Olivia. Ethan was forced to take a paternity test, proving he is in fact the father. Em and Kimiko were shocked when they heard, but I can't say it floored me. Ethan revealed enough duplicity that weekend to make even this revelation unsurprising. Confirming his paternity is a good thing, since now a portion of Sadie's vast fortune will go toward child support. Amy and Olivia have their own place, a cute little cottage in Bellingham. We can only hope for the best. I know Amy has her own demons to grapple with, but getting away from the toxic MacTavish web has to be a step in the right direction.

Kimiko's still got her cannabis dispensary, and from what I hear, business is picking up. She started making cannabis-infused baked goods that are quite the hit with the stoner crowd and cancer patients alike. Kimi always did have a knack for tasty treats. We talked on the phone last week. She told me the loan from Sadie hasn't been mentioned by the family lawyers; they've got so much on their plate right now, it's not surprising they can't be bothered with something so insignificant. Her son got out of juvie, and he's doing really well, apparently. She says he's been nagging her about smoking too much weed; we had a good laugh about her twelve-year-old drug counselor.

Em studies me. She's splayed out on her charcoal couch. I'm perched on the love seat across from her, a marble coffee table between us. The evening light casts her face in an apricot hue. Leo calls this "Italian light," the flattering, rosy glow that gilds a landscape as the sun sinks low. Behind Em, jasmine trails from a jade-green planter, scenting the air.

"How are you feeling about all that?" She watches me, her dark eyes calm.

Surprisingly, Em and I haven't talked about that weekend all that much. We made a tacit agreement to put it behind us. When we were younger, the sheer drama of such an event would have been irresistible; we would have rehashed it ad nauseam. It's one of the perks of aging, I suppose—an eagerness to release the baggage that doesn't serve you. I know this goes against common wisdom; our therapy-obsessed culture seems to think old wounds must be reopened before they can heal. I'm not sure I agree.

I take another sip of my wine. "It seems unreal, to tell you the truth. It feels like it happened to someone else."

"I know what you mean." Em's cat, Mr. Bojangles, leaps into her lap.

I feel a wave of sadness, thinking about Sadie. "It's hard to believe Sadie's really gone. We were never that close, but it still feels like there's a big hole where she used to be."

Em adjusts her legs under Mr. Bojangles, running a hand over his gray fur as he settles into her lap. "We all had mixed feelings about her, obviously, and what went down that weekend eclipsed everything else for a while. Now that the shock has worn off, I find myself thinking about her a lot, combing through memories we all shared."

One of the things I love best about Em is her ability to put into words the hazy swirl of emotions I can't quite articulate. I've been doing a lot of remembering, too. More and more, the Sadie I picture isn't the manipulative, high-strung puppet master I saw in action during the last few days of her life. Now I think more often of the Sadie I knew in college—the feisty, confident, competitive nemesis who pushed me with her very presence. We were always destined to be frenemies, I suppose, but we were part of a circle that managed to nurture and support one another even as we vied for supremacy.

In the last couple of months, I've found myself reaching out to Em, Kimiko, and Amy more often than I did before. That weekend pushed us all to our limits, revealing ugly truths and buried resentments. It also showed me just how valuable these women are to me. They're the people who share my memories and helped shape the person I've become. There's a depth and a history there that can't be created from scratch. Maybe that's another thing you learn, as you get older—the value of people who know your secrets, who understand not just your present-tense persona but the younger, more reckless, more innocent version of who you used to be.

I stare at Mr. Bojangles, not quite able to meet Em's eye. "What's going on with Sadie's book?"

Em shakes her head, a cloud passing over her expression. "I don't know. Nothing's been said about it in the media, so I'm hoping that means it won't be published."

"What will you do if it comes out?" I ask.

She scratches Mr. Bojangles behind the ears, and he purrs in approval. "It would suck, but I think I'd find a way to make peace with it. That weekend forced me to realize how much that secret was weighing me down. I was sixteen, hormonal, confused. My relationship with my mom was totally unhealthy. I thought I was in love, and Johan took advantage of my vulnerable, screwed-up, sixteen-year-old self. It's time I forgive myself for making a series of really bad choices."

This is the most she's said about her relationship with her mother's boyfriend since that weekend. I feel encouraged to wade in a little deeper, conscious not to overstep. "Does Reggie know?"

"Yeah. We went away for the weekend, and I found myself telling him the whole sordid tale. I explained about Johan, my mom, all of it." She reaches for her wine and takes a long sip. "It felt like something I needed to do, whether or not that stupid book ever sees the light of day."

"And your mom?" I ask, my voice gentle.

She shakes her head. "That's a conversation I'll never be ready for. Hopefully I can go on avoiding it forever."

I sense she doesn't want more questions, so I let the silence linger.

"How's it going with Leo?" she asks, her tone brightening.

"Good." I shoot her a sheepish sideways glance. "We're talking about moving in together."

She jerks upright, her voice rising. "Wait, what? How am I just now hearing this?"

I laugh. "We're still trying to figure out what we're doing."

"Meaning?"

"It's the definition of complicated."

When I don't elaborate, she leans forward, prompting Mr. Bojangles to give her an affronted sniff. "I've given you tons of space with this. I knew you weren't

ready to talk about it. I'm sorry, though—'it's complicated' doesn't cut it."

I sigh, propping my bare feet on the coffee table. "I
love him. He says he loves me."

She squeals.

"But—and this is a huge but," I go on, trying to reel
in her excitement, "he's still mourning the loss of his
son. It's no small thing. If we're going to be together,
we've got to take it slow. I'm talking ice-age slow. The
jury's still out."

She covers her mouth. "Oh my God. That's fantas-
tic."

"Don't get ahead of yourself." I swill the last of my
wine and hold my glass out for a refill.

She obliges, filling it with a generous pour. "Finally,
after all these years, you're going to be with someone
who deserves you. You ever talk to Pete?"

"Never." I watch a plane trace a white line across the
perfect blue sky. "One thing I'll say for the emotional
maelstrom of that trip: it sure was an effective way to
get my mind off my cheating ex."

Em grins. "This is it for you. Leo's the one. I can
feel it."

"Oh, you can, huh? And does your 'feeling' say anything about how we're going to navigate his tragedy?"

She shrugs. "You'll figure it out."

"What makes you say that?" If I'm being honest, I
desperately want her to be right. It's something I try not
to admit, especially to myself. "I don't have the great-
est track record."

Em sheds any trace of flippancy. Her eyes lock with

mine, her voice going low and serious. "You've never been more open, June. That trip really changed you."

I look out over the city. The sun sparkles on the water, glints off the Bay Bridge, catches on the glass of skyscrapers in shards of gold. A horn honks in the distance; a seagull circles overhead, hunting for scraps. I sip my wine, feeling the warmth of it gathering in my chest.

"It did, I think." I realize how much lighter and less resentful I feel, now that I've stopped comparing my life to Sadie's. It wasn't just Sadie, either—it was the overwhelming sense that other people were so much healthier, happier, more successful than me.

"What do you think shifted?" Em asks.

I sigh, leaning back against the cushions. "I guess I finally learned to focus on what I've got, not the sparkly things just out of reach."

She beams at me. "It's made all the difference. I can tell."

I picture Leo's whiskey-colored eyes and smile. "I hope I've changed enough to get it right this time."

"You're already getting it right. You're just scared." She's smug again.

I change the subject, not wanting to jinx anything by overthinking it. "You think we'll ever attempt another girls weekend?"

"God," she says on a sigh. "I don't know. You up for it?"

"Not for a few months, at least." I can already feel my stomach squirming at the thought. These are people I need in my life, though, and phones can only do so much to keep you connected. "Next summer, maybe? We could meet halfway, in Oregon—Ashland or Portland—find a good rental? We should meet Olivia before she becomes an obnoxious toddler."

Em looks a little surprised, but she flashes a smile that tells me she's proud of me. "I think that sounds like a great plan."

"Bet you never thought *I'd* suggest it though, huh?" I give her a knowing smirk.

"The old June? Never." She nudges my foot with her own. "The new June is full of surprises, though."

I shrug, accepting the compliment.

With one hand, she raises her glass. "To old friends and new love."

As our glasses clink, a golden warmth spreads through me.

It feels suspiciously like hope.

* * * * *

ACKNOWLEDGMENTS

I AM DEEPLY indebted to the vast network of people who helped bring this book to life.

First of all, a huge thanks goes to my savvy and supportive agent, Jill Marr, whose faith in me never wavers. Chelsey Emmelhainz, my brilliant editor at Crooked Lane Books, saw enough potential in my lumpy, misshapen manuscript to push me further and deeper than I ever thought possible. A big thanks to everyone at CLB for your tireless work on my behalf, especially Melissa Rechter, Ashley Di Dio, and Rachel Keith.

As always, early readers provided me with notes that helped me find the story I needed to tell: Rose Bell, Wendy James, David Wolf, Ginny Buccelli, Cameron Lund, Zac Simons, Sherry Garner, Marion Deeds, and Ed Gehrman. You all helped me see the plot holes and how to fill them. Without you this book would be languishing in my proverbial sock drawer.

Lastly, a huge and heartfelt thanks to one of my oldest, dearest friends, Laura Parsons. Our time together in Deception Pass, Fidalgo Island, and Port Townsend helped with so much more than just fleshing out the setting. Our many adventures over the years have shaped who I am today. Thank you for letting me back into your world with such grace and generosity.